LEADER OF BATTLES (II): ARTORIUS

By David Pilling

More Books by David Pilling
Leader of Battles (I): Ambrosius
King's Knight (I)
The White Hawk (I): Revenge
The White Hawk (II): Rebellion ·
The White Hawk (III): Restoration
The White Hawk (IV): Redemption
Caesar's Sword (I): The Red Death
Caesar's Sword (II): Siege of Rome
Caesar's Sword (III): Flame of the West
Robin Hood (I)
Robin Hood (II): The Wrath of God
Robin Hood (III): The Hooded Man
Nowhere Was There Peace
The Half-Hanged Man
The Best Weapon (with Martin Bolton)
Sorrow (with Martin Bolton)

The John Swale Chronicles
Folville's Law & 12 mini-sequels

Follow David at his blogs at:
www.pillingswritingcorner.blogspot.co.uk
www.davidpillingauthor.com

http://www.boltonandpilling.com

Or contact him direct at:
Davidpilling56@hotmail.com

Index of place names

Glossary

Angon – short Saxon javelin or throwing spear

Buccelari – elite Romano-British cavalry

Ceorl – a free Saxon peasant

Comes Britanniarum – commander of Romano-British field army

Comes Litoris Saxoni – Count of the Saxon Shore

Comitatenses – Romano-British field army

Dux Bellorum – 'Leader of Battles'/commander-in-chief of Roman forces in Britannia

Dux Britanniarum – Senior Roman officer in charge of defence of the North of Britannia

Gesith – early form of Saxon thegn, indicating a man ranking between a freeman and a king

Magister Militum – Master of Horse/Cavalry

Magister Militum – Master of Soldiers

Saex – Type of Saxon dagger

Scop – Saxon poet or bard

Spatha – Long-bladed Roman cavalry sword

Vicarius – Roman term for a high-ranking government official

"Then Arthur fought at that time against them in those days along with the kings of the Britons, but he was their leader in battles..."

- *The Historia Brittonum*

Alt Clut, 470 AD

They were hunting him again. He could hear the frantic baying of the hounds, not half a mile to the north, and the scarcely less excited shouts of the huntsmen.

Gwrgi pictured the hounds. Lean, hairy bodies straining at their leashes, eyes rolling in bestial rage, foam drooling from yellow jaws. As soon as he was sighted, the handlers would release them, and Gwrgi would have to fly for his life with the animals snapping at his heels.

He ran, gliding across the hard, frosted ground as though it was marble. Gwrgi moved with the speed and grace of a dancer. Speed, along with knife-sharp instincts, kept him alive.

Terror coursed through him, rising to exhilaration as he leaped over a fallen bough and splashed through the shallow bog that lay beyond. He ran in a sort of half-crouch, like an ape, and resembled a spider as he scrambled up a steep bank, using his long arms and powerful, tapering fingers to seize hanging branches and propel himself to the top.

The deep forests of the kingdom of Alt Clut were his territory. His refuge. Whenever danger threatened, he would vanish into their depths, where only the bravest dared seek him out.

Gwrgi Wyllt, the Wild Man-Dog, was a dark legend among the local tribes. A lone hunter, a shadow, a monster in human form. At night he would come greedily prowling from his bogs and marshes and mist-shrouded forests to snatch lambs and chickens, or even young children, and carry them back to his lair. There he would feed, devouring the raw flesh of his wriggling victims, gorging on hot blood, cracking bones in his strong jaws and sucking them dry of marrow.

Such was the legend. There was some truth to it. Gwrgi was fond of human flesh, especially if young and tender. It was hard to get. The children in these parts had learned to be wary of the Man-Dog, and rarely ventured into the woods save in groups or the company of adults.

The noise of the hunt was dwindling slightly. Gwrgi leaned against the withered trunk of an ancient oak to collect his breath. It was a grey morning in late October, the air still and cold, but still the sweat cascaded down his brow. He dashed the worst of it away with the back of his hand.

Getting older, he thought. How old was he? Gwrgi didn't know. He had lived like this since his youth. Since the warriors came to his village and drowned it in blood.

Gwrgi survived the massacre by running away and hiding in a cave. He had cowered in the darkness for hours, like a terrified animal, listening to the thunder of his own heartbeat. When night came, he crept back to the fire-gutted ruins of the village.

The warriors had killed everyone, taken everything of value, and burned what they could not carry. Gwrgi was left with nothing to eat.

After two days the hunger pangs became unbearable. To stave them off, he gnawed one of the maimed corpses of his kin.

How often have I run since? How many times have I been hunted like a wild beast?

Gwrgi slid on his backside down the further side of the bank, scattering loose stones. He jumped across the narrow gulley at the bottom and loped up a shallow incline, through a waist-high sea of undergrowth. Frosted brambles like dead fingers snatched at the filthy woollen smock that was his only garment. In his haste he ignored them, and the stinging pain of the cuts on his naked arms and calves.

He grinned as he ran, exposing an uneven fence of teeth filed to points. Gwrgi deserved to be hunted like a beast, for he was one, as wild and pitiless as any predator in the forest.

Lately he had started to believe in his own legend, and become over-bold. He tried to take a little girl while she was playing in a meadow behind her parents' cottage.

Foolish.

The girl had screamed, and writhed in his grip with surprising strength for one so young. Her father, a shepherd, came rushing out of the cottage, followed by his sons.

Gwrgi had dropped the girl and fled, racing through the woods while the enraged cries of her father and brothers faded behind him. That was not the end of it: the shepherd had gone to his lord, a sub-king of Alt Clut named Meirchion. Meirchion called out his warriors and led them into the woods to put an end to the Man-Dog once and for all.

Now the hunt was nearing its conclusion. Gwrgi reached the edge of a fast-flowing river and slid easily into the shallows, gasping at the icy shock of the freezing water. He let the current take him for a few seconds, towards some swirling rapids marked by a series of shining black rocks, and then jack-knifed, his body darting with smooth, powerful strokes through the boiling white waters to the opposite shore.

He dragged himself out and plunged into the thickest of the woods. His thin mouth twisted in a snarl. Let the hounds try and follow his scent now. They would lose hours picking up his trail again, assuming they ever did, by which time he would be safely hidden inside one of his many bolt-holes.

The winding note of a hunting horn seared through the forest to the west. Panic ignited in his breast. They were already across the river! Or else a separate band of huntsmen had taken a separate route to the first, hoping to pen their quarry.

Gwrgi dropped to a crouch, staring around wildly, frantically searching his memory.

Hide. He had to hide. There was nowhere close by. The cave he was making for still lay some two miles away. He could hear the dogs. Almost smell them. Their infernal baying echoed and re-echoed through the winter forest. They would be on him long before he reached sanctuary.

All he could do was run. Gwrgi broke cover and sped south. He had no destination in mind. All he could do was match his pace against the hounds and offer up prayers to the dimly-remembered God of his youth.

His feet were unshod, their pads hardened by years of making his way barefoot through the world. They leaped and skidded over the ground, at times barely touching it. Sure-footed as any fleeing deer, Gwrgi never stumbled or checked his pace. To do so now might prove fatal.

There was no cave for miles around unknown to him, no potential refuge he had not found and made his own. Or so he thought. He uttered a sharp cry as the ground suddenly gave way under his left foot, and then his right as he tried to leap clear. The forest vanished as Gwrgi plummeted into the darkness beneath the earth.

The fall was long enough for him to turn in the air. He landed on his back with a jarring thump, and lay there for a few seconds, wincing in anticipation of broken bones.

Gwrgi was fortunate. Save a few minor bruises, he was unharmed. His right hand quickly explored the ground under him, and found soft brown soil.

Light poured through the hole he had plunged through, far above. Grey walls rose sheer around him. The cavern was roughly circular, and looked man-made. Some old mine, perhaps? If so, there should be a tunnel leading back to the surface.

The distant barking of hounds jerked Gwrgi out of his shock. He sat up and jerked his head left and right, straining to see through the gloom.

His eyesight, honed from years of moving through darkness, was superb. He spied a deeper shadow in the darkness to his left, and scrambled towards it.

There was a waist-high fissure in the rock, just wide enough for him to squirm through. The prospect of crawling blindly through a restricted passage under hundreds of tons of rock might have appalled another man, but Gwrgi had no fear of confined spaces. He dropped to all fours and crept inside.

The floor was smooth, and the jagged rock of the ceiling scraped against his back. The passage narrowed further until Gwrgi was forced to lie flat on his belly, inching along by force of will and the wiry strength in his arms.

His back was bleeding. The breath was being crushed from his lungs. The musty air threatened to choke him.

"I am not dead," he whispered, "I am alive. I will live. Nothing can kill me. Not steel, nor stone. Not fang, tooth or claw."

The passage started to widen. A hint of fresh air wafted across his face. Gwrgi dragged himself forward until there was enough space to rise to his hands and knees. Still there was no light. He groped through pitch darkness, one hand outstretched before him.

Soon he was able to rise to a standing position. Careful exploration revealed that the ceiling was now little more more than a hand's breadth above his head. The space between his body and the walls was about the same. Gwrgi broke into a jog. With each step he took, the air became fresher.

The passage ended suddenly, opening onto a round chamber, dimly illuminated by pale grey light filtering through another passage immediately to Gwrgi's left. A third lay to his right. The entrance to the latter was dark, and doubtless led further into the bowels of the earth.

Gwrgi thought for a moment. The way to the left would almost certainly take him back to the surface, though God knew where it came out.

Most men have a devil inside them, working at their thoughts, trying to steer them down dark paths. A whole host of devils resided inside Gwrgi. They turned him now, away from the safe course, into the velvet darkness to his right.

This new passage was short, and opened onto the largest cavern yet.

No, Gwrgi corrected himself as he stepped inside, *not a cavern. A temple.*

The temple was a perfect circle, definitely man-made, though he could only guess at the labour required to hack out such a place from solid rock. There were stone tiles on the floor, rough squares of uneven size, painted with mercifully faded images that hurt his eyes to look upon.

Light streamed in from six vents built into the walls. The shafts of light fell upon a man sitting in the exact centre of the chamber. His head was bowed, hidden under a tattered hood made of some coarse black stuff, and his slender body hidden under a robe of the same material.

"You," said Gwrgi, his voice echoing hollowly inside the chamber, "speak."

No reply. Intrigued, he shuffled closer. Some kind of priest, maybe, lost in meditation?

Then he saw the skeletal feet protruding from under the skirts of the robe.

Gwrgi exhaled, and straightened up. There was nothing to fear. The man was quite dead.

He reached out and flicked back the hood. A rotting face gazed sadly back at him, the flesh much decayed but still clinging to a long, narrow skull. Scraps of grey hair lingered on the scalp. The eye-sockets were empty. Sniggering, Gwrgi poked his finger inside one and wiggled it around.

From the looks of it, the man had suffered an exceedingly painful death. Possibly self-inflicted. His bony jaw rested on his knees, which were drawn up under him. A thick leather shawl or belt was wrapped tightly round the back of his neck and under his knees, forcing him to stay in this agonising hunched position forever.

It seemed the priest or hermit, if such he was, had deliberately suffocated himself to death. Gwrgi had encountered hermits before, holy men who took themselves off to live in wild places and commune with God. He had killed one or two, and taken the food and clothing left for them by awestruck local peasants. This one had probably been a worshipper of some long-forgotten pagan god. There were many such gods in Y Hen Ogledd, the Old North, once, before the light of Christ came and burned them out.

Gwrgi squatted on his haunches before the corpse. His fear of the hunt had quite gone. Meirchion's warriors would never find him down here. Let them and their accursed hounds run around in circles until night fell. He was quite safe.

"Why?" he asked, his voice echoing around the chamber, "why did you choose such a death? Did it help you see your gods?"

He laughed. The god of the temple was still here. Gwrgi's sharp eyes had picked out a tiny figure lying among the rubble of a shattered tile at the dead man's feet.

His long fingers seized the figure and held it up to the light. It was a crude bone carving of a man, made of bone, but with the head of a dog.

The dog-head was cast in some kind of shiny metal, untarnished with age. Gwrgi gazed in wonder and a growing sense of excitement at the long snout and rows of serrated teeth.

Gwrgi knew almost nothing of gods, or how his fellow men interpreted them. But he knew something now. He knew he was meant to come here. Some power beyond his little understanding had guided his steps.

The dead man's eyes gazed vacantly at him. Gwrgi lashed out with his left hand and knocked the skull from its shoulders.

"Mine," he taunted as the skull hit the ground and shattered into countless pieces, "your god is mine now."

A deeper truth struck him. Eyes widening, Gwrgi stared down at the object resting in the palm of his hand.

"No," he whispered, "not mine. We are one."

2.

Morgana slept. She lay on a heap of dirty blankets in a wretched tumbledown cottage built into the side of an ancient barrow. The barrow lay inside a marsh, hidden among the haunted, mist-laden woods of the far west of Britannia.

None would disturb her. The previous occupant of the cottage, a half-starved hermit named Blaise, had willingly given up his home to the Seer of Britannia, and become her servant. While she slept, he sat outside the doorway armed with a sling and a pile of stones, ready to chase off wolves and other unwanted intruders.

Free from the cares and restraints of the body, Morgana's mind roamed. She turned her Sight east, to the city of Londinium, and the crowning of the new High King.

Londinium prospered. Just a few years previously, the capital had been virtually abandoned and left to rot, the remainder of her populace huddled inside the western quarter. Now, thanks to the efforts of Ambrosius Aurelianus, the late Vicarius and Dux Bellorum, it had flowered again. Overseas trade had resumed, the streets thronged, and people were flooding back in from the countryside, looking to take advantage of the city's newfound wealth.

Morgana watched the High King, a slender young man with hair the colour of burnished gold, riding through the crowded streets towards the praetorium at the head of his bodyguard. His men looked magnificent in their shining mail and blood-red cloaks, the tips of their lances dripping with bunches of spring flowers, but even they paled next to the royal splendour of their master.

The king rode a high-stepping grey mare, no more than four winters old, sleek muscles rippling under her smooth skin, a tubular gold bit in her mouth. Her rider was loaded down with finery. He held a long spear tipped with silver in his right hand, and a gold-chased shield with an ivory rim strapped to his left arm. A gold-hilted sword in a scabbard of red velvet hung from his thigh. He wore a long purple cloak, a symbol of supreme authority derived from the Romans. On his brow rested the crown, a laurel wreath forged in gold.

The people loved him, and the city rang to the sound of his name.

"Constantine! Constantine!"

Morgana twitched in her sleep. Constantine, eldest son of Cadeyrn, late King of the Durotriges.

Cadeyrn had been murdered by the followers of Hengist during the massacre remembered as the Treachery of the Long Knives. An ineffective and grotesquely fat man, unable to keep the peace in his own war-band or defend his coasts against Saxon pirates. His impotent reputation was only enforced by the sight of him being carried about in a chair by a team of slaves.

His son was a much more forceful character. As soon as he came of age, Constantine had taken his murdered father's place on the Council of Britannia, and immediately set about expanding the borders of his kingdom.

After the torpor of the previous reign, Constantine's furious energy caught all by surprise. He whipped his recalcitrant warriors to heel, drove off the pirates threatening his lands, reduced rival kings to sullen obedience. Using a potent mixture of threats, bribes and promises, he bought the votes of many of his fellow councillors: enough to secure his election as High King.

It pained Morgana to look at him. Strong, powerful and ruthless, an ideal ruler in many ways, he was the wrong choice.

Constantine should not be king, she thought, *the Council allowed themselves to be bullied...the land will not flourish under*

*him. He will not protect us from our
enemies.*

Her gaze moved on, sweeping down the
line of red-cloaked guards and the splendid
retinues of the kings, lords and magistrates
of Britannia that followed in their wake. The
parade seemed endless, a tide of banners and
horsemen, marching columns of infantry,
thumping drums and squealing bugles,
flowing all the way back to the western gate.

The rear of the procession – the position of
honour or disgrace, depending how you
looked at it – was brought up by a company
of fifty horsemen. They looked drab beside
the retinues of the kings, and rode in
disciplined silence with little fanfare or
display.

Their standard bearer carried a dragon
banner. The long cloth tube attached to the
back of the gaping dragon's head rippled
feebly in the slight wind. In front rode the
officer of the company. He wore a plain
russet cloak, and his face was almost
completely hidden behind a cavalry helmet
with a nose-guard and long cheek-pieces.

*Artorius. The rightful High King. The
Dragon of Britannia. He was destined to
follow Ambrosius, to take the crown that the
last of the Romans refused to wear.*

He also refused his duty.

Morgana shuddered. Once a nun, she had deserted her convent to serve the ancient spirits of the land, the small gods of forests and rivers, worshipped in Britannia for centuries before the coming of Christ.

Little gods now, mere breaths on the wind, their names all but forgotten: Belenos and Agroná; Andrasta the Invincible One, Goddess of War; Brigantia and Nemetona. Many others. Morgana was drawn to their ancient places of worship, the sacred groves deep in the forests, ruined and ivy-grown temples, time-weathered stone circles. They were neglected now, shunned by all right-thinking Christian folk and visited by none save Morgana and a few like her.

Her Sight was a gift from the old gods, bestowed in exchange for her service. It enabled her to see the world in spite of her useless eyes, ruined by a childhood illness. And more. Morgana had learned to control her dreams, to direct her Sight to anywhere in the land, and to interpret the confusing images of prophecy.

Now she focused on Artorius. There was nothing grand or ostentatious about him. If he harboured any pretensions to kingship, he kept them well-hidden behind the plain garb of a soldier.

He had allowed the greatest prize to slip from his hands. When Constantine was elected High King, Artorius freely surrendered to him all the fortresses in the western part of Dumnonia, including Ambrosius' old headquarters at Mons Ambrius. Thus Constantine became ruler of the largest kingdom in Britannia.

Artorius had moved west, to set up a new court at Caerleon in Gwent. The King of Gwent, Caradog Freichfras, was a friend, and permitted him to settle in the old hill-fort beside the Roman town.

In gratitude Constantine allowed Artorius to retain his rank of Magister Militum, and keep three hundred cavalry for his own retinue. The remainder of the comitatenses, the British field-army, was taken by the High King to fill the garrisons of his newly acquired forts.

Morgana was able to see much in her dreams, but never into the hearts of men. She could not understand why Artorius had freely surrendered the power that was his for the taking, and taken himself off into a form of semi-retirement. He was meant to succeed Ambrosius as the defender and ruler of Britannia, but had instead chosen exile.

She watched him lead his men at a sedate trot down the street leading to the praetorium, past a semi-ruined Roman temple and complex of public baths. The latter were also fallen into ruin, but recent attempts had been made to patch them up with plaster and thatch.

Immediately behind Artorius rode two of his closest companions, red-headed Cei and darkly handsome Bedwyr. Morgana concentrated on their voices.

"...not safe..." she overheard Cei say, "we are riding into a trap."

"Tut, man," Bedwyr replied scornfully, "you think Constantine means to cut our throats? What for? He owes Artorius his throne."

Cei stabbed a finger at his childhood friend. "Precisely. He knows Artorius could have challenged him, and still retains the loyalty of the army. Who led the soldiers when Ambrosius was too ill to fight? It wasn't Constantine. Our new king likes to pose as a great warrior, just because he chased a few sea-wolves off his land and burned their ships. I tell you, he knows nothing of war."

Bedwyr shrugged. "That is hardly his fault. He is still young, and can learn. Only a fool would set aside Artorius. From what I have seen of Constantine, he is no fool."

Cei snorted in derision, but his response was cut off by Artorius.

"What a poor couple of spies you two would make," he said without turning his head, "Cei, you whisper with the subtlety of a cow in season, calling for the bull. Keep your tongue behind the wall of your teeth, before it leads you into trouble."

Cei grumbled a little – his words escaped Morgana, though she could guess at them – but he and Bedwyr knew better than to defy their chief. Artorius kept a tight rein on his followers, even those he counted as friends.

Morgana watched the parade move on to the praetorium, the old Roman governor's palace, where the High King would be crowned.

The palace was a suitably imposing building, constructed on a steeply sloping hillside above the Tamesas. To the north of the central garden court was a massive hall, with another of almost equal size adjoining it to the east. The halls and surrounding terraces were made of brick, with impressive ragstone foundations, and had tiled roofs. Much of the smaller east and south wings were taken up by residential quarters, including a small bath-house, one of the luxuries brought to Britannia by the Romans and still enjoyed by the noble elite.

Constantine and his retinue dismounted before the steps of the palace. They marched in solemn state through the colonnaded gallery leading to the central court, preceded by a troop of grey-robed monks, who made the lofty corridors echo to the sound of their plainchant.

At their head was Patricius, the Bishop of Londinium. He cut almost a splendid figure as the king, scarlet and gold robes billowing around him as he strode purposefully towards the great hall, white beard bristling, silver-topped shepherd's crook gleaming in his hand.

The interior of the hall was huge, similar to the nave of a cathedral, its arched roof supported by twin rows of marble pillars. These formed a central gallery ending at a dais, specially constructed for the ceremony, upon which rested the throne. This was a high-backed chair made of solid oak, once occupied by the late and unlamented Vortigern.

Hundreds of miles to the west, Morgana seethed with impotent fury. The powers bestowed on her by the gods were strictly limited. She could see and hear events, but do nothing to influence them.

Let me strike down that old fool, she begged silently, tortured by the sight of Dubricius leading the assembly in prayer as Constantine slowly climbed the steps to the throne, *let me stop his heart with a snap of my fingers. Spirits of old, the Sight is not enough!*

Constantine turned and lowered his rump onto the throne. He sat, silver-tipped spear in one hand and sword in the other, his face pale as death as the liturgy washed over him.

Morgana could have laughed. The elaborate ceremony of the coronation was a farce, its solemn rites and procedures invented by Dubricius mere weeks beforehand. When Vortigern took the crown, there was little in the way of ceremony. His troops had marched into Londinium and threatened a bloodbath if the Council refused to acknowledge him as High King. An enormous feast followed, and Vortigern had to be carried to bed, swine-drunk, his crown askew and royal robes stained with vomit.

There was little chance of Constantine making such an exhibition of himself. He was far too self-possessed, acutely aware of his royal dignity. After the chanting had died away he rose to his feet, tall and proud and handsome in a cold sort of way, his shining golden crown and carefully groomed and powdered blonde hair lending him the appearance of an angel.

Silence fell over the hall. The kings of Britannia filled the front rank of the assembly, lesser men crowded behind them. Artorius, who held no lands and no title beyond his military rank, stood at the very rear alongside Cei and Bedwyr, almost in the doorway.

Dubricius rapped his staff against the floor. "Constantine the First, High King of Britannia," he boomed, "will you hold and guard by all proper means the sacred faith as handed down to Christian men of the true faith, abjuring all heresy?"

Constantine was heard to clear his throat before replying. "I will," he cried in a high, nervous tone.

"Will you be the faithful shield and protector of Holy Church and her servants?"

"I will."

"Will you uphold and recover those rights and territories of the Kingdom of Britannia that have been unlawfully usurped and stolen by the heathen men, the enemies of Christ?"

"I will."

"Will you protect the poor, the fatherless and the widowed?"

"I will."

"Will you pay due submission to the Roman Pontiff and the Holy Roman Church?"

"I will…"

Morgana groaned, and allowed the vision to slip away. She could watch no more.

Her eyes fluttered open. The splendour of the great hall in Londinium was gone, replaced by the musty thatch and mud walls of the hermit's miserable little cottage.

Blaise heard her groan as she woke and hurried inside, the tattered fringe of his robe flapping against his bare calves. .

He was a slack-witted creature, too stupid to realise that he had given his dwelling over to an apostate. He seemed to think that Morgana's powers derived from Christ. So had the abbess at the convent, believing them a consequence of the blessing given to Morgana as a child by the holy Germanus, Bishop of Auxerre.

"Water," she croaked, holding out her hand, "my throat is dry."

He nodded and ran outside to fetch water from the stream running through a hollow behind the cottage. It was fresh, and untainted by the marsh.

While he was gone, Morgana sat on the edge of the bed and concentrated on clearing her head. The images she had seen gently faded away, along with the voices of the gods, until nothing remained but a vague murmur on the edge of consciousness.

Morgana waited patiently for guidance. Slowly, it came to her.

Constantine could not be permitted to reign for long. He would bring nothing but ruin and death to Britannia. Under him, the land would fail, and its enemies gather strength.

He had no enemies among the Britons, or at least none with the power to unseat him. Morgana briefly considered seeking out Artorius and pleading with him to lead a rebellion against the High King.

No. My brother will not be persuaded into treason. If he will not embrace his destiny, he must be driven to it.

The duty fell to Morgana. Like her father before her, she was the only one who could save Britannia.

Blaise returned to find her weeping.

"My friend," she said, knowing he would not understand or even remember, "to save our country, it seems I must first betray it."

3.

Seven days of feasting followed the coronation of the High King. Artorius and his followers were keen to depart, but Constantine wouldn't hear of it.

"You can't vanish into the west just yet," he said, smiling, "men must see the love and friendship that exists between us."

His smile had no real warmth to it, and his eyes were hostile as they fixed on Artorius, weighing him up.

"As you wish, lord king," replied Artorius, hiding his frustration.

Artorius loathed taking orders from this chilly upstart, several years his junior. He had seldom deferred to the authority of anyone save Ambrosius, and already chafed under the new regime.

I only have myself to blame, he thought as Constantine and his entourage left him, heading towards the palace gardens.

To avoid civil war in the land, and shouldering a burden he was not ready or willing to bear, Artorius had allowed Constantine to take the crown. His friends warned him he was making a mistake. Even his favourite concubine, Ganhumara, gave him the benefit of her opinion. Artorius would not listen. He was a mere soldier, so he liked to claim, who knew little and cared less of the business of government.

Secretly, he was frightened of the responsibility. Once, when he was younger, he had craved a kingdom of his own, but Ambrosius refused his demands.

"No lands," his adoptive father had said, "yours will be a roving commission, and I don't want you tied down to one part of the country."

The life of a captain of horse, the Magister Equitum, suited Artorius perfectly. During the last years of his adoptive father's rule he had ridden up and down the country at the head of his buccelari, fighting invading Picts and Saxons. His martial existence gave him little time to learn how to rule men as well as kill them.

"All I want," he said to his friends as they played at dice together on the seventh morning after the coronation, "is to be allowed to continue soldiering. Is it not the best life a man could wish for?"

"Young men, possibly," said Cei in his usual grumbling, sullen tone, "and we are still young enough. But age will creep up on us. I do not intend to be dragging my old bones from one end of the land to the other when I am fifty."

"You won't reach thirty, the way you stuff and swill," remarked Bedwyr, who was fastidious in his diet, "one fine evening you will burst and shower us all in gore."

"I'm not cleaning up the mess," said Gwalchmei, "the dogs can lick up Cei's blood, assuming it doesn't poison them."

"Turd," Cei snarled, snatching up one of the dice and throwing it at him. Gwalchmei laughed as he ducked. The exchange of insults had caused no offence. They were all used to Cei's moods, and his sharp tongue.

Artorius paid little heed to their good-natured bickering. His thoughts were turned inward, contemplating a range of possible futures. None of them were very bright. Constantine was a difficult man to love, and would not tolerate any potential rivals. He had shown that already by the ruthless way he crushed his enemies in Dumnonia.

I will be allowed to live, for now, because I am useful. Once my usefulness is expended...what will it be? A knife in the back, one dark night? Poison in my drink?

Artorius grimaced. That was how Ambrosius died, choking to death after some wretch had tampered with his wine. The culprit was still unknown, though many suspected Pascent, third and only surviving son of old King Vortigern.

Pascent had moved quickly to align himself with the new regime. He already stood high in Constantine's favour. Artorius found this this suspicious, and often wondered if he and Constantine had conspired to murder his father.

"The truth will never be known," he muttered under his breath. Gwalchmei overheard him.

"What's this, lord?" he asked lightly, "you are not yourself tonight."

"He's missing his woman," jeered Cei, "the fair Ganhumara, with the raven-black hair. Not missing her bairns, though, I'll wager. Squealing, wriggling little brats, making the hall at Caerleon foul with their noise and dung."

He wagged a finger at his comrades. "I tell you," he said solemnly, "boys are best left with their mothers until they are old enough to hold a spear. Before that, they are mere spawn. Mindless, stinking little creatures."

"Thank you, Cei," said Artorius, "but my sons show much promise. When I last saw Medraut, I offered him my sword-hilt. He reached his hand up out of the cot and grasped it."

"He will make a fine warrior," he added cheerfully, "and so will Llacheu."

"What of your eldest, Cydfan?" Bedwyr asked. With the exception of their chief, they were all married men. Artorius preferred to dally with his stable of concubines, but was expected to make a wife of his favourite.

Unlike the other girls, Ganhumara had borne him sons. Three healthy bastard boys. Had Artorius chosen a different path, they might have been heirs to his kingdom.

Artorius frowned. "Cydfan may be for the church, sadly," he replied, "Ganhumara allowed the priests to get to him. He's only three, toddling around on fat legs, but he already speaks more Latin than his father. I tried to put a wooden gladius in his hand. He wouldn't take it. Prefers to carry a little crucifix. A son of mine, aping priests!"

They laughed, and Cei yelled at the slave waiting by the door to fetch some wine. It was still early, but there was little else to do save drink, gamble and argue until sundown, when Constantine would stage the seventh – and hopefully last – of his ceremonial feasts.

Come the evening, the four men stumbled down the maze of corridors leading to the great hall. The rest of Artorius' followers were quartered in the barracks outside the palace. Constantine had insisted on this, claiming there was no room to house them inside, a move that had done nothing to quell Cei's fears of treachery.

They reached the garden court, which was open to the elements and dominated by an elongated central pool, enclosed in concrete.

To the north and south were smaller pools inside semicircular recesses with domed roofs. Inside each were alcoves containing statues of Jupiter and Venus: ancient Roman gods, worshipped by no-one now and only kept for their decorative value.

The court was full of people, soldiers and courtiers for the most part, milling to and fro and speaking in hushed tones. Despite the wine sloshing around inside him, Artorius detected the excitement in the air.

"Something's happening," he said thickly, "look, the doors to the hall are closed."

He nodded at the great hall, the towering oak-panelled doors of which were firmly shut, guarded by a troop of red-cloaked spearmen.

A huddled group of courtiers heard his voice, and turned to stare at him. Silence fell over the court as more eyes fell on Artorius. They were lesser lights, these men, clerks and minor freeman officials and the like. The kings and great lords would be gathered inside the hall.

While I am excluded from their august company.

"Well?" he said fiercely, "what are you all gaping at? Let me pass."

He and his friends marched towards the doors. Cei glared belligerently at the people in their way, who fell back hurriedly, forming a lane through which Artorius marched with slightly drunken arrogance, eyes fixed on the captain of the guard.

"General Artorius," said the captain, bowing his head, "the High King was about to send for you."

"Was he, now?" Artorius replied, "then open the doors and get out of my way."

The captain nodded and signalled at his men, two of whom put their shoulders to the great doors. They were unbarred and slid inward smoothly, filling the shadowy interior of the hall with light.

Artorius folded his cloak over his left arm and marched inside, careful to hold himself straight and betray no hint of the effect of a day's drinking.

The babble of voices inside the hall died away. As he suspected, the vast chamber was filled with the great men of Britannia, while the greatest sat on his throne at the far end in imperial state, robed in purple, gold wreath flashing on his brow.

Artorius recognised most of the faces, but not all. Three strangers stood below the royal dais, soldiers from the look of them, middle-aged, neatly bearded and unsmiling. Artorius noted the quality of their glistening shirts of scale mail, and the gold-hilted swords in leather scabbards at their hips.

"Artorius," said Constantine, his voice echoing in the vaulted ceiling, "your timing is commendable These men are envoys from Rigotomos, King of Amorica."

The bearded faces lost something of their taut, suspicious look when his name was announced. All three of the envoys bowed in unison.

"Lord," said the one in the middle, who appeared to be the eldest, "your fame has travelled across the Narrow Sea. It is an honour to meet you."

Artorius hiccoughed, and quickly smothered it. "Honour is mine," he replied lamely, "lord king, why are these men here?"

Constantine smiled thinly, and shifted position, folding one elegant, well-turned leg over the other and resting his chin on his hand.

"The plain-speaking military man," he drawled, "and none the worse for that. Let us speak plain, then. Rigotomos has sent these men to ask for our aid in fighting the Visigoths in Gaul. Under their chief, Euric, these pests have overrun much of the province and are threatening the borders of Amorica."

Artorius knew most of this already. The Visigoths were perhaps the largest of the vigorous Germanic tribes descending to feast on the remnants of the Western Empire. Euric was a particularly ruthless and aggressive prince of their race. Having murdered his predecessor, Theoderic, he had set about expanding his power from the lost Roman province of Hispania into Gaul.

"If Rigotomos has sent these men to ask us for soldiers," Artorius said bluntly, "then he asks in vain. We have barely enough men to defend our own territory. No more sons of Britannia should have to die on foreign soil, attempting to prop up a diseased and dying state."

"Well said!" exclaimed Cei. There were a few shouts of approval from the assembled nobles. Constantine stilled them with a glance.

"You forget, Artorius, who rules Britannia," he said in a soft tone, smooth and deadly as steel, "I am king. I decide our policy."

Artorius cursed. The wine had got hold of his tongue. "Of course, sire," he mumbled, looking down, "I have not forgotten it."

Mollified, Constantine waved languidly at the envoys. "Repeat the details of your message, for the benefit of General Artorius," he ordered.

The eldest spokesman cleared his throat. "My master recently received a message from Rome," he began, "the Western

Emperor Anthemius offered to join his forces with ours against the Visigoths. The remaining Roman territories north of the Liger are under threat from these barbarians, and cannot hope to resist them alone. Our united armies would be able to meet the Visigoths in the field and drive them like sheep, all the way back to Hispania. Thus spake Caesar."

"Then Caesar is an optimist," said Cei, "the Visigoths are all over Gaul like flies on a carcase. I thought Anthemius was occupied with fighting his own son-in-law?"

"Quiet," Artorius snapped, though Cei had a point. The Emperor's throne was shaky, and all knew the real power lay with his Magister Militum, Ricimer, who had married his daughter. Ricimer had already set up and disposed of two puppet Emperors, and there were rumours he was already dissatisfied with the third.

The envoy was clearly a practised diplomat, and ignored the interruption. "King Rigotomos has mustered an army of five thousand men," he went on, "their ranks bolstered by the recent exiles from Britannia."

He spread his hands. "My lords," he said imploringly, looking around at the assembly, "hundreds of your fellow countrymen will serve in this campaign. Will you not help them? Will you stay at home and do nothing, while they risk their lives fighting under the banner of Christ to drive out the Arian threat?"

Many of the nobles looked ashamed, and would not meet his eye. Constantine slapped the arm of his throne.

"We will send aid," he announced confidently, "I have decided it. A thousand men, horse and foot, will sail from Londinium before the month is out."

It was warm inside the hall from so many close-packed bodies, yet Artorius felt a sudden chill steal over him. "Where will you find them in so short a time, lord king?" he asked, though he could guess.

"From you, General Artorius," replied Constantine with a triumphant smile, "you shall hold the title of Dux Bellorum, as your father did before you, and lead our men to victory in Gaul."

4.

The onset of summer brought with it oppressively warm weather, and Llacheu's first teeth. His lower gums were sore and red for days, which meant sleepless nights for himself and most of the folk in Caerleon.

His mother, Ganhumara, did her best to alleviate the boy's discomfort, rubbing ointment on his gums and giving him a teething ring made of bone, cooled in water before gently inserted into his mouth. She sat up with him all night in her bedchamber, gently rocking the tiny body in her arms and singing childish lullabies.

Ganhumara liked to keep her babies close. Cydfan, the eldest, slept in her bed, while Medraut and Llacheu each had separate cots nearby. It was a way of alleviating her loneliness.

One bright, clear-skied morning, she sat by the window of her chamber with Llacheu nestled on her lap, gazing out at the landscape. From here, she had a good view of the town of Caerleon and the soft green hills lying south-east of the ancient hill-fort her lover had chosen to make his new home. Between the town and the countryside lay the broad ribbon of the Afon Wysg, its glittering blue waters flowing down from the north towards the sea.

The town was largely deserted and falling to pieces, having been abandoned by the Romans sometime in her great-grandfather's day. It was dominated by the huge, decaying fortress of Isca Augusta, built as a permanent fortified camp for one of their legions.

Ganhumara found something awesome and terrifying about the deserted fort. Big enough to house over three thousand soldiers, it was like a self-contained town, with all manner of buildings inside its crumbling stone walls: a hospital, bathhouses, barrack blocks, a fine house for the legate, workshops, granaries, even a small amphitheatre, where men and beasts had once fought each other to the death for the amusement of the soldiers.

All empty now, peopled by nothing save the faint ghosts of the imperial past. Most of the buildings were falling into ruin, used by local peasants as a source of dressed stone. Artorius' workmen had taken some of the of masonry from the outer walls to buttress the ramparts of his new home.

Isca was far too big to defend, which was why Artorius had chosen to occupy the hill-fort instead. His three hundred cavalry, even with their families and slaves, amounted to less than a thousand souls. Nowhere near enough to fill the town.

"What were they like," whispered Ganhumara, planting a soft kiss on Llacheu's head, "the people who dwelled in that great stone palace? Were they cruel, do you think? They must have been, to force men to kill each other for entertainment. Lions and bears, too, and other beasts."

She recalled even darker stories of the horrors once practised at Caerleon. There was a church in the middle of the town, relatively new – that is to say, merely a century old – containing a shrine to two Christian martyrs, Saint Julius and Saint Aaron. In the days when the Empire was still officially pagan, these two unfortunate men had been martyred there.

"Put to death," she breathed, staring at the distant marketplace, where the terrible event was supposed to have occurred, "made to suffer all kinds of horrible tortures, before the headsman put an end to their sufferings."

Ganhumara was a devout woman. "Not once did either of the saints renounce Christ. No matter what the Romans did to them. They called on the Lord, and died with courage and dignity."

She gently lowered her baby to the floor. He crawled away to his twin, Medraut, who was playing with a couple of wooden soldiers. Llacheu snatched one from his plump hand, and excited screams filled the room as Medraut tried to claw it back.

The soldiers were barely recognisable as such, being roughly hacked from a lump of timber by one with no talent for carving, but Ganhumara regarded them as precious. Artorius had made them with his own hands, and the effort was worth more than the execution: a rare demonstration of love for his sons.

"God grant he returns before the autumn," she said, returning to her vigil of the window, "safe and hale, ready to make me his wife."

She had great hopes of marrying Artorius. As the only one of his five concubines to bear him sons, her chances were high. She enjoyed the privileges of sharing his bed and sitting by his side at meals in the feasting hall, while her rivals were kept out of sight, given lodgings in some of the less decayed buildings in the town.

Of her rivals, Ganhumara only feared one. This was Lisanor, a slender, whey-faced redhead who had borne Artorius a stillborn daughter. Lisanor was a few years older than Ganhumara, and fast dropping out of favour. Artorius rarely visited her now.

She smiled, and ran a hand through her lustrous black hair. The other girls were silly, unintelligent creatures, incapable of holding his interest for long.

"He will choose me," she said confidently, "he must, and soon."

As a Christian, it was unseemly for Artorius to remain unmarried for much longer, much less keep a stable of glorified whores. His habit of fathering bastards was frowned upon by the priest of the shrine, not that Artorius cared for the old man's opinion. He cared little for what anyone thought.

Ganhumara didn't love him, but her feelings were unimportant. Born the daughter of slaves in a noble household near Glevum, she had caught Artorius' eye while serving him wine at table in the palace of Eidol Cadarn, his friend and ally.

"That one with the black hair," she overheard him saying to Eidol, "I want her. Give her to me."

"Maybe I want her for myself," the other man said, "she's a pretty enough thing, under the grime. You have a good eye."

Artorius chuckled. "I know your wife, Eidol. She would cut your balls off if you so much as looked at a slave-girl. Come, name your price."

"Oh, very well. You can have the girl in exchange for that chestnut brown mare of yours. What is she, three or four winters old? A fine animal."

"And, unlike the girl, one you can ride in safety," Artorius quipped.

The bargain was made, and Ganhumara taken to Caerleon to serve as Artorius' new bedmate. She was no virgin, which was just as well, though he was never cruel, nor insisted on his pleasure. Even so, Ganhumara knew what was required of her. In return she was given fine clothes and jewellery, a roof over her head, and the promise of being married off to one of his warriors when he tired of her.

Her fertility had changed all that. Cydfan, Llacheu and Medraut might be bastards, but they were strong. There was no reason why Ganhumara might not bear more. At just seventeen, she was young yet, and prepared to endure further agonies of childbirth in order to secure her place as Artorius' wife.

She sighed. A secure life, but a dull one, especially when the men were away at war. There was no-one to talk to. The wives of Artorius' warriors shunned her company, regarding her as a jumped-up whore, and the female slaves were excessively timid in her presence. She was kind to them, but still they cringed, as though expecting a whipping at any moment. Lisanor, she knew, had been over-liberal with the whip in the days when she basked in Artorius'

45

favour. The slaves now distrusted all his concubines on principle.

A sudden shriek made Ganhumara wince. Ever the peacemaker, Cydfan had tried to intervene in the brawl between his brothers, and taken a bang on the head for his pains. The crude swords held by the wooden soldiers were blunt, but still Medraut hit him hard enough to draw blood.

"Enough," she snapped, striding across the softly carpeted room to grab Medraut's wrist, "you three are always fighting. Can you not love each other a little? You will have need of each other when you are grown."

Their nurse, Gwawr, a skinny young woman with mouse-brown hair, appeared in the doorway. Beyond lay the shadowy vastness of the hall, dark and silent these days, but a place of light and warmth and noise when the men were home.

"I heard Cydfan scream, lady," she said, avoiding Ganhumara's eye, "and thought you might need me."

"I do," replied Ganhumara, scooping Cydfan up in her arms, "wash the cut on his scalp, will you, and take him for a walk outside. He can't be around his brothers at the moment."

Cydfan obediently offered his hand to Gwawr and allowed himself to be led away.

He was a meek, biddable child, nothing like his father in that regard, though they shared the same fair hair and ruddy colouring.

She would never say as much to Artorius, but Ganhumara secretly liked the idea of having at least one son destined for scholarship rather than the bloodstained life of a warrior. To that end, she had asked the priest in Caerleon to teach Cydfan his letters, and fill his head with the glory and mystery of the gospels.

With Cydfan gone, Ganhumara was able to bring Llacheu and Medraut under a semblance of control. They were identical twins, just over a year old, and had inherited her dark looks and black hair. Lively and aggressive, they promised to be the opposite of Cydfan. Nothing like their sire to look at, but his mirror image in character.

When they were calm again, she left them at play and ventured into the hall. There was something oppressive about the huge space, with its rows of empty chairs and empty tables, and nothing but cold ashes in the central hearth.

Ganhumara's heart leaped as she heard a sudden noise above her, in the shadows of the rafters. She looked up, one hand to her breast, and sighed with relief when a sparrow flew out of the darkness and vanished through the open door.

From outside there came the sound of spears thudding against shields. Not all the men were gone. Artorius had left a small garrison to guard the fort in his absence. Most were young men, not yet blooded in war, with a handful of grey-headed veterans to keep them in line.

"Get your shield up quicker, Pwyll, unless you want my spear in your throat! Faster – God help us, are you asleep? Move your feet! Is that another hit to me, then? You will be a patchwork of bruises tonight, my friend."

Ganhumara blushed. The voice was familiar, as was its tone of sneering mockery. They belonged to a youth named Melwas.

Melwas. The mere thought of his name brought the blood rushing to her face.

He would be sparring in the yard outside the hall, showing off in front of the other young warriors. None of them were as lightning-quick as he with sword and spear, though there was always some fool willing to take him on.

Ganhumara soft-footed to the doorway and peered outside. She couldn't afford to be seen gawping at Melwas. Tongues would wag, and some of the gossip might eventually reach Artorius.

She was willing to take the risk. Melwas was the most beautiful young man she had ever seen, almost girlishly pretty with his red lips, startling blue eyes and long, soft auburn hair. He had only been in Caerleon for a few days, having come alone to to offer his spear to the depleted garrison.

Currently his hair was soaked in sweat, as were the glistening muscles of his upper body. He was stripped to the waist, the better to show off his perfect sinews and flat stomach, long ash spear whirling and stabbing in his right hand, almost too fast for the eye to see.

His unfortunate opponent, Pwyll, was struggling. Heavier-built than Melwas, with a head of curling brown hair, his neck, chest and shoulders were spotted with livid purple bruises. Had Melwas' practise spear been tipped with sharp iron instead of blunted, he would be on the floor already, his life's blood gushing into the earth from a dozen wounds.

Both fighters carried large round shields strapped to their upper left arms. Pwyll was slow at using his, and Melwas exploited the weakness mercilessly, jabbing his spear over and under the rim, leaving a fresh mark with every thrust.

"You're a brave lad, Pwyll," laughed Melwas, "even if you can't fight properly."

Pwyll's bracae were drenched in sweat, his breath coming in labouring gasps. Perspiration dripped over his brow, blinding him. While he swallowed and fought for air, Melwas spun in a circle, holding his spear and shield aloft, soaking in the ironic cheers of the little group of warriors watching the combat.

"Never gloat over a wounded foe," growled the eldest of them, a battered veteran with a scar where his left eye used to be, "it's dangerous and dishonourable. Put him down first, make sure he isn't going to get up again, and then boast as much as you like."

Melwas laughed again – his laugh rang like a bell in Ganhumara's ears – and turned gracefully to finish off his opponent.

There was no need. Pwyll was already slumped to his knees, breath whistling in his throat. Blood dribbled from his nose and ears. He would have collapsed, but two of the warriors rushed forward to lift him up by his arms and drag him away for treatment.

"I dedicate my victory, and all my victories to come," declared Melwas, standing on his toes and pointing his spear at the hall, in the direction of Ganhumara's bedchamber, "to the fair Ganhumara, lady of Caerleon!"

Ganhumara darted away from the door and

pressed her back against the wall, heart fluttering against her ribs.

"No, please," she moaned, trying to will away her emotions.

She was in love. And it terrified her.

5.

The Narrow Sea

"Anthemius is an Emperor," said Cei, "you can't trust emperors. All they do is murder each other and marry their sisters."

His face had an unhealthy greenish tinge as he clung to the rail of the foredeck. Formidable on land, Cei was a hopeless sailor, and since the fleet put out from Londinium had divided his time between complaining and retching up his breakfast.

He bent double as a fresh spasm coursed through him. "You can't trust kings either," he moaned when it had passed, wiping his mouth, "all crowned heads are liars. Constantine has deliberately sent us on a fool's errand. He wants us out of the way. No, more than that – he wants us dead."

Artorius was only half-listening. The Dux Bellorum gazed south, legs braced against the roll of the ship, shading his eyes under his gauntleted hand as he tried to catch a first glimpse of Amorica.

He had never been at sea before, and was grateful to discover the sickness didn't affect him. The same could not be said for a good number of his warriors, including Cei and Bedwyr. Only his foolish, stiff-necked pride was holding Cei upright, while Bedwyr had long since retired below, where he could nurse his groaning belly in peace.

"A fine day," he remarked, glancing up at the wind billowing the red and white striped foresail, "we're making good speed."

Artorius' flagship cut through the water like a shark, easily outstripping her fellows. She was, fittingly, the finest vessel in the fleet, a single-deck war galley left to rot in the harbour when the Romans left Britannia. Constantine had ordered her refitted. Britannia no longer had a standing fleet, but within weeks Constantine had managed to scrape together over thirty galleys, merchant vessels and longboats. Enough to carry the army, including horses and fodder and provisions, over the Narrow Sea to Amorica.

Artorius turned to look at Cei, who was a thoroughly wretched sight, feeble, grey-faced and sweating, all his high colour drained away.

"God help us if the Visigoth fleet finds us," said Artorius, "not one man in three can keep his food down, or raise a hand in his own defence."

"Lost at sea," Cei panted, "or slaughtered on land, what difference does it make?"

He snatched at Artorius' cloak. "Please, lord," he said in a whining tone that was most unlike him, "give the order to turn about, and sail home. Nothing good can come from this hopeless sortie."

Artorius swung around. "You are too pessimistic, Cei," he said, "Rigotomos is a faithful ally to Britannia. His father took in many of our people when they fled across the sea from the wrath of the Saxons. Constantine could hardly ignore his plea."

"Horse dung," snarled Cei, "you said it yourself, we are not obliged to send the flower of our menfolk to die in the defence of a foreign kingdom. At best, we could have maybe offered him a few auxiliaries to help defend his borders. But a thousand men? I tell you, it is sheer folly."

Artorius said nothing. Arguing with Cei was a futile pastime, and he privately had some sympathy with his views.

What are Constantine's true motives? he wondered, while the ship surged under him, *does he want me to meet with death, or merely fail? To be defeated, and crawl back home with a handful of survivors?*

Such a defeat would damage, if not ruin, Artorius' hard-won military reputation. Constantine would be justified in stripping him of his title and casting him into permanent disgrace and exile. It was one way, though an extreme one, of disposing of a potential rival.

Artorius had done all he could to demonstrate his loyalty to the young king. He should have listened to his doubts, and realised that Constantine regarded him with suspicion: as another Ricimer, far too popular with the soldiers, and in a position to make and break kings as he pleased.

Still, if his envoys spoke the truth, Rigotomos had assembled a considerable army. Six thousand men, combined with the Roman forces of Anthemius, should be enough to match anything the Visigoths brought to the field.

Rigotomos' envoys were also aboard the flagship. Before the fleet sailed, they had informed Artorius that their king had already marched into Gaul, and was busy destroying the Visigoth settlements that had spread along the Liger. Like their kin, the Saxons, it seemed Euric's people were intent on making the land their own after driving out the natives.

"I advise you to land here, lord," said the senior envoy, whose name was Valerian, pointing at a map showing the coastline of Amorica, "and march inland to join with our king's forces as they move into Visigoth territory."

Artorius looked where he pointed, a section of the western coast near the city of Portus Namnetum. To reach it meant sailing around the western tip of Amorica and marching deep into central Gaul.

"If you think it best," he said, scratching his jaw, "your king means to goad the Visigoths to battle by invading their territory, then?"

"Just so," nodded Valerian, "Euric has seized the town of Vicus Dolensis" – here his hand traced a line east of Portus Namnetum – and made it his headquarters. Once my lord has joined up with your troops and those of Anthemius, we shall march together on Euric and challenge his entire host to battle. The favour of Christ, allied to the strong right arm of our warrior king, shall give us the victory!"

Artorius looked sideways at the envoy, whose voice was trembling with fervour. He and his colleagues always spoke of Rigotomos with adoration.

"A brave strategy," said Artorius, "how large is the Arian host, and how many troops will Anthemius bring?"

Valerian beamed at him. "Our scouts report some twelve thousand of the enemy gathered at Vicus Dolensis. The strength of the Romans is so far unknown, but Anthemius will surely bring a force equal to ours, if not greater."

"And where is the Emperor?" asked Artorius, who disliked these vague answers.

"At Arelate, the last I knew," Valerian replied, gesturing at a town disturbingly far to the south, "but that was before I left for Britannia. He will have advanced north to the Liger by now, for certain."

"Certain?" said Artorius, "nothing is certain in war. You had best be right about the Emperor's progress, otherwise Rigotomos is marching straight into the lion's mouth."

The fair weather held, and the British fleet sailed undisturbed around the western coast of Amorica, down past the Gulf of Morbihan and the Rhuys Peninsula. They anchored off the coast near Pornic, where Artorius insisted on sending men ashore to scout out the land before disembarking.

"I know nothing of this country," he said to Valerian, who wanted the Britons to land as soon as possible, "except that it is foully hot and full of barbarians. What if Rigotomos has already engaged them in battle, and met with defeat?"

"That is impossible," Valerian replied stiffly, "my king is as canny as he is brave. He will only give battle on ground of his choosing, and on his terms."

"Then he and I are of like mind."

In spite of Valerian's protests, Artorius sent a longboat with a party of eighteen men ashore, and barges to ferry their horses. The

terrified animals had to be coaxed from their
stalls below deck and lifted on cranes into
the landing craft, and made life hell for the
luckless crewmen tasked with getting them
aboard.

From his flagship, half a mile out to sea,
Artorius watched his men lead the horses
through the shallows onto the wide expanse
of flat, golden beach stretching up and down
the coastline. Valerian had chosen a good
spot to land, with more than enough room
for the small British army to camp on the
sands.

Beyond the beach he could see a dark line
of forest, and smoke rising from a hill-fort a
mile or so to the north.

"The fort is occupied by a local tribe," said
Valerian in response to Artorius'
questioning look, "I'm not sure which.
There are so many. Possibly the Pictones, or
the Venetii, maybe even the Redones,
though they tend to dwell further to the
north…"

Artorius raised a hand. "Enough," he said
firmly, "I don't care who lives there, so long
as they leave us alone."

The scouting party split into three groups
and vanished into the forest. Artorius was
condemned to an anxious wait, striding back
and forth on his foredeck while the late
afternoon sun slowly dipped in the sky.

Sweating in his light tunic and thin woollen cloak, he was grateful when the oppressive heat started to ebb a little.

Cei and Bedwyr, who had recovered somewhat by now, joined him in his vigil.

"A beautiful country," remarked Bedwyr, still pale and red-eyed from his illness, "reminds me of home."

"Home is where we should be," said Cei.

The scouts emerged from the trees at dusk, just as the setting sun was forging a red-gold haze on the horizon under a band of violet cloud.

"We saw nothing of the enemy," reported their captain after he had climbed aboard the flagship, "the forest peters out a few miles to the east, and there is a road, a rutted highway leading straight across the countryside. We saw a couple of small villages, but no towns."

"There is no settlement of any note until Portus Namnetum, some twenty miles away," said Valerian.

Artorius gripped the rail with both hands and peered towards the shore. The onset of evening had lent the distant forest a sinister, menacing look, full of hidden dangers.

"We shall land tomorrow," he said, "and march east as quickly as we may."

After spending a night aboard ship, the Britons disembarked the following dawn, swiftly and without fuss, and marched east towards Portus Namnetum.

After days at sea, Artorius was relieved to be in the saddle again, riding along a surface that didn't pitch and roll alarmingly with every step. A good number of his men, still weak from the effects of sea-sickness, offered up fervent prayers of gratitude for having survived their ordeal.

It was high summer, and his spirits rose as the army delved further east, following the track through the forest discovered by the scouts, eventually joining with the road in open country.

"You are seeing our land at its best," said Valerian, riding to his left, "for much of the year Amorica is cold and damp, much afflicted by winds sweeping in from the sea. Now everything is in bloom. The sun shines on you, general. A clear sign of God's favour."

"Let us hope so," Artorius replied distractedly. He had sent Bedwyr ahead with a troop of thirty horsemen to scout out the land. More riders were despatched to cover the flanks of his line of march. The land ahead seemed peaceful enough, the wide highway cutting directly through a series of gently rolling green hills, with patches of woodland, but he was taking no chances.

The scouts reported nothing amiss, and by noon Portus Namnetes was within sight. Built on the north bank of the Liger and protected by a stone wall built by the Gallo-Romans, the town was an impressive and prosperous place, a wealthy trading port with direct access to the sea via the river.

Rigotomos was not in the town, according to Valerian, but would be found some distance to the south-east, following the line of the river towards the Visigoth headquarters at Vicus Dolensis. Exactly how far away the king's army was, he had no idea.

"The governor of the town will know," Valerian said complacently, "he is a firm ally of the king, and gave him troops and supplies for the campaign."

The governor, a hard-faced veteran of many wars, proved a far more reassuring figure than Valerian, and told Artorius what he needed to know.

"I have men shadowing the army's advance," he said promptly after riding from the town to greet the British commander, "two days ago they had reached Loudon, a village twenty-five miles to the west of here. Rigotomos is advancing slowly, waiting for yourself and the Romans to come up and join him."

He grinned and pointed his spear west, at the faint wisps of smoke visible against the deep blue coverlet of the sky. "All you have to do is follow the signs of slaughter. Our men have left a trail of burned-out encampments and dead barbarians behind them. The Visigoths are in full retreat."

Encouraged, Artorius pushed his troops west, skirting the northern walls of the town. Thanks to heat and lingering sickness, the infantry were struggling to keep up, so he decided to leave them behind.

"Bring them up as soon as you can," he ordered Gwalchmei, who he left in command of the footmen, "but don't force the pace too much. They will have to fight a battle, probably soon, and need to be rested before then."

"Yes, lord," replied Gwalchmei. Artorius took comfort from his stolid, competent presence. The ex-slave turned soldier could be relied on not to do anything rash.

He took his cavalry on at a fast canter, their hoofs kicking up clouds of dust from the highway. They encountered no traffic. The land was at war, and the local peasants had made themselves scarce, melting away into the hills and forests, leaving their villages empty and the pastures stripped of livestock.

Much of the day passed riding through this eerie, deserted landscape. Artorius allowed just one rest to water their horses on the banks of the Ligris. He kept the river close to his right flank at all times. Bands of scouts rode ahead and to his left. At any moment he feared the sight of Visigoth banners on the horizon, and the distant thump of barbarian war-drums.

The trail of the Amorican army was not difficult to follow: the road was in a poor state, and in places ran out completely. The muddy ground was churned up by the passage of thousands of men and horses, along with wheel-marks from the baggage train.

Shortly after midday Bedwyr came galloping back with the news Artorius hoped and expected to hear.

"Rigotomos is just two miles to the east," he said excitedly, "thousands of spearmen marching in column, light horse on the flanks, mailed lancers to the fore. I have never seen finer cavalry. The legions themselves can have looked no better!"

Artorius wanted to see for himself. He took his men on at the gallop, and was soon rewarded by the sound of drums, echoing through the hills, accompanied by the steady tramp of marching feet.

Then he glimpsed the banners of the Amorican rearguard, colourful streamers and pennants fluttering on the ends of the lances of their horsemen.

Artorius reined in a little and threw up his hand, signalling his buccelari to slow their pace. Ahead of him, not half a mile to the east, a long column of mounted lancers was jogging along behind a line of supply wagons.

The breath caught in his throat. "You're right, Bedwyr," he said admiringly, "they are the finest cavalry I ever saw. God grant they fight as well as they look."

Every one of the Amoricans wore a coat of scale mail reaching to his knees, glistening like the skin of a salmon. They carried long lances, of the type the Romans called a *contus*, over twelve feet in height and meant to be used two-handed in combat. Their heavy round shields were painted white, and they wore snowy white cloaks flowing from shoulder to ankle.

"Look at their horses," Bedwyr said admiringly, "every one a pureblood. From Hispania, I'll be bound. They breed the best horseflesh there."

Artorius needed no telling. His adoptive father, Ambrosius, had struggled for years to obtain horses from Hispania for his cavalry. Rigotomos clearly experienced no such difficulty. There were at least five hundred men in his rearguard, and their mounts were indeed of the best. He could even afford a startling indulgence – every horse was either pure black, or pure white.

"Don't feel envious," muttered Artorius, patting the neck of his own coal-black mare, Llamrei. She was the finest horse in his stable, but even she looked rather commonplace next to the sleek, muscular, high-stepping beasts ahead.

The Amoricans were marching through a valley floor, with the river to their right and steeply rising ground to their left. Beyond the rearguard, Artorius could see a forest of banners and spear-heads. The sun flashed from the spears like heaven's lightning, and the earth trembled under the weight of their host.

"Such an army," remarked Cei, "could storm the gates of Hell."

"You think better of our chances now, then?" Artorius said wryly, smiling at him, "there are even more of the Visigoths, you know. If Valerian is to be believed, Euric's host outnumbers Rigotomos two to one."

Cei slowly shook his head. "This is a war between giants. How are we, with our paltry little band, supposed to make the difference?"

"The King of the Amoricans will no doubt tell us," said Artorius. He had spotted a group of horsemen galloping down the line of the army, led by a gigantic figure on a snowy white stallion. This man wore the same gear as his men, but with additional trappings: a gold-hilted sword at his hip, a silvery breastplate over his mail, and a purple fringe to his streaming white cloak.

This was Rigotomos. Tall and sinewy and handsome in a fleshy, square-faced sort of way, with a square black beard, luminous blue eyes and a bluff, hearty, slightly boorish manner.

Artorius struggled to like him. The King of the Amoricans laughed too much, and too loudly, and made too many confident assertions. He was also rather too free with his big, powerful hands, insisting on repeatedly embracing Artorius and slapping him on the back in an overly friendly manner.

Above all else, Artorius loathed flattery, but Rigotomos seemed determined to grease him with the stuff.

"General Artorius," he boomed when they first met, "the famed Dux Bellorum, champion of the Britons, chief warlord and first sword of the Island of the Mighty! Who will stand against us, eh? Who will dare face our combined might?"

He threw back his head and unleashed another bellow of laughter. The sixteen lancers who served him for a bodyguard laughed with him.

"Euric will," replied Artorius, wondering if the man was drunk, "and his twelve thousand warriors."

Rigotomos slapped his gauntleted hands together. "Mice!" he spat contemptuously, "or should I call them rats, these vermin who infest Gaul and think to grow fat on the remains of empire. The Visigoths shall rue the day they chose to creep out of their stinking northern forests. We shall school them in war, you and I, and send Euric's head back to his foul kinsmen in a basket."

"Us, and Anthemius," said Artorius, who refused to be swept along by the king's enthusiasm, "we need the Romans, lord king. Where are they? Have you received any word from the Emperor?"

Rigotomos grinned, displaying thick white teeth. "I have. Yesterday I had a letter from the Praetorian prefect of Gaul, Arvandus. It assured me that Anthemius is racing north with all his power. Have no fear. Caesar shall join us before we make our final advance on Vicus Dolensis."

This made sense. When Aetius had reconquered parts of northern Gaul for the Western Empire, some twenty years gone, he also revived the office of prefect. The letter was reassuring, though Artorius would have preferred Roman troops to Roman promises.

His cavalry joined the Amorican vanguard as auxiliaries, and once the army had marched beyond the valley Rigotomos called a halt for the night. "We are in no hurry," he said with another of his toothy grins, "I follow the old Roman ways. Tonight we shall rest in safety behind a deep ditch and a strong palisade. The barbarians shall never catch me unawares. Come they early, come they late, they shall find Rigotomos at his gate!"

Artorius was grateful for the halt, since it gave Gwalchmei time to catch up with the British infantry. Rigotomos was excessively complimentary as he watched the column of tired, dust-spattered spearmen and archers trudge into camp, praising them as though they were crack legionaries.

"Fine men," he brayed, "soiled and footsore from a long march, true, but I'll wager every man is worth three Visigoths, eh?"

Artorius was not so sure of that. His infantry numbered just seven hundred men, as well-drilled and prepared as he could make them, but the real strength of the Britons lay in their cavalry. These were his pride, many of them hardened veterans he had inherited from Ambrosius.

"They might look rough-hewn, compared to the splendour of your Amoricans," he said as he and Rigotomos shared a flagon of wine in the king's pavilion, "but they fight like demons."

He turned to practical matters. "Tell me more of the Visigoths," he asked, "do they use cavalry? The Saxons and their ilk mostly fight on foot."

Rigotomos stifled a belch. His eyes were heavy, and Artorius had noticed him drink more wine than was sensible at dinner.

"Plenty," he muttered thickly, "they make good horse-soldiers too, damn them. Good enough to beat the Huns, even. It was Visigoth cavalry that stopped Attila at the Catalaunian Plains. Euric has hundreds of heavy lancers and horse-archers."

He thumped his hand on the table. "I have the battle all planned out. We shall fight on the defensive, and invite the barbarians to break their teeth on us. Our spears shall form a wall in the centre of our line – so."

Rigotomos tore up the remnant of a loaf of bread and started arranging the pieces. "Heavy cavalry in reserve," he went on, losing some of his befuddled look, "my men and yours, mixed with the Roman foederati, Sarmatians and Alans and Heruls and the like. Excellent fighters. Light horse and archers on the flanks, to drive away Euric's damned horse-archers."

He winked slyly at Artorius, and tapped the side of his nose. "I know his way of fighting. He's a mad dog. Show him an enemy, and he will lunge at it, teeth bared. Let him lunge. We shall beat back anything he throws at us. And *then* –

He never got to finish. A bugle screamed outside, making both men start in their chairs. The slit of the tent was flung aside, and one of the king's guards, his face as white as his cloak, almost fell into the pavilion.

"Lord king," he said, "forgive the interruption. Our sentries have seen banners to the east. Horsemen, moving fast towards our camp."

Rigotomos almost knocked over his chair in his haste to stand. "Anthemius, at last!" he cried.

He staggered outside, brushing aside the guard.

"My lord," the latter protested nervously, "I...I don't think..."

The king ignored him and vanished into the night. Artorius followed, snatching up his sword-belt from where it hung over the back of his chair. Caledfwlch, the ancient gladius given to him by Morgana, the self-styled Seer of Britannia, lay snug inside the wooden sheath. He touched the hilt for luck before hurrying outside.

Rigotomos was striding through the encampment towards the western ditch. He walked confidently, back straight, all trace of his drunkenness gone. Whatever his flaws, he knew how to appear and conduct himself as a king in public.

Lesser men scattered before him, while his white-cloaked guards scrambled from their tents, buckling on shields and helms.

The soldiers ordered to dig the ditch and build the palisade had not yet finished their work. Many had stopped, leaning on their picks and shovels, to watch the approach of the horsemen.

It was still light, and the line of hills to the west shimmered in a haze of tawny yellow. The river valley opened out onto a broad, flat plain, with little in the way of cover.

"There," said Valerian, who followed his king everywhere like a faithful hound, "do you see their banners, my lord?"

He pointed a trembling finger west. A troop of horsemen were visible, gathered on a hillock about half a mile from the camp.

"I count two score," muttered Rigotomos, straining his eyes, "difficult to tell in this light. Are they Romans, or Visigoths?"

"Vicus Dolensis is still over four day's march away, lord," said Valerian, "Euric cannot possibly know of our presence. Unless…"

"Unless our position has already been betrayed. Spies, by God! Filthy spies in our camp!"

Spies, or traitors?, wondered Artorius.

The horsemen came no closer. A strange quiet fell over the field. Hundreds of soldiers, Amorican and British, stood in silence, waiting for God to reveal their fate.

"Drums," said Bedwyr, standing to Artorius' left, "and war-horns too, I think. Listen."

6.

The noise was on the very cusp of hearing. Artorius tried to will it out of existence. Slowly, undeniably, the steady throb of beating drums rolled across the landscape. Then the ominous boom of war-horns, the tramp-tramp-tramp of marching squadrons of horse and foot, column after column, regiment after regiment.

Artorius knew the sound of those horns. He had heard them many times in the bleak fenlands around Lindum, heralding the advance of Saxon war-bands. Visigoth horns sounded no different.

"Lord king," he said quietly, trying to keep his voice calm, "the enemy is almost upon us. This camp is not defensible. What are your orders?"

Rigotomos' face was ashen. "It is only an advance party," he said hoarsely, "a few hundred barbarians, nothing more. Insolent wretches. I shall send my guards to scatter them!"

The handful of horsemen to the west were fast multiplying. More and more riders appeared, spreading out in neatly ordered divisions until they covered much of the width of the plain. They were too far to pick out in detail, but the sun flashed from their iron helms and mail shirts, glimmering across the bristling rows of lance-points.

"Euric is here in force, lord," Artorius said, more urgently this time, "what are your orders?"

The other man's Adam's Apple bobbed up and down, his bloodless lips moved, but no sound came out. His eyes glazed over. He seemed paralysed, frozen in shock.

Artorius gave him up for lost. "Bedwyr," he said, swinging around, "muster our horse. Get them out on the plain to the north. Battle array, two wings and a reserve. Quick!"

Bedwyr took off like a greyhound. Artorius looked for Cei and Gwalchmei, and saw them among a knot of Amorican officers.

"Cei, go with him," he barked, "Gwalchmei, rouse the infantry – I want a shieldwall, three ranks deep, archers behind. You men, why do you stand idle? Don't you know your duty?"

This was aimed at the Amoricans. Their king's paralysis had spread among his officers, who seemed at a loss without Rigotomos to guide them. Artorius raised his voice.

"To your commands, at once!" he roared, striding towards the nearest man and grabbing him by the throat, "get the men out of this death-trap and muster them on the plain – move, you fools, before the Visigoths come down upon us! Do you want your skulls to adorn Euric's table tonight? *To arms!"*

Somewhere in the camp a bugle sounded, and the spell broke. Artorius thanked God for the bugler. The Amorican officers came to life again, men rushed for their weapons, horses screamed and whinnied as they were dragged from their temporary pens.

Artorius was desperate to go to his own men, but Rigotomos was still lost in a daze.

"A king must lead," Artorius raged at him, "your soldiers rely on you. Speak! Act!"

He lost patience and let fly with his fist. Rigotomos' head snapped to the left and he fell sprawling in the dirt, his white cloak tangled around him. His conical helmet, gleaming silver and adorned with a bunch of swan's feathers, spun out of his hands and rolled away.

Four of the king's guards sprang forward, eyes blazing, half-drawing their swords. Artorius dropped into a fighting crouch and reached for Caledfwlch.

"Wait!" shouted Rigotomos, his voice somewhat muffled, "leave him be. He has brought me to my senses."

The guards stepped back, glowering, while Artorius reached down and helped their master to his feet. Rigotomos rubbed his jaw with his free hand, blood trickling from the corner of his mouth.

"I have lost a tooth," he said, staring at Artorius with a new respect, "no-one has dared strike me since I was a child."

"There are thousands of Visigoths over there willing to repeat the offence," Artorius said brusquely, "for God's sake, lord king, get to your men!"

Rigotomos nodded. "My horse," he shouted at his guards, "fetch him, quickly. Damn you all, where is my helm?"

One of his men snatched up the fallen helm and thrust it into his hands. Rigotomos jammed it on his head and ran back towards his pavilion, soiled cloak flying about him. His guards sprinted after him, one or two giving Artorius evil looks as they went.

He was concerned solely with his own command. The doleful roar of enemy war-horns was almost deafening now, and the earth shook under the hoofs of their cavalry.

Artorius' eyes widened in horror as he turned and saw the lancers of Euric's vanguard plunging straight towards the camp at a reckless gallop, screeching war-cries, horse-tail banners rising and falling, their armour shimmering in the haze like a wall of mirrors.

"Christ save me," he muttered. There was nothing to stop them. It was too late to run.

They would be on him in moments, leaping the pathetic little ditch to trample him into oblivion.

His fingers closed on Caledfwlch's ivory grip. At least he could die well.

Old words, spoken to him years ago by Ambrosius, coursed through his mind. *"Men talk of dying well in battle, my son. Don't be deceived. I have seen many men die in battle, and none died well. They died in fear and agony, shitting their guts out and calling for their mothers."*

"Lord!"

He looked to his left. Cadwy, the young warrior who served him for a squire, was running towards him with Llamrei. The glossy black mare was bitted and saddled, and neighed in recognition of her master.

For a big man, Artorius could shift when needed. He ran at Llamrei, seized her reins and vaulted into her saddle. As he righted himself, he reached down, grabbed Cadwy by the scruff of the neck and hauled him aboard as well.

Fortunately the youth was light, and Llamrei strong enough to carry them both. She wheeled and bolted, galloping away at the limit of her speed towards the open plain to the north, where the allied army was frantically trying to deploy.

Artorius peered through the chaos of men and horses, and glimpsed his dragon banner, away to the north-west. Llamrei, ever responsive, swerved in that direction when he gave a twitch on the reins.

Behind him, terrifyingly close, he could hear the deep-throated roaring of the Visigoths. He didn't dare look back. They would be in the camp by now, overturning tents and wagons and butchering anything that moved.

Christ's blood, what a mess!

Artorius was himself a master of the swift ambush, sudden raids under grey pre-morning skies at the head of his cavalry, wreaking as much carnage as possible before retreating, leaving the enemy dazed, confused and terrified.

Now he was on the wrong end of the same strategy – all because of the fool Rigotomos, and his idiotic faith in the Emperor! Where in hell were the Romans? How had the Visigoths come to learn of the location of the allied army?

There was treachery here, as black as the Devil could make it, but Artorius had no time to ponder. He guided Llamrei through a mob of leaderless Amorican spearmen, bellowing at them to stand clear, and then the arrows hit.

One whipped past Artorius' helmet, so close it scraped the metal. Screams erupted around him. The spearmen wore little armour, and were easy prey for the vicious, black and yellow-striped shafts falling among them like poison rain.

He twisted his neck and saw the arrows were coming from a band of horse-archers, galloping forward in a loose skirmish line to spread more chaos among the allies. A few scattered units of Amorican bowmen were shooting back at them, plucking a few from their saddles.

Cadwy, who sat behind Artorius, gave a sudden shriek and fell away. Artorius looked around and saw him rolling on the ground with two arrows in his back.

He made a snap decision, and a hard one. Cadwy had saved his life. By rights, he was honour-bound to return the favour, but the boy was most likely dead already, and Artorius had an army to save.

The call of a bugle summoned him to his duty. He spotted his infantry being hustled and bawled into three ranks by Cei and Gwalchmei, while the archers scrambled into position behind them. The hail of wasp-like arrows fell among them too. Here and there a man screamed and went down, clutching the deadly shaft sticking from his body.

"Shields!" Cei was bellowing, "get your shields up!"

Artorius put his head down and dug in his spurs, steering Llamrei's head towards the dragon banner. Bedwyr had drawn up the British cavalry into two wings on the flanks of the shieldwall, with himself at the head of the reserve.

Another arrow skipped under Llamrei's hoofs, but Artorius reached his men unscathed. His cavalry cheered the sight of him.

"Lord," shouted Bedwyr above the din, "what are your orders? Do we hold here, or withdraw?"

Artorius wheeled Llamrei about to take in the situation. His spirits plummeted at what he saw.

The order and discipline of his veterans made for a dire contrast to the rest of the allied army. Men were streaming out of the half-finished encampment, many of them fleeing in blind panic, deaf to the shouts of their officers. The camp itself was completely overrun. Visigoth horsemen rode through and over it at will, slaughtering terrified fugitives without mercy, putting all they found to the sword.

He switched his gaze to the east. No comfort was to be had there. A moving forest of spears was advancing steadily across the plain, filling the horizon from end to end. Euric's infantry were on the march.

Artorius swallowed. There were ten thousand at least, a mighty and remorseless tide of barbarian warriors. More cavalry advanced before them, squadrons of lancers supported by horse-archers – Artorius had never seen the latter before – moving at a steady trot. The King of the Visigoths, it seemed, was in no hurry to clinch his triumph.

"We hold our ground," he shouted, "if Rigotomos can form some kind of battle-line, we could yet hold off these savages until…"

Until what? Until the Romans came to rescue them?

"Anthemius is not coming, lord," Bedwyr said grimly, voicing his master's doubts, "Rigotomos has been played for a fool. So have we all."

"Nevertheless, I will not desert him," said Artorius, "we cannot withdraw, even if I ordered it – look there!"

He had spotted the auxiliary cavalry on the flanks of the Visigoth host, light lancers and horse-archers, burst forward and surge around the edges of the plain. While the Amoricans struggled into line, Euric had sent his auxiliaries to cut off their line of retreat.

Artorius was caught in two minds. If he led his cavalry forward to repel the Visigoths, who enjoyed a three or four to one supremacy in numbers, he risked being trapped and destroyed. His infantry would be left without cavalry support. If he remained where he was, the allies would be surrounded, caught inside a rapidly tightening noose.

There was no help for it. The risk had to be taken. He turned in the saddle, opening his mouth to order his bugler to sound the charge, when a sudden roar and a barrage of galloping hoofs drowned him out.

"The king!" shouted Bedwyr, his voice cracking with excitement, "see, lord, the king has taken the field!"

Mouth still hanging open, Artorius looked, and the image of the great sea of Visigoth horsemen pounding towards the allied lines remained forever engraved on his memory.

So did the sight of the King of the Amoricans, at the head of his white-cloaked guards, wheeling out from the jumbled chaos of his army and launching a charge straight at the flank of the Visigoths bearing down from the left.

They didn't expect it, Euric's men, and were too slow in avoiding the shattering impact of five hundred mailed troopers on heavy horses, striking right and left with their long lances. Artorius blinked, and in a second the Visigoth squadrons had crumpled into a bloody and bewildered mass of shrieking beasts and tumbling riders, cut down, impaled and driven into headlong flight. The Amoricans pursued, extracting a heavy toll of lives.

Artorius uttered a wordless cry of triumph, and saw Cei shake his spear at the mob of fleeing Visigoths, but Rigotomos had only delayed the inevitable. A few hundred light horse had been routed, nothing more. Even as the King's silver-armoured figure turned about and led his men back to their lines at a canter, the crushing weight of the main barbarian host was rumbling forward to engulf his doomed army.

The shouts of the overwhelming mass of Visigoth infantry rolled across the field as they stormed forward, spearmen and axe-men preceded by waves of skirmishers flinging javelins. By now the Amorican officers had managed to assemble a fair imitation of a battle-line, arranging the best of their infantry into a shieldwall, three ranks deep.

The Britons had formed up on the extreme right of the allied line, close to the gory ruin of the encampment. Cei and Gwalchmei rode up and down behind the third rank of

British infantry, exhorting the men to stand firm.

Artorius gritted his teeth as the barbarian tide crashed against the patchwork allied defences. The triple wall of shields before him gave ground, thrust back by the sheer force and impetus of the Visigoth charge.

"If the shieldwall breaks, we charge," he said to Bedwyr, "if I fall, get the men off the field and back to the ships."

Bedwyr gave a sharp nod, his handsome face taut with concentration, eyes fixed on the vicious struggle raging just a few feet ahead of them.

The line was holding, just, as the allied infantry fought back with the stubborn fury of despair. Break now, allow the Visigoths to tear through the gaps, and they were all dead men.

Artorius was a horse-soldier. He had rarely fought on foot, and never in the hell of a shieldwall. It was close fighting of the most brutal and pitiless sort, a place of sweat and cramp and blood and gut-twisting terror. Two lines of warriors locked together, barely inches apart, stabbing at exposed faces or gaps in the enemy shields, looking into the eyes of the men they killed.

Cei's hoarse voice rose above the clamour of fighting and dying. "Look at those gutless bastards!" he raged, "running away without striking a blow!"

He stabbed his spear to the left, where the allied line had suddenly collapsed. Three squadrons of mounted Amorican lancers were broken and streaming away in rout, leaving the spearmen on foot isolated, flanks and rear hopelessly exposed.

For a sickening moment Artorius thought all was lost. Having broken the line, the Visigoth infantry stormed through, baying like hounds as they set about carving up what remained of the Amorican left flank.

Flushed at such an easy victory, many of the Visigoths blundered after the fleeing horsemen. All order in their tight-knit ranks dissolved as they gave chase, hungry for more blood.

The Visigoths had been tricked. Trumpets sounded among the Amorican cavalry. They turned about, re-formed, clapped in their spurs and charged with lances dipped at their startled pursuers.

A feigned retreat. Artorius had never seen the manoeuvre attempted, though he was familiar with it from his lessons in military history as a child. The Alans, fierce, warlike people from far Scythia and beyond, were said to have used it to great effect against the Roman legions. Artorius could only assume that Rigotomos, or one of his officers, had read the same histories.

The Amorican horsemen were well-drilled. Forming into a wedge, they ploughed into the hapless Visigoths, slaughtering many and sending the rest fleeing in panic. A few of the barbarians doggedly stood their ground, but their valour did them no good as they were swiftly mown down, speared and chopped into oblivion, bodies trampled under-hoof.

Again the Visigoth assault was turned back, again their dead carpeted the earth like autumn leaves. The cavalry returned to their position on the left, driving away the Visigoth skirmishers and shoring up the Amorican flank.

It was all in vain. The bulk of the enemy host still raged and howled against the thin allied lines. Apparently careless of casualties, the pick of Euric's warriors hurled themselves onto the bloodied spears, sacrificing themselves to make space for their comrades.

Euric can afford to waste the lives of his men, thought Artorius, *he has reserves. We have none.*

He glanced desperately to the south. If Christ was merciful, Roman banners would soon appear over the horizon, and their foederati thunder over the distant hills to take the Visigoths in flank.

There was nothing. The land to the south was empty and silent. For all Artorius knew, the Emperor was still in Rome, chuckling quietly to himself as he imagined the armies of the West destroying each other.

The truth dawned on Artorius, cold and terrible. Anthemius had betrayed the Amoricans, tempting their impetuous king to attack Euric with false promises of support. Rigotomos could not win on his own, but would kill plenty of Visigoths before his army was driven from the field.

Once the Amoricans and the Visigoths have nigh-on destroyed each other, Anthemius will march from Rome to take back Gaul for the Western Empire.

While part of his mind grappled with the ruthless, blood-stained politics, another remained focused on the battle. Bedwyr shouted a warning, but Artorius had already seen the danger: having ravaged the encampment to their heart's content, Visigoth cavalry were pouring out of the flimsy stockade to threaten the Britons. They moved fast, mounted spearmen and more of their accursed horse-archers.

"Stay with the reserve," he ordered Bedwyr, turning Llamrei about and galloping to the cavalry formed up on his right.

Their captain was Llwch Llemineawg, a young half-Scotti savage from Venedotia, hard-faced for all his tender years, with the whitening skull of a Saxon gesith hanging from his saddlebow by its long red hair. The gesith had been his first kill, slain during a skirmish in the marshes around Lindum, and he carried the grim trophy as a mark of pride.

"Follow me," shouted Artorius as he galloped past Llwch and his standard bearer. Without looking back, he ripped Caledfwlch free of its sheath and drove Llamrei straight at the Visigoths.

He picked out one of their captains, a massive brute with a triple-forked yellow beard flowing down over his golden scale mail, silken black cloak fastened at the shoulder by a copper brooch forged into the sinuous shape of a dragon. Blue eyes spat joy and hatred at him in equal measure from under an iron helmet topped with a spike.

This one looked worth the killing. In an instant their blades met, clashing like cymbals while the tide of horsemen swept past, yelling as they closed with the Britons.

The Visigoth had a slight advantage in height and reach over Artorius, and was his equal in skill and aggression. They fought in silence, hacking at each other's heads, parting, wheeling their horses and closing again.

Artorius tried using the hilt of his sword, punching at the Visigoth's face. The other man was wise to the tactic and got his shield in the way.

"Bastard," Artorius snarled as he skinned his knuckles on the iron rim of the shield. He got his own up in time to deflect a savage sword-cut that would have cut deep into his neck, the solid thump of steel against wood jarring down the length of his arm.

Teeth gritted against the pain, he cut at the Visigoth's sword-arm. This time his aim was true, and the thick chopping edge of the spatha sliced into the crook of his target's elbow, shearing through the leaf-shaped plates of his scale armour and the cloth and flesh beneath.

The Visigoth squealed in agony. The cut wasn't quite enough to sever his forearm, but hacked through the sinew, leaving it attached by a bleeding strip of flesh and bone.

His sword dropped from suddenly nerveless fingers. Lost to pain, he made no effort to dodge or defend himself as Artorius smashed him again with the hilt, breaking his nose and several teeth and knocking him half-out of the saddle.

Artorius quickly sheathed his sword as the man fell, and reached out to grasp the dragon brooch. He twisted it free, letting the black cloak flutter to earth even as its owner tumbled from his horse, hitting the ground with a rib-crunching thud.

He stuffed the brooch into his belt. Like Llwch, Artorius was fond of taking trophies from beaten opponents. Ambrosius had thought the practice barbaric, and tried unsuccessfully to dissuade him from it.

Visigoths and Britons swirled around him, locked in combat, stabbing and hacking at each other. He glimpsed Llwch through the press, spearing a Visigoth horse-archer, before a sudden rush of bodies hid the youth from view. Artorius tried to reach the young officer, laying about him at bearded Visigoth faces, taking their blows on his shield. All around him were men shouting and cursing, steel clashing, the screams of terrified horses, banners rising and falling.

The chaotic, frenzied melee only seemed to last a few seconds, and then the Visigoths were breaking away, turning to retreat back towards the camp. They were only light cavalry, with no mailed lancers among them, and could not stand against the British veterans for long.

Artorius found himself surrounded by riderless horses. Dead and dying men lay strewn about the ground. Most, to his relief, were Visigoths.

"Hold," he shouted at his men as a few of them gave chase to the fleeing enemy, "get back, you fools!"

Thankfully Llwch had seen the danger and ordered his bugler to sound the recall. One or two hotheads ignored the summons, but most reluctantly gave up the hunt and trotted back to their standard.

Artorius had no time to draw breath. Fresh fighting had broken out to his left, where the triple line of British spearmen had all but vanished under waves of Visigoth infantry.

"Christ's death," cried Artorius, "there is no end to these pigs. Llwch, sound the charge! Where in God's name are Bedwyr and Gwaeddan?"

These two were in command of the rest of his cavalry, and should have been protecting the hopelessly outnumbered spearmen.

Even as Llwch yelled the order to re-form and charge, Artorius looked around frantically for the dragon banner at the head of his reserve. Had it fallen? Was Bedwyr slain?

The allied line was breaking up. Everywhere the overwhelming numbers of the Visigoths was telling. Their warriors poured through the ever-widening gaps in the shieldwall, doing terrible execution with spear and long-axe, sword and dagger. Euric's horse-archers hovered on the edges of the fighting, thinning out the Amoricans with constant flights of arrows, darting in to isolate and butcher stranded groups of infantrymen, swiftly retreating before they could be snared in a counter-attack.

There! The dragon banner briefly floated into view, waving bravely above a throng of fighting horsemen. Bedwyr's men were engulfed, struggling to repel many times their number of Visigoths.

Artorius cursed. While he was fending off the attack on the right, Euric's cavalry had swept through the disintegrating fence of shields and hammered into the British reserve. Gwaeddan's men were also embroiled, surrounded and fighting for their lives.

Llamrei was already at the gallop, head down, surging fearlessly towards the cluster of barbarians trying to bring down the dragon. Artorius struck three men from their saddles before they even knew he was there, and exchanged savage cuts with another Visigoth officer while Llwch's men fought to rescue Bedwyr and relieve some of the pressure on the spearmen.

The officer went down, blood pouring from the deep gash Artorius had opened from his left eye down to his chin. He was almost in touching distance of Bedwyr, who wielded his spear with calm, lightning-quick precision.

The British standard bearer was dead, so Bedwyr had picked up the fallen banner and held it aloft in his left hand. By far the most skilled of Artorius' warriors, he was lethal in combat, and had already brought down seven Visigoths. Their twitching bodies lay under the hoofs of his horse, but still more came, jostling each other in their fury to get at him.

Artorius would not let his standard fall, much less be taken: to see the Visigoths make off with it would be an unbearable disgrace. He fought by Bedwyr's side, hacking at the enemy until his wrist ached and the contorted, snarling faces melded into a blur. Sweat cascaded down his brow, while hot blood from a cut on his cheek trickled down his neck.

After a time – he had no idea how long – the Visigoths gave back, growling like dogs, denied their quarry for the present. Artorius wiped his face with the back of his leather gauntlet, itself slick with blood, and blinked away the sweat in his eyes.

"Oh, God," he breathed, "we are finished."

His spearmen were dying by inches, the dwindling band of survivors forced to shuffle together in a ring around their standards. Their comrades lay in heaps, mixed with their fallen enemies, a reeking pile of human wreckage. Some of the bodies still moved, feebly trying to crawl away, or extricate themselves from the crushing weight of those lying on top.

The Visigoths had fallen back. Now the shieldwall was broken, they could safely pick off the surviving Britons from a distance. Groups of horse-archers galloped in circles, shooting a perpetual rain of arrows down on the heads of the British spearmen.

Artorius saw the Visigoth lancers regrouping, preparing for another attack. One last charge, sweeping over the doomed and outnumbered British cavalry, sending them all to the long house.

A kind of peace descended over Artorius. If he was doomed to die here, on foreign soil in the service of a foreign king, at least he would die among friends.

"Where is Cei?" he asked, "does he live? I would not step into the next life without him at my side, complaining all the way and picking a fight with the angels."

"He lives, lord," replied Bedwyr, smiling as he pointed at a bloodied, bare-headed figure mounted on a Visigoth pony, "he killed the owner of that beast with his bare hands."

Together they waited for the end, while the arrows fell and men died. The Visigoths seemed uncertain, wary of pressing their final attack. While they hesitated, a shout rippled down the length of the ruined field, a last wail of despair from Amorican throats:

"The king has fled! The king abandons us!"

Artorius stared to his left, and his heart broke inside him as he saw the royal banner, a huge square piece of cloth displaying a spreading black tree against a white field, moving away from the field.

"Rigotomos has quit the field," said Bedwyr, "we are no longer honour-bound to remain."

"I will not abandon my soldiers," Artorius replied stubbornly. Bedwyr laid a hand on his shoulder.

"Our infantry are done for," he said, "but we can get the cavalry out. Now, before the Visigoths close in again. Would you sacrifice all your men this day, or save as many as you can?"

Bedwyr was right. For the second time that day Artorius was required to make a hard decision, knowing the guilt would haunt him for the remainder of his days.

The alternative was death, and the destruction of his entire army.

"We will retreat," he said.

*

The survivors of the British forces followed Rigotomos, whose guards closed up around him as he departed the battlefield. He too had chosen to leave his infantry to their fate.

Artorius expected be pursued relentlessly, hunted across the fertile, low-lying landscape of central Gaul, but the Visigoths made little effort to give chase. Some of their horse-archers galloped after the Britons as they fled in the wake of the royal banner, picking a few men from their saddles with well-aimed shots. After a mile or so they halted and withdrew, summoned back to the field by the bellowing of war-horns.

The unexpected reprieve gave Artorius little comfort. Shame and guilt warred inside him. His thoughts were dominated by the faces of the men he had left behind, to be slaughtered or enslaved by the barbarians. He had never suffered a defeat before in battle, never been obliged to turn his back on an enemy.

Bedwyr tried to reassure him. "Every general, no matter how great, suffers defeats," he said, "even Hannibal and Julius Caesar had to concede the field on occasion. At least this loss was not of your making."

"That's right," growled Cei, who had been sorely wounded in the fighting and wore a blood-soaked strip of cloth around his head, "blame Constantine. I warned you not to trust him. He sent us here to die, the conniving bastard."

Artorius would have rebuked him for uttering such blatant treason, but lacked the will and the energy. Stubborn as he was, obnoxious and foul-mouthed, Cei only spoke the truth. It seemed obvious now.

Anger boiled over inside him, drowning all the other emotions. A personal betrayal was one thing, but Constantine had also betrayed his men. Hundreds of Britons lay dead, slaughtered in a battle they had no business fighting and no hope of winning.

Brooding over his thoughts, Artorius paid little attention to the country were passing through. It was pretty enough, verdant fields thick with waving crops, shining red-gold in the light of the setting sun. Following the clouds of dust kicked up by the fleeing Amorican cavalry, they galloped past a number of hilltop villages guarded by strong walls of stone or timber, and the occasional lonely farmstead. Rigotomos and his men were travelling along the old Roman roads that criss-crossed this part of Gaul, though Artorius had little notion of what sanctuary might lie to the north-east.

The evening sky was deep blue fading to purple when the frantic pace of the Amoricans slowed. They halted in the middle of a wide patchwork of fields, with a broad river shining a half-mile or so to the west. Far to the north, a single triangular spire silhouetted against the sky was the only sign of occupation.

Artorius went forward with Cei, Bedwyr and a handful of other men to seek out Rigotomos. The king's guards, bloodied, dust-stained and weary, glanced bleakly at him as they rubbed down their exhausted horses and led them to the edge of the river to drink.

They found Rigotomos sitting on the side of the road, held upright by a group of weeping officers. The mangled ruin of his silver helmet lay nearby, its swan's feathers trailing in the dust, one side smashed in by some terrific blow.

The man cradling his head looked up at the newcomers.

"Valerian," said Artorius, "I thought you were lost in the fighting."

The envoy's face was smeared in dirt and blood and sweat. Slow tears plodded down his cheeks, carving runnels in the grime.

"I wish I had died," he whimpered, "I wish I could die a thousand deaths, if only my lord would live."

One look at Rigotomos was enough to confirm he wished in vain. The king's face was a gory ruin, his left eyeball shattered, probably by the same blow that stoved in his helmet.

God was cruel, and had allowed Rigotomos to live on a while longer in unspeakable pain and torment. His remaining eye sparked with life as it took in Artorius, and he made a whining noise in his throat, as though trying to speak.

Artorius slid down from the saddle and knelt before him. "Lord king," he said gently, clasping the dying man's hand.

"He would never have quit the field," Valerian said fiercely, "if not for his wound, he would have stayed to the end! But we had to get him away, lest he was taken prisoner. My king could not be captured. Euric, would have paraded him through the streets in chains."

Artorius nodded impatiently. He leaned closer, trying to hear the words Rigotomos was straining to mumble.

"Treachery...Arvandus..."

He released the king's hand and stood up. Arvandus, the Prefect of Gaul: the one who had sent honeyed promises to Rigotomos, assuring him that the Romans would march to his aid against Euric. Artorius could only wonder what other messages had passed between the scheming Prefect and the High King in Londinium.

Some day he would find out, and there would be a reckoning. "Where were you heading?" he asked Valerian, "I know nothing of this part of Gaul."

Valerian bowed his head, too lost in misery to respond, so another officer spoke for him.

"To Avallon," he replied, "a fortified town on the Via Agrippa, held by the Burgundians. This is their land. They are allies of ours, and will give our lord shelter."

Or a tomb, by the looks of him, Artorius thought. The King of the Amoricans was not long for the world. His breathing was increasingly shallow, his life's blood staining the earth. He would likely be dead long before his retinue reached Avallon.

"Perhaps that is why Euric did not pursue us," suggested Bedwyr, "he was reluctant to trespass on Burgundian territory. His men also suffered in the battle, and would scarce be in a fit state to fight another so soon."

"Perhaps," said Artorius, gazing north. Somewhere beyond the broad fields and green forests of Gaul lay the Narrow Sea, and home.

He had brought a thousand men to Gaul. Less than a quarter of that number would return. His worst fears had come to pass: public disgrace would be the inevitable consequence of defeat. At best, Constantine would remove him from the Council and condemn him to perpetual exile, a life of irrelevance, stripped of power and dignity. At worst, he would face trial. The ride home might well end on the gallows.

So be it. Artorius would not shy away from his fate, or spend the rest of his days wandering the lands of the Western Empire as an exile, offering the services of his dwindling war-band to foreign kings. He would see Ganhumara again, however briefly, and his sons.

"Come," he said, turning back to his men, "we have a long journey ahead of us."

7.

Caerleon

The seduction of Ganhumara by Melwas was slow, and all the more effective for it. All through the long, hot summer, while the gently crumbling ruins of Caerleon drowsed in the heat, he chipped away at her resistance.

Ganhumara was young and impressionable, but no fool. She knew his intentions. When he served her at dinner, catching her eye as he poured her mead, or offered her the best cuts of meat on bended knee, she looked back at him stonily, giving no outward sign of interest.

Nor did she flinch or look away. Ganhumara made the mistake of thinking it was all a game to him, one he would soon grow tired of.

"I expect he has bedded every desirable girl for miles around," she told her sons in the privacy of their shared bedchamber, "and has fathered a host of bastards among the local village girls. Soon the land will be stocked with pretty redheads!"

She giggled at the thought, and clapped a hand to her mouth. This was no laughing matter. If Artorius should ever find out, he would kill Melwas. Of that she was certain. He had always treated her kindly, according to his lights, but she had glimpsed flashes of his temper, the savagery that lay beneath his thin coating of education and civilised behaviour.

He was a barbarian, after all. Artorius seldom talked of his true ancestry, but she knew from whispers among his warriors that he came from north of the Wall. Born into some minor tribe or other, orphaned at a young age, and picked up by Ambrosius during one of the latter's infrequent visits to the far north country.

"Sheer chance," she murmured, stroking Cydfan's blonde curls, "if Ambrosius had not spotted him, he would have spent the rest of his days in barbarian squalor, and probably died on some dim northern battlefield. You and I, my babies, would not have known each other."

Cydfan gurgled happily, showing his pearly white teeth. He was her favourite, sweet-natured and mild as a lamb. Llacheu and Medraut, the dark-haired twins, were quiet for once, watching with obvious jealousy as Ganhumara fussed over their elder brother.

Feeling guilty at neglecting them, she set Cydfan down on his still-unsteady legs and held out her arms.

"Come, Medraut," she said, smiling at him, "and you, Llacheu. Come to me."

The twins took some coaxing – no child could sulk like Medraut – but eventually they nestled in her arms, while she rested her cheek on Llacheu's head and sang softly to them.

"The hall of your father is quiet tonight,
Without laughter, without joy,
But for thee, who will keep me company?
The vault is dark, without candle, without light,
Longing for you comes over me…"

She stopped. Longing for who? Not for Artorius. Her thoughts were for the younger man, all whipcord and lean muscle, his blue eyes under the mop of auburn hair laughing at her, beckoning to her, yearning for her.

Melwas. His name was like a kiss. Ganhumara groaned and covered her face.

"Keep him from my thoughts, lord," she prayed, "send him away from me, so we may not fall into sin."

God was deaf to her entreaties. For the next few days she suffered sleepless nights, her mind torn between Artorius and Melwas.

There was no news of her lover's progress in Gaul. The High King had despatched him across the Narrow Sea soon after the coronation, with no time for Artorius to return west and bid her farewell. For all she knew, he was already dead, and all his men with him.

She prayed it was not so. Without Artorius to protect her, she would be nothing, a dead man's concubine. What would be her fate then, and that of her sons? What man would take her for husband? Ganhumara would be reduced to slavery again, or even beggary. She had no kin, no-one who would take her in.

Consumed with fear and exhaustion, she resolved to stay away from Melwas. He was death, sent by the Devil to lure her to destruction.

Melwas would not be deterred. Though young, he was senior to most of the other remaining warriors at Caerleon in rank. His father was ailing, and Melwas liked to boast of the lands he would inherit one day, in a part of Dumnonia called the Summer Country.

"My father's court is hidden among the mists and reeds," she overheard him saying to his cronies one night at dinner, "only the men of our blood, or those in their service, can find it."

He grinned and stabbed his eating knife at the drunken youths gathered around him. "If one of you blockheads tried, you would soon get lost in the marsh," he jeered, "led in circles by evil spirits, until you drowned in a bog or were devoured by the Old Ones."

"What are the Old Ones?" asked one of the boys, his brow furrowing.

"An ancient people," Melwas replied in a low voice, "similar to men, but of a different race. They were here long before our ancestors crossed the sea and claimed this island for their own. The Old Ones tried to fight them, but were too few, and their weapons were crude things made of bronze. They retreated to the wildest and most inaccessible parts of Britannia."

There were few diners in the hall, which was built to house almost a hundred warriors. Ganhumara fancied the shadows in the corners started to lengthen as Melwas spoke, and the fire in the hearth burned low.

"Some of them live on," he added, "in the depths of the Summer Country, and other such places, where men cannot reach them. Vile and degraded creatures, barely recognisable as human. They don't bother us, though. My family have a drop or two of the ancient blood in our veins, and the Old Ones think of us as distant kin."

Ganhumara sat alone at high table, the place of honour, usually reserved for Artorius and his closest followers. She looked up from her fish stew to find Melwas staring directly at her.

His blue eyes possessed a riveting, almost hypnotic quality. "Do not be afraid, lady," he called out, "you would be a welcome guest in the Summer Country whenever you wished. With myself for an escort, the Old Ones would not dare to lay their scaly fingers on you."

A gasp rippled around the gloomy, echoing vault of the hall. Ganhumara felt the blood rushing to her face.

"I've warned you before, boy," snarled Cilydd, the one-eyed veteran, "watch that tongue of yours. If Artorius had heard you speak thus to his lady, he would have ripped it out."

Melwas leaned back in his chair, balancing it on two rear legs, and gave Cilydd an insolent smirk. "If Artorius was here, I would not have said it," he said carelessly, "really, Cilydd, do you think I'm stupid? I meant no disrespect."

"I won't listen to any more," said the older man, rising from his seat near the fire, "you've drunk too much mead, Melwas. Take a word of advice from one who has survived fifty-three winters, and go to bed. Now."

Melwas took a defiant swig from his cup, and reached for the flagon. "You go to bed if you wish, Cilydd. Old men need their rest. I will stay awhile."

Scowling, Cilydd bowed to Ganhumara and limped out of the hall. Most of the younger warriors bedded down inside the hall, but he and his wife dwelled in one of the roundhouses inside the stockade.

"Poor Cilydd," said one of the youths, "you should show him more respect, Melwas. He has seen more fighting than any of us. They say he was lamed by a spear-wound to his leg, fighting for Ambrosius."

"To the seven hells with him," sneered Melwas, "limping old bore. Why Artorius keeps such relics, instead of putting them out to pasture with all the other blown horses, is beyond me."

He gulped some more mead and stared at Ganhumara over the edge of his cup. "You look lonely on that dais, my lady," he said, "why not come down and play at dice with us?"

Ganhumara avoided his eyes. "My thanks," she replied, trying to sound stiff and formal, "but I prefer to remain where I am. This is my proper place."

She stared into her bowl, painfully aware of him contemplating her like a choice bit of meat.

"Come down, my lady," he repeated, slowly and deliberately, "and play at dice with us."

"Melwas..." one of his friends said nervously, but fell quiet when Melwas raised his hand.

They are all frightened of him, thought Ganhumara, *not only because he is good at fighting. There is something about him, under the easy smiles and careless insolence. Something bad.*

Ganhumara was also frightened. She was suddenly grateful for the presence of the spearman behind her chair, and his comrade standing next to the purple curtain behind the dais, hiding her bedchamber from view. Artorius had left these two competent, hard-faced veterans to guard his family during his absence.

"I have eaten my fill," she declared, wiping her mouth with a cloth, "and will retire for the night. Dice and drink for as long as you like, friends, but not too loudly, else you will wake my children."

The tension lifted, and the handful of warriors bade her a respectful goodnight as she pushed back her chair and padded down the steps of the dais.

All save Melwas. He said nothing, legs crossed before him on the table, his eyes fixed on Ganhumara. Even when she showed him her back, she could still feel their hot gaze drilling into her.

Three days after this comfortless evening, news finally arrived from Londinium. The messenger was a youth named Cacamwri, one of Artorius' freeman servants, left behind in the capital to await his master's return from Gaul.

Cacamwri was made welcome at Caerleon, and given his fill of hot peppered chops and a brimming flagon of wine. Ganhumara sat impatiently while the man ate and drank, desperate to know of her lover's fate.

"Well, now," Cacamwri said at last, brushing crumbs from his moustache, "it is good to know the courtesy of my master's hall has not lessened in his absence."

He paused to belch. Ganhumara's fingers twitched, longing to seize the man by his neck and wring the words out of him

"You may be comforted, my lady," he said, as though sensing her agitation, "Artorius is alive, and unharmed. His ships sailed into Londinium seven days ago."

Ganhumara closed her eyes in a silent prayer of thanks, while the warriors gathered around her banged the tables with their feasts and shouted for joy.

As usual, the exception was Melwas. He sat, dark and silent, his eyes hooded, studying the backs of his hands.

Cacamwri gave a nervous cough. "Alas, that is the end of good news," he said when the noise had died down, "there was no victory in Gaul. It seems Rigotomos was betrayed by the Emperor, and lured into fighting a battle he could not win against the Visigoths. He is dead, and most of his army with him."

Some of the men exchanged horrified glances. "Is Gaul lost?" asked Cilydd, "and Amorica with it?"

"Not so," replied Cacamwra, "Euric holds the south of Gaul, but his advance has halted, at least for now. His army may have won a victory, but was severely mauled in the fighting. Rigotomos was careful to leave his borders well-guarded, so his kingdom should be safe for a time."

He paused to swallow down the last of his wine. "Much of our army was lost," he said sadly, "almost eight hundred men, including all the infantry. Artorius hired five merchant vessels at Caletum to carry the survivors home. No more ships were needed."

Dead silence fell, and Melwas chose this moment to speak up. "Artorius may not be dead," he drawled, "but he is surely disgraced. The High King does not strike me as a very patient man. Certainly not one to tolerate such a shameful defeat."

Cacamwra scowled at him. "Artorius bears no shame," he said hotly, "the shame, if any there be, lies with Rigotomos for believing in the lies of the Romans."

"I regret to admit that Constantine did see the matter differently," he added after a moment's reflection, "the king met Artorius outside the steps of the palace, and there publicly stripped him of his titles. Our master is no longer Dux Bellorum, or even Magister Equitum. He has lost his seat on the Council of Britannia. 'No longer', the king declared, 'shall you have any say in the governing of this land, General Artorius.' Such is the gratitude of kings."

Ganhumara could never love Artorius, but it was impossible for her not to pity him a little as she listened to this. She knew him for a proud man, all his self-worth invested in his strength as a warrior, his right and ability to lead other men in war. Such a public humiliation, inflicted by the king he had sworn to serve, would have been a spear to his heart.

"That was the limit of his punishment, thank God," said Cacamwri, "a few of the councillors called for Artorius to be placed on trial, but Constantine would not hear of it. Not, you may be sure, through any sense of mercy. He wants Artorius to live on as a man shamed before the world, a symbol and reminder of the fate of those who fail the High King."

He spat on the rushes. "Damn Constantine. He is no king of mine. I piss on his crown, and his fine robes. Damn the councillors as well. Cowardly swine. Not one of them would dare meet my master's eye, and yet they are more than willing to slide knives into his back."

"Have a care," said Melwas, "you have just spoken enough treason to put your neck in a noose."

Cacamwri responded with a rude gesture. Some of the other men laughed, and Melwas looked furious at being insulted by a mere servant. His hand flew to his dagger.

Ganhumara intervened before he had a chance to draw. "What will Artorius do?" she asked softly, "surely he must come home?"

"Yes, lady," replied Cacamwri, resuming his normal smooth, courteous manner, "he has some affairs to attend to in Londinium, but will return as soon as he may. After all" – he spread his hands – "where else should he go? All he loves is here."

She smiled at the compliment, though it filled her with foreboding. The prospect of living forever in Caerleon with Artorius, a disgraced and increasingly embittered man, was not an attractive one. Shorn of his duty, with nothing to do but hunt, drink and pick quarrels with his neighbours, she could imagine him degenerating into a monster.

She feared for him, and herself, and their sons. What might they become, with such a father for an example?

Ganhumara shuddered. The hairs on the back of her neck prickled. Melwas was watching her again with his steady, unblinking gaze.

All her desire for Melwas was gone, replaced by a creeping fear of the young man, and what he might do. Save for Cacamwri and Cilydd, everyone was scared of him, or held him in a kind of awe.

The news of the catastrophe in Gaul, and the disgrace of Artorius, made him grow bolder. In the following days his arrogant and overbearing nature, always ill-concealed, came to the fore. He strutted about the fort as though he was the lord of Caerleon, followed by his cronies, taking it upon himself to oversee the preparation for Artorius' return. Slaves who dawdled in their work were brutally flogged, and Melwas often wielded the whip himself.

Ganhumara avoided him and stayed inside as much as possible. "Forgive me, O Lord," she begged in her prayers, "forgive me for the sin of lust, and fetch Artorius home. I vow to be a good wife to him."

Cydfan and Llacheu clung to their mother's legs, frightened by her obvious distress, and the sound of the cruelties being inflicted outside. Medraut reacted differently. He squatted beside the curtain dividing her bedchamber from the hall, tiny fists balled, face creased into an angry grimace.

"Will you protect me against Melwas, little warrior?" she said, smiling through her tears, "I fear you have some growing to do yet. Still, we have two good spearmen outside."

Night came, and cast a blanket over the terrors of the day. All was peace, save for the usual comforting noises: goats bleating as they were herded into their pens, the distant neigh of a horse, snatches of laughter and conversation. Ganhumara fastened the shutters, knelt beside her bed and said her evening prayers. Cydfan, who grew more devout by the day, knelt beside her.

"Little priest," she said fondly, tousling his soft red hair.

She rose and doused two of the three lamps on the bronze tripod standing in a corner. She preferred to keep one burning through the night as a comfort against the darkness.

"Time for bed, my brave one," she whispered, scooping up Medraut and lowering his plump body into the cot at the foot of her bed. He offered no resistance, his big dark eyes fastened on the curtain.

She stripped to her shift and climbed into the large bed. It was spread with red wool blankets and a fur rug, the pillows stuffed with goose down. Cydfan and Llacheu were already asleep, their little bodies lying next to each other. Sighing, Ganhumara lay down next to her sons, draped one slender, pale arm over them, and closed her eyes.

She woke to the sound of a child shrieking, and a powerful hand clamped round her throat.

Unable to move her head, she kicked out wildly, but froze as the cold tip of a dagger was pressed against her temple.

"Come play with me, my lady," the sibilant voice of Melwas hissed in her ear, "you will accept my invitation this time."

His hot breath, thick with lust and wine, wafted over her face. Heart racing, she saw Cydfan and Llacheu had vanished from her side.

The shrieks came from Medraut. His high-pitched yells of childish fury and despair filled the room

"My boys," she moaned, "what have you done with my boys?"

Melwas ignored her. "Christ's wounds, shut him up!" he roared at someone Ganhumara couldn't see.

There was the sound of a blow, a final terrible scream from Medraut, abruptly cut off, and then silence.

8.

Artorius made his way back to Caerleon with a heavy heart. The memory of his public disgrace at the hands of Constantine was still fresh, like a wound that refused to heal. For much of the journey he was silent, exchanging few words even with his closest comrades, and sat apart at night, gazing blankly into the camp fire while men spoke in low voices around him.

He was not wholly given over to misery. Both his fathers – his birth father, Uthyr of the Selgovae, and Ambrosius, the man who formally adopted him as a child – had taught him to fight until his last breath. Setbacks were just that. They could be overcome, provided a man held his nerve.

Thus he contemplated the flames at night and mulled over recent events, pondering how to turn them to his advantage.

The defeat of Rigotomos in Gaul had been pre-arranged. He was certain of this. A plot, cooked up between Constantine and the Prefect, Arvandus, who in turn was probably acting on behalf of his imperial master in Rome. Their motives were clear enough: Constantine wanted to destroy Artorius without getting his own hands dirty, and the Emperor wanted to fool Rigotomos into launching a suicidal attack on the Visigoths. Though Euric had won, both armies were severely mauled, giving the Romans an opportunity to march into Gaul and drive out the survivors.

The treachery of the Emperor was breathtaking. Rigotomos and his troops were fellow Christians. They had deserved better. Now the King of the Amoricans was dead, his body lapped in stone and lead at Avallon, thousands of his men left on the battlefield as food for crows.

Artorius wondered who had first suggested the plot to Constantine. He had his suspicions. When the High King harangued him from the steps of the palace in Londinium, Pascent was foremost among the herd of richly-dressed courtiers standing behind Constantine.

Vortigern's youngest son had gazed down at Artorius with undisguised triumph and hatred. These days he basked in royal favour, a trusted servant and confidante to the king. Some whispered of a darker connection between the two: neither were married, and Constantine showed remarkably little interest in women. Pascent was still a handsome young man, and would not be the first to have acquired power between the sheets.

Now his revenge is complete, thought Artorius, *he never forgave Ambrosius for defeating and slaying his father. He poisoned Ambrosius, and waited for his chance to strike me down as well.*

No. Not quite complete. I still live. In that respect, their plan failed.

Constantine had tried unsuccessfully to draw Artorius' last remaining teeth. "Soldiers," he cried, addressing the survivors of the British army, "your commander has been stripped of his rank, and you are no longer oath-sworn to follow him. If you choose to leave his service, and God knows there will be little honour or reward in it for you now, you would be welcome to join my household guards."

Of all the indignities the High King chose to heap on Artorius, this was the worst. A blatant attempt at further humiliation, taking away his buccelari and leaving him friendless and alone.

Constantine misjudged the quality of the men he tried to bribe. Every one had fought alongside Artorius for years in the endless campaigns against Britannia's enemies. Hard-forged bonds of loyalty existed between the men and their captain. It would take more than cheap promises of gold, and a comfortable berth in the royal guard, to break them.

Artorius had not wept since his early childhood, when his unloving mother beat him for leaving a fire untended. Still, his eyes misted when he recalled the reaction of his followers to the High King's shameless offer.

"Artorius!" bellowed Cei, his head still swathed in a rough bandage, raising his spear, "God for Artorius!"

The rest followed suit, and the drab skies above Londinium echoed to their furious shouts.

"Artorius! Artorius! We will have no other chief! Artorius!"

The memory of this test of loyalty was a salve on Artorius' wounded pride. His battered spirits slowly recovered as he led his men further west, away from the snake-pit of Londinium and back to the gentle green country he knew and loved. Though a northerner by birth, the west was his true home, where he had learned to fight and ride, and met the woman of his heart.

His old friend Eidol Cadarn welcomed him at Glevum, and feasted him and his officers inside the hall of his palace, a crumbling old Roman fortress built on some rising ground above the river.

"That for the High King's judgment," the old magistrate said contemptuously, snapping his fingers, "if he decides to punish me for receiving you, well, let him try. These walls have stood for hundreds of years. It will take more than our upstart king and his lackeys to knock them down."

Artorius sipped his indifferent wine, poured into an ugly goblet of smoked green glass made by some ham-fisted local craftsman, and looked around fondly at the hall. The pleasant smells of roasting meat and wood smoke filled his nostrils.

"This was where I first saw her," he said, "the woman I intend to make my wife. I bought her from you for the price of a horse. Do you remember?"

"I still have the horse," replied Eidol with a grin, "one of my sons rode her into the ground, and now she's a broken-winded creature, good for nothing save ambling about and cropping grass. You got the best of that bargain."

"Ganhumara is everything I want in a woman," Artorius said seriously, "she should have been born a queen, not a slave."

Eidol's eyes were mazed with drink as he leaned in closer. Artorius feared he was about to say something conspiratorial. The paunchy old man was as subtle as a hammer, with a voice that carried across a crowded room like a war-horn.

"She could yet be a queen," he husked, the hot spice of his breath gusting over Artorius, "if she was the wife of a king."

Artorius clenched his jaw. "Enough," he said curtly, staring into his cup, "save your wind. I have no designs on the throne. All I ever wanted was a hall of my own, some good land to go with it, and to live and die as a soldier. I am a base-born northerner, with no more royal blood in my veins than a swineherd."

Eidol swayed a little in his chair, fumbling for speech. "No man can fool himself forever," he hissed, "God has marked you out for greatness, Artorius. You cannot escape. Nor do you want to, deep down. If all you craved was a damp hall in the west, and a litter of bairns crawling at your feet, why did you accept Caledfwlch? Caesar's sword, man! Only kings and emperors are fit to wield such a blade."

Artorius put down his glass. The wine tasted sour in his throat. "You forget, Julius Caesar was first and foremost a soldier," he said, "I accepted the sword as a gift from his shade. One military man to another. A symbol of my good faith, my duty to defend Britannia, and whoever rules the land."

Eidol sniggered and broke wind. "Horse dung," he said cheerfully, "you were fated the moment you took Caledfwlch from Morgana, and you knew it. Where is the witch, anyway?"

"I have seen or heard nothing from my sister since I met her at the stones," Artorius replied truthfully, "she walks strange paths, down which none can follow."

"She did you no favours by offering you the sword. Constantine dearly wants the accursed thing for himself. By giving Caledfwlch to another man, she was insulting him, saying he was unworthy to defend his kingdom. Unworthy to wear the crown."

"Mind you," he added, reaching for a chop from the heap on the platter before him, "she was right. Only a fool would have set you aside, the best soldier in the land, and worked so hard to make an enemy of you. I suppose he has put one of his toadies in charge of the army."

"He has appointed Geraint, the captain of his personal guard, as Magister Militum," said Artorius, "he will lead the fight against the Picts and the Saxons, while Constantine remains in Londinium."

"Where he is free to debauch himself," Eidol snorted, "and you wallow in self-pity and baby shit at Caerleon. God help us, the Saxons must be rubbing their hands."

"Listen," he said, cocking his grey head, "listen hard, and you may hear the laughter of Hengist."

After bidding Eidol a warm farewell, Artorius left Glevum the next morning, nursing a sourness in his guts and a persistent ache in his head.

"Damn that wine," he moaned, rubbing his belly, "Eidol always did keep a cellar full of piss."

"Take heart," said Bedwyr, who was in a similar condition, "soon you will be in the comfort of your own hall, where the wines taste sweeter."

They did indeed. Caerleon was no longer used as a port, since the town was ruined and the river largely silted up, but some of the goods of its previous wealth remained. The last merchants to reside there had left in a hurry, abandoning their houses and well-stocked wine cellars. Artorius had found a small private store of Falernian wine, from the best Italian vineyards on the slopes of Mount Falernus in Campania, and taken it for himself.

He had other comforts in mind. As they headed south-west from Glevum, following the Roman road into the forested hill country of the Kingdom of Gwent, his thoughts were full of Ganhumara. Strangely faithful in his way, Artorius had lain with no other woman since leaving Caerleon.

As so often, Bedwyr seemed to guess his thoughts. "Shall we have a wedding to celebrate, before the summer is out?" he asked slyly, glancing sidelong at his chief.

Artorius rubbed his brow with the heel of his hand, and smiled for the first time since returning from Gaul. "Maybe," he replied gruffly, "if my damned head has cleared by then."

They skirted the ruined town of Caerleon, home to nothing but ghosts and a handful of squatters, and made for the hill-fort looming over the decaying amphitheatre.

Something of the weight lifted from Artorius' shoulders as he saw the puffs of smoke rising from the thatched roof of his hall. Soon he would be warming his bones by his own hearth, listening to Ganhumara's chatter while his sons vied for his attention. Later, when the feasting was over and the fires burned low, he would lie next to her warm body. Perhaps even plant another son inside her. Why not? A man could never have too many sons.

The main entrance to the fort lay to the west, so Artorius led his men around the southern flank of the hill, following the line of the outer ditch.

A lone horseman rode down from the gateway to meet them. Artorius recognised him immediately.

"Cacamwri," he called out, pleased to see one of his most loyal servants, "you survived the journey from Londinium, then. I felt guilty at sending you back alone."

His good humour faded. "This is a poor homecoming," he added, frowning, "where is Cilydd, and the other men I left to guard my hall? Why don't they come out to welcome me?"

Cacamwri was a stocky, pot-bellied young man with a round face, usually a cheerful sort, with a great store of filthy stories. Now he looked sombre, and there was fear in his eyes as he reined in his pony.

"What's the matter with you?" snapped Artorius as Cacamwri appeared to struggle for words.

A sudden chill struck him. "Is it my boys?" he said, making the sign of the cross, "has one of them taken ill, or had an accident?"

Cacamwri swallowed. "Not...not taken ill, lord," he stammered, "but..."

He stared at Artorius hopelessly, and then the words came tumbling out. "Ganhumara is gone, lord. Melwas has taken her.

Twenty-one of your warriors have gone with him. The others, including Cilydd, are dead. Melwas and his traitors murdered them. Your sons live, but Medraut…Medraut is hurt. He screamed when his mother was taken, and suffered a blow to his face. Elias has attended him since, day and night, and done his best to patch up the wound. He…he fears the boy will be marked for life."

Elias was a doctor, a travelling Frank from the northeast of Gaul who had seen much of the world in his time before washing up in Caerleon. Pickled in wine, he still retained much of his skill, and knew more of the mysterious arts of medicine than most of the native leeches.

Artorius' knuckles turned white as he twisted the reins in his hands. He recalled Melwas, a promising young warrior with an insolent tongue and a roving eye.

"Melwas," he muttered, rolling the name around his mouth. Artorius had never suspected him of such treachery. He had barely thought about him at all. The lad was a mere pup, yet to ride in his first war-band, always courteous in the presence of his elders.

This is how it happens, he thought, *when a man loses the respect of his followers, they turn away from him. Insult him. Betray him. The rot has begun.*

It had to be stopped. "Speak truthfully, Cacamwri," he said, striving to keep his voice calm, "was she taken, or did she go willingly?"

The other man would not meet his eye. "I…I don't know, lord," he answered, "I was in bed when it happened, and it was all over when I got up to the hall. There were bodies strewn about, and Cilydd lay dying in one corner, his throat slashed. He and Ganhumara's spearmen tried to stop them, but there were too many. The slaves, though, they say…"

"They say what?"

"Just kitchen talk, lord. You know how slaves gossip. But there are rumours. They speak of a…of an understanding between Ganhumara and Melwas. Nothing was seen to happen, but…"

An understanding. Artorius took in a deep breath. His men knew his moods, and were eyeing him warily.

Should he be surprised, though? Ganhumara was just a girl, left alone for months with three young children to look after. She and Melwas were of an age, and he was handsome, and personable, with a talent for making himself pleasant…

And he has killed my men, and caused others to turn traitor, and hurt my son.

His dreams of a comfortable homecoming were shattered. Betrayed, disgraced, humiliated and maybe even cuckolded. It was too much to bear. A more peaceable man might have wondered why God had chosen to heap such miseries on him. Artorius was a fighter. His way was to strike first and examine the reasons later.

"They have gone to the Summer Country, lord," said Cacamwri, "to his father's court, well-hidden among the mists and bogs."

"Let them hide where they will," snarled Artorius, "I will smoke them out, wherever they may be, and show the world what it means to insult me."

9.

Artorius chose sixty of his best men, leaving the remainder to guard Caerleon, and rode back east to delve into the Summer Country. This lay in the very heart of Dumnonia, a place of misted hills and crooked valleys, dark forests and ancient, forbidden magic.

Driven by anger, Artorius cared nothing for crossing into Dumnonian territory, the ancestral realm of the High King. He knew the northern part of the kingdom well, having lived there for years under the tutelage of Ambrosius, but had never ventured close to the borders of the land within a land, where this world was said to merge with Annwn, the Otherworld.

Those borders shifted, and seemed to vary greatly depending on who was looking for them. Artorius knew enough, from listening to tales in his youth, to always keep the massive range of hills that dominated the landscape in the north-west of the kingdom to his right as he rode south. Eventually, depending on the whim of whatever mysterious powers guarded access, he would come to the gates of the Summer Country.

None of Constantine's scattered garrisons tried to bar his path. His following was too large, and he knew the garrison of each fort would likely number no more than fifty men: Artorius knew, since he had once owned the forts.

"What a fool I was, to give up the chance of power when God offered it," he confessed to Cei and Bedwyr as they pushed further south, through a land of fertile, low-lying meadows and little rivers, "since then I have known nothing but defeat. The Lord resents his gifts being spurned."

"I thought God was supposed to value modesty," said Cei, "plenty of men have craved power, and slaughtered each other for a crown. Not many have turned one down without a fight."

He grinned, creasing the fleshy, raw-boned features of his face into a hideous grimace. "I reckon God is confused. He prefers meek little priests who do what they're told, not a band of northern savages like us. My grandfather was a pagan, and I still remember him showing me the secret places of the old gods when I was young."

"When it comes to you, Cei, there is no confusion," remarked Bedwyr, who could be relied on to take few things seriously, "your rotten soul will baste in Hell. Mine, no doubt, will baste with you."

The cultivated land gradually petered out, until they descended into a valley with a little stream coursing through the middle. It was desperately hot. Artorius cursed the necessity of wearing so much leather and iron in high summer.

A heat haze, like a fine yellow mist, hung over the valley. It was thinly wooded on both flanks, and the trees were silent, with no sound of birdsong or animal life.

Artorius instinctively knew where they were. The knowledge rose from somewhere deep inside him, from the blood and the bone.

"We are here," he said, slowing Llamrei to a walk, "the edge of the Summer Country. The stream is the gateway."

He hesitated. All knew the tales of Annwn, a land of spectacular delights and hellish cruelties, where men walked as gods and fought with demons for mastery of their unknowable, ever-shifting realm. It was said that the gates to Annwn lay inside streams and rivers. If Artorius and his men ventured into the water, might they be dragged down to the Otherworld, never to return?

Cei dismounted and led his horse towards the bank. He peered with exaggerated care into the fast-flowing water, and dipped his spear in it. The spear only sank a foot or so before scraping against the bottom.

"Seems safe enough," he said, winking at his comrades, "shall I cross first? If I vanish, tell my wife I love her."

Artorius laughed, as did some of the other men, but the others remained tense and silent, watching anxiously as Cei climbed back into the saddle and urged his horse into the stream.

He reached the other side without incident. Slightly ashamed at his own timidity, Artorius was the first to follow. Eventually all the men crossed, with the faintest hearts bringing up the rear.

Beyond lay deep forest, dark and tangled and thickly wooded, with few obvious paths. For a while they led their horses through the eerily silent wilderness, hacking through dead branches and twisting barriers of thorn and bramble. The sky had faded from blue to a lowering, washed-out grey, but the heat was worse than ever, beating down mercilessly from a sun that was scarcely visible now, hidden behind the yellow haze that hung over the forest: a stifling vapour, leeching all the moisture from the air and strangling the breath in their lungs.

Artorius led the way, and was the first to see the pool, a circle of grey, brackish water set in the middle of a glade.

"We'll rest here," he said, taking a swig from the leather flask he carried at his belt. Using his cloak to dab at the sweat streaming down his face, he knelt beside the pool.

The water looked undrinkable, clotted with filth and rank with dead flies. No wind rippled its surface. Artorius stared down at the vague outline of his reflection. A weary, hollow-eyed man with an untidy mess of dirty yellow hair and beard stared back at him.

He sighed. *I am not twenty-four, and look twenty years older.*

When he blinked, his reflection vanished, and was replaced by another. A remarkably ugly one, a devil's face, little eyes flaming under prominent bony brows, pointed chin, hooked nose and wide grinning mouth, teeth reduced to blackish stumps. Its hair was grey and scanty, mere wisps of fluff clinging to a bald dome.

Artorius looked up, and saw the owner of this unlovely visage squatting on a rock on the opposite side of the pool.

A small man, barely half his size, with long, stick-thin arms and froglike legs ending in bare feet, a hint of webbing between the toes. Crude tattoos, swirling blue patterns and rough animal figures, were daubed all down the length of his arms. His skin was deathly pale, his meagre body clothed in a deerhide smock tied at the waist with a knotted length of cord. A knife carved from a single piece of bone was thrust into his crude belt. Otherwise he carried no weapon.

Artorius remained kneeling. The appearance of the ugly, dwarfish little man had not surprised him. This was an Old One – otherwise known as the Painted People or Hill Folk – descendants of the oldest inhabitants of Britannia.

He heard someone move behind him, and flung up his hand just as Cei was drawing back a spear to throw.

"No, Cei," he said quietly, "he is no threat."

Cei reluctantly lowered his spear. "The little rat could be one of Melwas' scouts," he growled, "we made more noise blundering through this accursed forest than a herd of oxen. Melwas must know we are coming."

The dwarf's face split in a gaping grin, and he uttered a hoarse coughing noise that might have been a laugh.

"Not oxen," he gasped in a wheezing, high-pitched voice, "a herd of pigs. You look like pigs to me, all fat and pink. I watched you cross the water, and followed you into the woods. These are the Dead Lands. Nothing grows here. Nothing lives. Why would men with iron come to such a place?"

"You heard my friend," said Artorius, "we came to hunt Melwas. He has taken my woman. You know him?"

The dwarf sucked on one of his few remaining teeth for a moment, his gnarled, weather-beaten face crumpling like an old sack.

"I know him," he wheezed, "I know his hall. It lies in the middle of this web. Among reeds, among dykes, among marshes. My people saw him ride through our lands. Him and the woman."

He snickered, and gave his long nose a pull. "You shall never get her back. No outsider can find his way through the Summer Country. Not without help."

"Your help?" said Artorius.

"My help. Why should I give it? Your people have been cruel to mine. You came to this island, long ago, with your strength and your iron, and drove us into the hills and bogs and wild places. It would give me joy to watch you walk around in circles until hunger took you, or your legs broke."

Now Artorius rose, and slowly drew Caledfwlch from her scabbard. "You know this iron," he said, holding up the sword.

The shrewd little eyes flickered in their bony sockets. "Yes," he replied, "Caesar's sword. Nennius gave it into our keeping, long ago. None should find the blade of kings, he said, so long as we kept it hidden. Then the blind seer came and took it from us. She could not be denied."

"The seer was my sister, Morgana. I am Artorius. She gave me the sword. If you wish to remain her friend, you will help us find Melwas."

"Artorius."

The dwarf hissed the name between his rotten teeth, eyes narrowing.

"She spoke of you," he said, rocking back and forth on his meatless haunches, "you will hold dominion over all the peoples of this island. Your name is engraved in the stars. The gods of old have chosen you. Your time is not yet."

"Help us," said Artorius, lowering his sword, "or bear my sister's curse. You know the power she wields."

Something like fear darted across the dwarf's ugly features. "Follow, then," he spat, hopping down off his rock, "look not to left or right, but keep your eyes straight ahead. Think not of the noises you may hear, the pleading voices, the painful cries, else you are lost. Stay on the paths. Above all, stay on the paths."

The dwarf gave his name as Nudd, and he took them out of the dead woods into a stretch of foul-smelling, mist-covered marshland, where the greenish waters sucked and lapped at the feet of the men as they tramped miserably through the mire, attacked by cloying heat and hordes of flies.

Nudd moved swiftly, striding confidently on his long legs. His spine was horribly twisted, forcing him to walk in a painful crouch, long arms dangling beside his ankles.

"My mother told me the Summer Country was a land of delights," panted Gwalchmei as he toiled through the mire, "of beautiful people and rich, rolling grasslands. The air was full of the scent of spring flowers. She never mentioned mud and flies."

"Your mother lied," sniggered Nudd, "there are no delights here. This is a place for the banished and the condemned, a refuge for those who have nowhere else to go."

They slogged through the marsh for what seemed like hours. Time had little meaning there, since the wan sun hung motionless in the sky, and the skies remained grey and featureless.

Gradually the dreary landscape started to break up. Scattered clumps of reeds appeared, straggling, feeble things at first, barely reaching to a man's thigh. The reeds grew thicker and broader, until Nudd was leading the Britons through a series of paths leading through walls of tall plants.

"Stay on the path," he wheezed, his lungs crackling with rheum, "no matter what you hear or see. Else you are lost, and I cannot help you."

A nervous silence hung over the procession. In places the path was so narrow they had to walk in single file, and the rustling of the reeds was like a constant whispering in their ears, ghostly voices just on the edge of hearing. The heat was unbearable, and the incessant flies crawled into the mouths and eyes of their horses, causing the beasts untold distress.

The crushing silence was occasionally punctured by a cry in the distance, a terrible strangled wail, like an animal in torment.

"Close your ears to it," said Artorius, "look ahead, and fear nothing. We are safe, so long as we keep to the path."

The cry sounded more frequently, and now took on a more human tone, the shrill, piercing scream of a woman or child in terrible pain.

Words formed. *"God save me...oh Jesu, no please...help me...help me..."*

"Don't be fooled," said Nudd, "mere spirits. Voices on the wind. They want to lure you deeper into the marsh."

"God aid us," Artorius heard Bedwyr mutter. One of the most lethal fighters in Artorius' war-band, he was also the most soft-hearted, and prone to take pity on the weak and defenceless. He was just the type to go haring off into the reeds, sword in hand.

"Courage, Bedwyr," said Artorius, though his own skin was crawling with fear, "Cei, Gwalchmei, keep a close eye on him. If he looks like running, knock him out."

At last they came to the end of the nightmarish fen. Flat green countryside stretched ahead, criss-crossed with innumerable small rivers and waterways.

Not half a mile away, perched on a small hillock rising from the wetlands, was a small timber hill-fort. Artorius counted eight or nine conical thatched roofs rising over the palisade, and caught the glint of light on spears and iron helmets over the gateway.

Nudd limped over to Artorius, and placed a clammy hand on his wrist. "See," he said, baring his foul teeth in an ingratiating smile, "there lies the hall of Melwas."

10.

Of her abduction from Caerleon, and the ride through the nightmarish depths of the Summer Country, Ganhumara remembered little. All was confusion, a meaningless jumble of images tumbling through the blackest vaults of memory, until Melwas guided his horse through the gates of his court.

"Welcome to Caer Thannoc, my lady," he murmured into her ear, "we shall be happy here, I promise."

Ever since she woke in bed at Caerleon and felt the edge of his knife pressed against her neck, Ganhumara's will had not been her own. Incapable of resistance, she had allowed herself to be dragged out of the hall and slung over his horse, where she only remained upright because he sat behind her, his strong arms encircling her waist.

To anyone watching, it may have looked as though she was allowing herself to be taken. Ganhumara knew how unpopular she was with the slaves at Caerleon, and how they would choose to interpret the manner of her leaving.

Something deep inside her rebelled now, as his horse clopped into the courtyard of Caer Thannoc. It was a poor and miserable-looking place, barely large enough to house fifty people, a far cry from the grand palace Melwas had boasted of. Unlike Caerleon, which always bustled with life, it was quiet and virtually empty. Two spearmen in rusting mail stood on the parapet over the gateway, and a slave in soiled and rotting clothing trudged about, carrying a bucket full of night soil. A few dismal, stringy cattle occupied a pen outside the mead-hall, much smaller than the one at Caerleon.

"My lover will hunt you down," she said, "and kill you. Artorius is not a man to cross."

Her voice sounded unnaturally loud in the silence. Save to answer Melwas' occasional questions in a dull monotone, she had barely uttered a word since her abduction. All through the dead forest and the stinking marshes and the rustling, haunted fens, she had remained mute and biddable, a mere puppet, sparking into life only when Melwas jerked her strings.

Melwas threw back his handsome head and brayed with laughter. "If Artorius ever finds this place," he said, sliding easily from the saddle, "which I doubt, he shall not find it so easy to kill me. This is my turf. The bones of my ancestors lie in the ground beneath us. I draw my power from them. Only a very foolish outsider would dare to challenge a prince of the Summer Country inside his own borders."

His complacent tone was hateful. Everything Ganhumara had once found desirable in him was loathsome now: his cocksure poise and arrogance, his lithe, sinewy body, the devilish sparkle in his eyes.

She would have spat in his face, but something about his expression dissuaded her. Melwas was a stranger to mercy, and wouldn't hesitate to strike down a woman if he thought it necessary.

"You hurt my son," she said quietly, "a baby boy, not yet old enough to walk. God damn you for that."

Melwas gave a careless shrug. "The little bastard should not have screamed so loud," he replied brutally, "his brothers had more sense. They stayed quiet. Be grateful I let Medraut live. He will bear a good scar for the rest of his days, as a reminder of the value of caution."

"Come, lady," he added impatiently, stretching out his hand, "I will not chop words with you out here. Let me show you my father's hall."

Ganhumara would rather have put her hand inside a lion's jaws, but he was right. This was his turf. He held the power here. Until Artorius arrived, she would have to do his bidding, if she wanted to live and see her children again.

She allowed him to help her down, and place her arm in his as he walked towards the hall. He didn't spare a glance for the men who had succumbed to his influence and followed them from Caerleon. They were deserters now, oath-breakers, beneath contempt in the eyes of all honourable men. Ganhumara might have pitied them, had they not aided Melwas in tearing her from hearth and home.

The hall was the largest building inside the stockade. Judging from the smell and the dirt, it also served as a byre for the cattle in bad weather, humans and animals huddling together for warmth. It was full of smoke from a guttering fire in the middle of the floor, most of which failed to escape through the inadequate hole hacked out of the roof. The floor itself was uneven, slippery with cow dung and urine mixed among the rushes. There were holes everywhere, obliging Ganhumara to watch her footing as Melwas led her, politely but firmly, towards a little group of people at the far end of the hall.

They were the oddest trio she had ever set eyes on. A very old man lay inside a narrow bed. His yellow, bony-knuckled hands lay folded over his shrivelled belly, while his rheumy, heavy-lidded eyes listlessly contemplated the ceiling. The only signs of life came from the gentle rise and fall of his chest, and the occasional blinking of the tired eyes.

At his bedside sat a hideously obese, white-haired hag, and a small, round, balding little man. Both were clenched in concentration over a game of gwyddbywll, the board resting on a stool between them. Occasionally the hag plucked some bits of dry twigs and holly leaves from the pile of chaff beside her chair and tossed them onto the fire, raising fresh plumes of smoke.

"There lies my father," said Melwas, nodding at the ruin in the bed, "he will die soon, if the gods are good, and I will inherit his kingdom."

"You call this a kingdom?" replied Ganhumara, with as much scorn as she dared, "this land of death and decay? You must be mad, to dream of inheriting such a waste."

Melwas smiled pityingly at her, as though she lacked all understanding. The hag and the bald man were still absorbed in their game and paid no attention to the newcomers.

"She was my nurse," said Melwas, referring to the hag, "the little man is my steward. He rules the Summer Country during my father's illness, and will call me lord one day."

At this the man glanced up from the board, and spat.

Melwas laughed. "Rough company, my lady," he said, stroking Ganhumara's arm, "the people of the Summer Country are only half-human. We observe different laws and customs. You will get used to us."

Ganhumara was repelled by his touch. "Not for long," she said stubbornly, pulling away from him, "Artorius will come soon, and put this pigsty to the torch."

He seized her arm and dragged her back. "You put too much faith in Artorius," he snarled, squeezing with his iron fingers until she cried out in pain, "even if he does find his way here, I shall kill him, and offer his heart on a platter to our gods."

"Whatever happens," she whispered, gazing without fear into his icy blue eyes, "I will not lie with you. Not willingly."

"I could make you do whatever I wished, lady," he said, his lips almost touching hers, "you would be powerless against my will. But I didn't take you for a slave. There is no joy in conquering one who cannot resist."

"Why do you want me so much?" she demanded, "what am I to you?"

His eyes glinted. "Artorius is not in the common roll of men. The blood of the Hill Folk runs in my veins. I have the Sight, and can see the greatness in Artorius, shining around him like fire. I want it for myself, to steal his power and make it mine. Snatching his woman is the first step. The next is to lure him to his destruction. If he has any pride at all, he will come for you, and place his own head in the trap."

Now Ganhumara understood. "You are envious of him!" she cried, "all this is jealousy – mere jealousy!"

His eyes widened, and for a brief second there was something truly animal about him, teeth bared in a hungry snarl, displaying over-long incisors. Ganhumara feared he might bury them in her throat, but instead he spun her around and shoved her towards a far corner, where an ox-skin lay draped over some dusty boards.

"You may sleep there tonight," he growled, "tomorrow night you will come to my bed. And the following night, and all the rest of your nights on earth. I wish you pleasant dreams, my lady."

He stalked away, vanishing through the tattered scrap of curtain dividing the hall from his private quarters. Ganhumara rubbed her arms – she felt cold, despite the warmth of the fire – and lay down in the corner. It stank of cattle and unwashed bodies, while the skin was rank with fleas. Exhausted by her trials, she did her best to ignore the fleas and curled up, using her soiled cloak as a makeshift pillow.

In spite of the stench and the discomfort, sleep came swiftly, casting her into a pit of dreams. She saw the sky over Britannia, bruised black by the smoke rising from burning towns and cities. A great crucifix hung in the sky. On it writhed the figure of Christ, thrown into fresh torment by the fires raging below. The land was burning, and the hosts of Hell ran amok, plundering and slaughtering at will. The banners of Christ were all thrown down, as were the banners of the kings of Britannia, lying among the heaped, blood-spattered corpses of her warriors.

She glimpsed the figure of Artorius, silhouetted against the horizon. In his right hand he grasped his spear Rhongymiad. Caledfwlch sparkled at his hip. He was a giant, godlike figure, scarcely recognisable as the man she knew. Instead of his usual plain armour and woollen cloak, he wore a coat of shimmering golden scales, and the crest on his helm was shaped like a dragon poised to lunge, wings outspread, jaws gaping, the precious gemstones of its eyes glowing a deep, smoky red.

The churning skies were split by the rumble of thunder and the flash of lightning. Ganhumara knew she was deceived. It was not thunder she could hear, but Artorius' war-band, advancing to battle; it was not lightning, but the gleam of sunlight reflecting off their spears.

Then the land was cloaked in a sweet odour, so heady and consuming it made Ganhumara feel drowsy, even though she already slept. The sweetness stemmed from the mead served to Artorius' warriors before battle, and the great virtue of that mead was that one man's stroke became as the stroke of nine, and no counter-stroke could oppose it.

The doleful booming of war-horns rolled across the hills and forests, signalling the advance of the warriors of the Island of the Mighty. Ganhumara twisted in her sleep as the horns grew ever louder, rising to an unbearable pitch, screaming in her ears like the howling of children...of her sons...

"Medraut!"

She woke with a yell, to find the hag standing over her, and the sound of a war-horn echoing through the hall.

The hag reached down with one grey hand and seized a handful of Ganhumara's black hair. Her grip was cruel. Ganhumara tried to wriggle free, but the other woman possessed enormous strength for her age.

"Come," the hag said throatily. Ganhumara struggled in vain as she was dragged up from the stinking ox-skin and out of the hall.

There was no way of telling night from day in the Summer Country. The same listless sky hovered overhead, the same pallid sun.

Most of the people of Caer Thannoc were gathered before the gate, summoned by the war-horn. There were even less than Ganhumara suspected, just nineteen guards and slaves, a dirty, unwashed rabble, their faces drawn and hollow-eyed. The slaves were barefoot and stood ankle-deep in mire, careless of the filth splattering their patched smocks.

Of the traitors who had brought her to Caer Thannoc, there was no sign. She imagined they were in hiding, or perhaps already gone, fearful of Artorius' vengeance.

Melwas stood on the timber rampart above the gate. For once he was dressed like the prince he claimed to be. A copper torc adorned his neck, and he wore a black woollen tunic and calfskin boots, with a jewelled dagger thrust into his belt.

He seemed to sense Ganhumara's presence, and turned to look down at her. He made a splendid figure, tall and sinewy and athletic, auburn hair bristling in the dead air, though she knew his fairness was only skin-deep.

"My lady," he called out cheerfully, almost skipping down the wooden steps beside the gate, "I owe you an apology. Your lover waits for us outside. One of the Hill Folk led them here, it seems. Damned traitors! And I regarded them as kin."

His tone was cheerful, as if he could have wished for nothing better. When he reached the ground, his people bowed before him, grovelling on their knees in the dirt. Even the little bald steward, who had previously spat in contempt of Melwas, knelt before him.

Only the hag remained standing, though she at least slackened her painful grip on Ganhumara's hair.

"My father died during the night," Melwas explained, "not before time. I am now the lord of Caer Thannoc."

He spread his arms wide, stretching until the joints in his shoulders clicked. "At last, life can truly begin," he cried, "I have great plans. First, I shall reduce the other lords of the Summer Country to obedience. Then the Hill Folk shall pay for their treachery. They will be smoked out, like bees from a hive, and ordered to find shelter elsewhere. Once these trifling matters are dealt with, I shall bend the whole of Britannia to my will."

"First, however," he said, "I shall kill Artorius. He seems so eager to die. It is a pity to keep him waiting."

Ganhumara found her voice. "What will you do?" she demanded, "hide behind your walls, like a coward, and wait for Artorius to come and get you? Or are you man enough to face him in the open?"

"Not a bad effort, my lady," he replied blandly, "but there is no need to try and goad me into crossing swords with your champion. I have already resolved to do so. It must be single combat between us. To the death. The winner takes the land…and, of course, the woman."

One of his slaves came limping from the door of a hut, carrying a long spear and a hatchet. It was the same spear Ganhumara had seen Melwas wield before, in his unequal sparring match with Pwyll.

"You will wear no armour?" she asked as Melwas took the weapons, tucking the hatchet into his silver-linked belt and hefting the spear in his right hand, "no helmet or shield?"

Melwas smiled mockingly at her. "Concerned for my safety, are you? Have no fear. Artorius will not leave a scratch on me. I told you, this is my turf. My strength is as the strength of ten here. No mortal blade can pierce my flesh. I shall be light on my feet, while Artorius lumbers about in his iron, sweating and bleeding his life into the earth."

She thought he was mad, and watched in disbelief as he ordered the gates to be flung open. His guards lifted the bar and dragged them inward, revealing the slope curving down towards the edge of the fen.

Ganhumara's heart leaped when she saw Artorius and his men gathered on the water meadow below, drawn up in three ranks. Artorius sat mounted on Llamrei just ahead of the front rank, staring up at the gate.

In his dull grey mail and soiled cloak, he little resembled the godlike figure of her dream. Even so, Ganhumara had never been so happy to see him, nor his companions. She quickly scanned the faces of the men behind him, and saw Cei and Bedwyr had also returned safe from the disaster in Gaul.

She thought Bedwyr – gentle, handsome Bedwyr, who any woman would be proud to call husband – smiled at her.

Melwas gestured at the hag, who gave Ganhumara a hard shove in the small of her back, pushing her towards the gate.

"You are part of the prize, lady," he said, "and should witness the death of your old lover at the hands of the new. I shall offer up half of his smoking heart to you, and the rest to the gods."

He strode confidently down the slope, spear balanced lightly in both hands. None of his warriors followed. They remained clustered inside the gate, pale and silent, apparently careless of their master's fate. Ganhumara walked quickly after him, aware of the monstrous old woman dogging her steps.

"Artorius," Melwas cried, "I feared you were not coming, or else the spirits of the marsh had swallowed you up."

He stopped near the foot of the slope, one man against sixty, and thrust the butt of his spear into the ground.

Artorius said nothing. The air was heavy and suffocating, like a prelude to a storm, as he raked Melwas and Ganhumara with his eyes. His face under the helmet was set in stone, mouth set in a firm line, heavy jaw clenched.

Ganhumara trembled. This was the Artorius she had never really known, Artorius the soldier, whose men feared and respected him in equal measure.

"Boy," he said eventually, his voice flat and hard, "you have stolen my woman, murdered my warriors and hurt my son. Make peace with your gods, for I will kill you now."

Melwas leaned nonchalantly against his spear, left hand planted on his hip. "Fool," he said with careless scorn, "you think to enter the Summer Country, and face me on my own ground? You are nothing here. I could kill you, and every one of those idiots behind you, without suffering so much as a graze. Your weapons cannot touch me."

Artorius slowly clambered down from the saddle. He looked weary from a long ride, splashed to the waist with fen mud. Next to the trim, youthful Melwas, he was a stolid, earthbound figure, older than his years.

"Your own ground?" he said, unfastening the brooch at his shoulder, "I have spent years fighting in the defence of this island. My blood has watered its soil. When I was young, Ambrosius prophesied that I would be Britannia's spear and shield. So I am."

His cloak fell from his shoulders. Iron hissed on wood as he drew Caledfwlch from its scabbard. The blade gleamed into life, absorbing the wan light and turning it into white fire, rippling up and down its length.

"I carry no ordinary sword," said Artorius, "look on Caledfwlch, Melwas. The Red Death, forged in the bowels of Mount Olympus. Your death."

Some of the colour drained from Melwas' wolfish features. "I have no fear of Caesar's pig-sticker," he hissed, "I will take it from you, and have my slaves use it to shovel dung."

He suddenly jerked his spear from the ground and ran at Artorius, leaping to stab at his face. Artorius flung his shield up, and the tip of the spear thudded harmlessly against the hide covering.

Melwas dropped into a crouch, waiting for the counter-thrust. It didn't come. Artorius stayed well behind his shield, holding Caledfwlch at stomach height.

"Slaughter the little bastard!" shouted Cei, to roars of approval from his comrades.

Ganhumara could only watch, and pray for God to smile on Artorius. She felt the press of sharp metal in her back. The hag was standing behind her with a knife, ready to stab it home if Ganhumara made any unwise moves.

Artorius was in no hurry. He kept his shield up, easily deflecting the other man's efforts to stab at his face and belly, making

157

no attacks of his own. The shouts and cheers of his warriors, urging him to make a quick end of Melwas, had no effect. For a big man, he was light on his feet, and kept his opponent at bay with ease, circling and backing away, perfectly composed.

"Fight me!" raged Melwas, his face crimson and dappled with sweat, "stop hiding behind that shield – your avoidance shames both of us!"

Artorius didn't react. He continued to back away, letting Melwas burn himself out.

The young man was a superb athlete, but even athletes tire. After one last futile thrust at Artorius' legs, Melwas roared in frustration and hurled the spear overarm, like a javelin.

It clanged harmlessly off the shield boss. Artorius stood still as Melwas sprang at him, red-faced and screaming in rage, hatchet whirling.

At the last moment Artorius stepped aside and let the hatchet cut through empty air. Off-balance, unprotected by any armour, Melwas was completely exposed.

Caledfwlch stabbed, once, its blade vanishing inside the young man's flank, just under his ribs.

It slid free, red to the hilt. Blood gushed from the neat slit in Melwas' guts. He dropped his hatchet and fell onto all fours, choking, eyes bulging, more blood dribbling from his mouth and nostrils.

Cei punched the air, and the roar of triumph from Artorius' warriors made the ground shake.

Ganhumara would have cried out for joy, but the knife pressed even harder into her back. She went rigid, expecting the hag to kill her out of spite for the death of Melwas.

"Let me live," she said, raising her voice above the din, "and I will beg Artorius to spare your life, and the lives of the people in Caer Thannoc. If you kill me, expect no mercy from him."

She got no response. Taking her courage in her hands, Ganhumara took a slow, deliberate step forward. Then another, and another, at any moment expecting the sharp kiss of the knife.

Nothing happened. The hag had let her go. She drew in a deep breath and muttered silent thanks.

Artorius was not done with Melwas. He might have finished off the fallen man easily. Instead he stuck Caledfwlch point-down into the ground, and picked up his opponent's hatchet.

The cheers of his warriors faded as he went to work. Silence followed, punctuated only by the wet thump of a heavy blade going into flesh, and the gasps and sobs of a dying man.

Ganhumara watched in shock. Her lover's earlier calm was quite gone. He hacked at Melwas with furious abandon, all his pent-up anger flowing out of him in an uncontrolled burst of savagery.

Finally he relented. "Kiss my foot," he snarled, and the shuddering, bleeding thing that had once been Melwas, would-be lord of the Summer Country, crawled over and pressed mangled lips to the toe of his boot.

Artorius raised his left hand and snapped his fingers. One of his youngest followers – Ganhumara recognised him as Gwaeddan, who had once sang sweetly for her during a hall-feast at Caerleon – dismounted and ran over, drawing his dagger.

He knelt beside Melwas and severed the big vein in his neck, putting an end to his suffering. A cry of horror went up from the people of Caer Thannoc, still huddled inside the gateway.

Artorius turned away from the ruin of his opponent and glanced up at them.

"See?" he said, holding up his red right hand, "there was no magic here. Your lord is dead. He was just a man after all. Your Summer Country is nothing but a dreary waste, peopled by ghosts and forgotten gods."

"None of you need die," he went on, "so long as you give up those men who betrayed me."

So far he had not even looked at Ganhumara. Fear and doubt entered her heart. She walked down to him, hands clasped before her.

"They are not here, lord," she said, "they chose to flee into the wild rather than face your justice. I thank God, and you, for my deliverance."

His eyes were cold, and his grim, closed-in expression belonged to a stranger. His armour, face and hands were smeared with fresh blood. He stank of the stuff. Of death.

"Fine words," he grunted, "they will not be enough to save you, Ganhumara. I was told you left Caerleon of your own free will."

"Whoever told you that is a liar!" she cried, suddenly angry, "I will swear any oath you wish. Melwas abducted me at knife-point."

He was unmoved, eyes narrowed to slits as they studied her. Words spilled out of Ganhumara, tripping over each other in their haste to be heard.

"My lord, what is this? Have I not always been true to you? You think I would abandon our children, our darling boys, for

161

the sake of that…that thing you have destroyed?"

Ganhumara almost went on her knees, begging him to see sense, but was too proud. His warriors were listening. She would not make a spectacle of herself for their entertainment.

Artorius seemed to relent a little. "No-one spoke in your defence," he said quietly, "not even Cacamwri. He says you were seen riding away with Melwas. All the while our son was lying on the floor of our bedchamber. His brothers were found cowering in a corner, weeping for their mother. Medraut lives, thank God, but shall be deformed for the rest of his days. One side of his face is crushed, though Elias managed to save his eye. What should I think? I came back from war to find my woman gone, my son disfigured, my warriors murdered or deserted."

Ganhumara opened her mouth to explain the strange influence Melwas had exerted over. Catastrophically, she hesitated, uncertain how to word it.

Artorius' eyes flashed with anger, and she knew her chance was gone.

"So," he said in a low, menacing tone, "that was the way of it. Now I, who would have gladly been your husband, must be your judge."

"My lord…" she began, reaching for him, but he waved her away.

"Hang her," said Cei, who had never been her friend, "once a whore, always a whore."

"Hold your noise!" Artorius shouted, and even stubborn, sharp-tongued Cei was cowed into silence.

Artorius turned back to her. "No, I will not execute you," he said, "not a woman I loved, and was fool enough to think she loved me in return."

"How can you expect love from a slave?" she responded, careless now, her natural bravery rising to the surface, "you took me, even though I didn't want you, and tried to mould me into something I was not. Oh, you were kind enough, in your way, but I was still your chattel. Your property, to be used as you liked."

He raised his fist. Ganhumara braced herself for the blow.

It didn't fall. Instead Artorius lowered his hand and dabbed some of the blood from his cheek. He stared at it, his face a mask of conflicting passions.

"We will let God decide your fate," he muttered, "God, and the elements."

11.

The Isle of Tanatos, Cent, Winter 472

The Saxons prowled ashore on the western edge of the isle, dragging their shallow-bottomed keels onto the sandy beach and swiftly dispersing into groups. The advance parties moved inland, while the remainder set about lifting their war-gear from the boats.

Hengist was among the last to set foot on land. Afflicted by a bad leg and creeping pains in his joints, he climbed out of the boat with difficulty, and splashed ashore through the creamy surf.

He was old now, with a liberal scattering of frost in his beard, but the vitality of youth throbbed in his veins as he stood on the beach and wrung out the water from his heavy wolfskin cloak.

All was reassuringly peaceful. No warning beacons flashed into life on the cliffs. He was right to land here. The coasts were poorly guarded. It seemed the years of peace had made the Britons complacent.

They did not expect to see me again, he thought, gazing over the flatlands of the isle, which at high tide was separated from the mainland. He had built a fort on the island, but after his flight the Britons under Ambrosius had destroyed it. Nothing remained save a few blackened stumps and post-holes.

They would have done better to refortify the place, and garrison it against my return.

Brushing aside the ghosts of the past, he swung round to watch his men disembark. Young men, most of them, greedy for plunder and slaughter, glory and land and women. All the things the scops sang of.

Plunder and slaughter, glory and land and women. Hengist had once desired all of these, as much as any man. Now his youth was flown, taking most of his desires with it.

He only had one ambition left. He wanted his land back, his kingdom of Cent, granted to him by Vortigern in exchange for his sister Rowena.

My land, he thought fiercely, *mine by right. Mine.*

Rowena was dead now, and Vortigern, killed by Ambrosius. Ambrosius was dead too, ushered into the afterlife, not by the sword, but poison.

Hengist despised the assassin, whoever he was. A man like Ambrosius had deserved a soldier's death. Only the worst kind of coward would serve his enemies poison, slaying them while they sat at meat and drink.

Still, he had to admit the death of Ambrosius had handed him an unlooked-for opportunity to recover what was lost. In place of their dead hero the Britons had crowned some western princeling, Constantine, who by all accounts preferred the pleasures of the flesh to the business of ruling.

Hengist was cautious. He had planned his return carefully over the years, slowly rebuilding his shattered war-band in his homeland of Germania, leading minor raids on the British coastline, probing their strength and will to resist.

Now he was back, and would not be shifted again. He would live and die here, defending his territory, with his sons at his side.

One of them lumbered over to him. Ebusa, his second son, stocky and thickset and fair-haired, brave enough, but not over-burdened with brains.

"There is no sign of any Britons, father," he said, "the beach and the land beyond is empty."

Hengist nodded. The advance parties had orders to go no further than half a mile inland before turning back. His first intention was to secure the Isle of Tanatos and make it his headquarters again. From there he could mount raids into Cent, spreading terror among the local towns and villages.

The High King would soon hear of his landing, and be obliged to either treat or fight. Hengist hoped he would fight. There was no British commander he feared, and the three hundred warriors he had brought with him could hold the isle for months against anything the natives threw at it.

More of his people were gathering across the northern seas, under the command of his third son Cerdic and his nephew Aelle. Only Hengist, and the pick of his young warriors, had dared to risk the crossing in the depths of winter. At the first hint of spring his reinforcements would sail in force, to join him and swell his war-band into an unstoppable army of conquest.

He checked himself. There was one British officer who gave him pause.

Artorius. But where is he? Vanished into the west, or the north. The rumours contradict each other.

The new High King had shown his mettle, and his wisdom, by banishing the one man who might have kept his kingdom safe from the Saxons. Sent him off on some hopeless sortie into Gaul, then stripped him of his rank and command.

Hengist smiled to himself. Perhaps if he waited a little longer, the leaders of the Britons would trip and fall on their own swords, thus saving him the trouble of killing them.

He looked up at the sky. Black clouds were scudding across the sky. Evening was coming on, and threatening to bring a storm with it.

"We'll camp here tonight," he said to Ebusa, "and look at the fort in the morning. See what can be salvaged."

"Yes, father," Ebusa replied obediently. He and his elder brother, Osla, seldom disagreed with their father.

The same could not be said for their half-brother Cerdic. Hengist frowned as he glanced to the west, at the glimmering, wine-dark seas, and wondered what was happening in Germania.

Cerdic had plenty of brains, no doubt of that, and ambition. Hengist preferred to keep him on a tight rein, but at the same time needed an able man back home, one who could plan and organise as well as lead. Aelle was every bit his father Horsa's son, good for breaking heads and dealing death in battle, but not much else.

He shrugged his heavy shoulders. If Cerdic chose to betray him, it would not happen yet. Not until the Britons were defeated, and a large part of Britannia safely in Saxon hands. Only then, with Constantine and the other British nobles grovelling at his feet, would Hengist think of watching his back.

Night draped her satin folds over the land, while the Saxons made camp inside the gutted ruin of a village near the remains of the fort. Their slaves had dwelled here, until the soldiers of Ambrosius came and destroyed the place.

The expected storm came, lashing the island with howling winds and pelting rain, while thunder growled among the clouds. White forks of lightning stabbed the distant seas.

"Thank the gods we didn't have to sail through that," remarked Hengist, huddled in his cloak inside the headman's hut. It still had part of its roof, a thick layer of rotting thatch, enough to protect him and his chief men from the worst of the storm.

Two of his men worked at getting a fire going. Like everything else on the isle, the wood was damp, and they quietly cursed as they worked the bits of kindling between their rough hands, trying to strike a spark.

"Osla is late in returning," said Ebusa, glancing out of the low doorway, "all the other scouts are back. I don't envy him, caught out in this filth."

"Perhaps he ran into some Britons," said Aesc, one of Hengist's gesiths, "and is busy killing them."

"Or being killed," added Ebusa. Hengist looked at him sharply. There was no love lost between the two brothers, who competed for their father's favour and the respect of the war-band.

He sniffed, and bit into a piece of salted meat. This was how it should be. He wanted wolves for sons, not lambs. Wolves might quarrel and snap at each other, but they would thrive in the days to come.

Osla and his little band of scouts returned shortly after midnight, tired and drenched to the skin and muttering darkly of the wrath of sky-gods.

They brought with them a captive. Hengist was surprised to see it was a woman, and apparently untouched. Osla was not known for his restraint in his treatment of female prisoners.

This one was unusual. She had somehow avoided being soaked, and her dark blue robe and hooded mantle were merely damp. Her hands were folded meekly before her, in the manner of a Christian priest or novice. They were delicate and pale, Hengist noticed, not the hands of one who worked the land for a living.

"Release her," he growled when she was shoved into the hut and made to kneel before the smoking apology for a fire, "why did you tie her wrists? You thought she might lash out suddenly, and strike you all down?"

Shame-faced, Osla drew his saex and cut the leather strap binding the captive's wrists. His saex was unusually large and broad-bladed, won from a Jutish chieftain at dice. Osla was equally skilled at gutting men and deer with it, and had earned the name Osla Big-Knife.

The woman knelt quietly on the earth floor, waiting. A fresh burst of thunder rumbled overhead as Hengist ran his single eye over her.

"We found her in the woods, not far to the east," said Osla, "or she found us."

Osla and Ebusa resembled each other physically, but the elder was the more intelligent. He gave his father a look full of meaning, and raised his left hand in the sign against evil.

"Let's have a look at you, then," Hengist grunted at the prisoner. He had picked up on his son's warning, and leaned back slightly, wary of what he might see.

The delicate white hands came up and slowly peeled back the hood, revealing a plain, thin-faced woman, no longer young, with skin the colour of fresh milk. Her hair was long and black, lightly salted with grey, and scraped back in a single plait. She wore a white silken cloth over her eyes.

"She's blind," said Hengist, "no wonder she didn't run. How did you lose your sight, woman?"

Her bloodless lips tightened into a smile. "Hengist the Saxon," she said in a low, surprisingly deep voice, "it is you who are blind. Blind to the danger that lies in wait for you."

"Danger," he scoffed, "what danger? Foolish cripple."

"No cripple, father," said Osla, "she could see her way in the dark, even with that cloth around her eyes, and needed no guiding to our camp."

Hengist irritably waved him into silence. "Eight miles to the north-east of here, an army of Britons is lying in wait for you," the woman continued, "the magistrate of Durovernum Cantiacorum was warned of your coming, and has raised as many levies

172

as he can. He means to ambush your men as they march further inland."

Hengist cursed, and threw his half-chewed lump of meat into the fire. If this witch spoke truth, the Britons must have had look-outs posted on the cliffs after all.

"Some five hundred men," she said, as though anticipating his next question, "mostly spearmen on foot. The magistrate is over-confident in his numbers. He has posted few guards, and thrown up no ditch or palisade around his camp."

Hengist looked past her, to the doorway. Outside was pitch dark, and the wind sounded like the shrieking of souls in torment.

Eight miles, he thought, *in darkness, in wind and rain...*

"The way to their camp is difficult," said the woman, "but I can guide you safely there. Through the forest. You could fall on the Britons while they sleep."

Such a victory would strike terror into the natives. On the other hand, if Hengist stayed where he was, and waited for the Britons to come to him, he risked being bottled up on the isle. This wretched magistrate had more men, and could afford to lay siege while reinforcements marched down from Londinium.

He ran a hand through his matted beard. "She could be lying to us, father," said Ebusa, "why should some British witch want to help us?"

There was a murmur of agreement around the fire. Hengist leaned forward. His fingers twitched, wanting to reach over the sputtering flames and tear off the silken bandage.

Something – perhaps fear, though Hengist never admitted to fear – stayed his hand.

"Answer him," he said softly, "why should you wish to give us aid, and betray your countrymen?"

"We are not a united people, Hengist the Saxon," she replied calmly, "the magistrate is the High King's man, and the High King is not my friend. It is...necessary for his men to be defeated."

"Tell me your name," he asked after a long moment, "since you are so free with mine."

"Morgana."

The name meant nothing to him. He pondered, staring into the fire while his mind raced.

Darkness had fallen early. His men were fit and young, and used to loping through the dense forests of their homeland like wolves. If guided through the unfamiliar country, they could easily cover eight miles before dawn.

His warriors were watching him, waiting for the old man to make a decision. None would dare speak again until he did. Hengist had them well in hand.

"Osla," he said eventually, lifting his head, "you will take the war-band, and follow Morgana. If she speaks true, attack the Britons where they lie, and kill as many as you can. Try to take their leader alive and bring him back here. We may be able to get a decent ransom for him."

"If she speaks false," he added, staring hard at Morgana, "kill her."

His men rose to depart. "Not you," he said to Ebusa, "you stay here with me. If I must risk my sons, I prefer to do it one at a time."

Ebusa scowled. "Why should Osla get the chance for glory?" he demanded.

"Because he is the eldest, and must earn a reputation for himself before I die. Otherwise men won't follow him. Be thankful you are a second son. They will follow you simply for who your brother is."

Their gazes locked. Ebusa broke first, and slumped back against the wall, muttering under his breath.

"Thank you, father," said Osla, grinning, and ruffled Ebusa's hair as he stepped past him to the entrance. The other men filed out after Hengist's eldest son, into the soaking darkness. Morgana rose and ghosted after them.

The storm rumbled on while Hengist and his remaining companions waited. Silence reigned inside the smoky little hut, broken by the occasional cough. Two of the older warriors, veterans from Hengist's first invasion of Cent, had also stayed behind. They sat together playing at dice, while Ebusa sulkily tended the fire.

Hengist sat and contemplated Morgana. He was as superstitious as any of his folk, and believed sincerely in the dark powers wielded by hags and witches.

Part of him regretted putting his men, and his eldest son, in the hands of such a one. It was a risk. Even now she could be leading them into the gates of some hellish otherworld, to be swallowed up by evil spirits. Or else she was merely a skilled liar, and would deliver his warriors into a trap laid by the Britons.

This is war, he thought, staring at the palms of his hands, *everything must be risked, if my people are to come into their own again.*

He would soon know. If his men did not return by noon of the following day, Hengist would have to go in search of them, or return to his ships with Ebusa and a couple of broken-down old spearmen. The journey back to Germania would be a sad one. How could he face his kin, and tell them of the latest failure? If Cerdic didn't seize the opportunity to slay him on the spot, Aelle surely would. All the younger men were chafing for power. Hengist's authority was fragile. One defeat might prove enough to bring him down.

Hours passed, the longest night of his long and brutal life. The veterans eventually fell asleep, curled up next to each other like a couple of old dogs. Ebusa drowsed, his head lolling against the wall, mouth hanging open.

Hengist prayed silently to his gods, though they were not usually the sort to listen. The likes of Woden and Thunor and Tiw, even his favourite deity Geta, who stole the secret of fire from the other gods and delivered it to men, were a selfish and careless lot. Far too embroiled in private quarrels and carousing with the shades of dead warriors in Valhalla, to care much for the troubles of one distressed mortal.

"Bring my son back safe to me," he muttered, fingering the crude iron amulet hanging from his neck. The amulet was engraved with the image of Geta, a man with a saex in either hand and curling ram's horns growing from his skull.

"Give him victory, and I shall make temples to you in every British town I conquer. The churches of the Christ shall be gutted, his shaved priests offered up as sacrifices, and statues raised in your honour in place of the nailed god."

Dawn arrived like a damp and wary stranger, cloaked in grey. When the first fingers of light groped through the doorway and the hut's single window, Hengist was roused from his doze by the distant echo of a war-horn.

He jumped up, cursing the cramps in his ageing body, and limped outside, ducking his head to avoid cracking it against the lintel.

Ebusa had also heard the sound of the horn, and staggered out after his father, followed by the two veterans. All four men blinked in the wan light of dawn, rubbing the sleep and wood smoke from their eyes.

"There," said Ebusa, pointing to the east. Hengist watched, heart thudding, as approaching spear-heads gleamed among the marshes.

His fingers tightened on the well-worn grip of his saex. If they were Britons, he was done for. Not that he cared to live much longer, since it would mean Osla was almost certainly dead, and all his warriors with him.

He spotted Morgana first, her greying hair unbound and blowing loose in the morning breeze wafting in from the sea. She walked at the head of the spearmen. It seemed the witch was indeed able to see perfectly well.

Hengist gave a deep sigh of relief when he saw Osla just behind her, struggling to keep up. His long fair hair and stocky build were easy to pick out. The men behind him were all Saxons, save a few miserable, bloodstained captives dragged along in the rear.

"We won, father!" Osla shouted as soon as he was within hearing, "the Britons fled before us like fire!"

Ignoring Ebusa's muttered curse, Hengist limped forward, throwing his arms wide to embrace his son.

"Good lad," he said, pounding Osla on the back, "I knew I could put my faith in you."

"I owe you a word of thanks," he added, glancing nervously at Morgana, "but expect no more."

The witch nodded, apparently satisfied. "I ask for nothing from you, Hengist the Saxon," she said.

Osla, still flushed with his victory, gestured at his men to bring one of the captives forward.

"This is the magistrate, their leader," he said, "the fool was squatting over a latrine pit behind his tent when we attacked. He barely had time to lace up his bracae before we were on them."

Hengist laughed, and turned to inspect the magistrate, a pot-bellied man in late middle age, the tufts of his remaining hair sticking up at comical angles. He had plainly been caught unawares, since he wore no mail and the leather scabbard of his sword-belt was empty.

"I knew you wanted him alive," said Osla, "he struggled at first, so we had to hurt him a bit."

Osla was too modest. The magistrate's fleshy face was covered in bruises, one eye closed, the flesh over it a livid shade of purple and swollen to gigantic size. His left arm dangled awkwardly, clearly broken in at least two places.

To do the man credit, he had courage. Confronted with the dreaded Hengist, a half-legendary figure and terror of the British race, he worked up some bloody phlegm and spat it at Hengist's feet.

"God curse you," he hissed between his cracked teeth, "curse you and your foul sons."

Osla reached for his saex, but Hengist gestured at him to leave it. Smiling, he stepped close to the magistrate and whispered a single word into his ear.

"Children."

12.

Two keels crawled north through icy, wind-
blasted seas, hugging the eastern coastline of
Britannia. There had been a third, but it
foundered and sank in a storm within sight
of Branadunum, the northernmost of the
Saxon Shore forts. When the storm abated,
the keel was gone, and all trace of the ten
Saxons who had crewed it.

Some of Aethelflaed's remaining
followers had pleaded with her to turn back
then, claiming she was tempting Thunor, the
God of Thunder, by persisting in the face of
his wrath.

"You may shift for yourselves," she
replied calmly, "for myself, I intend to go
on, even if I have to swim all the way."

Her calm courage shamed them into
silence, and put an end to their pleading.
Still, they took to praying rather more than

was fit for warriors, and casting fearful glances at the sky.

Aethelflaed cared nothing for the wrath of Thunor, or any other god. Born into a world dominated by men, she had long ago resolved to follow a different path to most of her sex. At the age of twelve, when she was expected to take a husband, Aethelflaed had stood up before her father and his advisors and declared she would stay unmarried.

"I will take no husband," she said, "but learn the art of spear and knife, sword and dagger."

She locked gazes with her father, willing herself not to tremble before him. Instead of anger, Hengist's single eye had glowed with pride, and he beckoned his daughter close so he could place his hand on her flaxen head.

"I thought I had three sons," he said, chuckling, "now I see I have four, though one is in a woman's guise."

Female warriors were rare, but not unknown among her people. As the daughter of a chief, and a great chief at that, Aethelflaed was granted more freedom than most young girls, and scandalously indulged by her otherwise stern and flint-hearted father.

Now, aged seventeen, she had insisted on accompanying Hengist when he followed the swan's path once more to Britannia. In this, and so many other things, he was incapable of denying her wish.

"Your mother would have wept to see you with your hair shorn, and wielding a sword," he said ruefully on the eve of their departure from Germania, "Aeleva was a soft-hearted creature, gods rest her."

Aethelflaed was secretly rather ashamed of her mother, who had died of a chill when she was still a baby. Hengist always made her sound like a weak creature, little more than another of his slaves, though she had been the daughter of a freeman. Aethelflaed had inherited her slender frame and fair looks, but nothing else.

"I am your flesh," she replied to her father, "steel straight, blade true. Give me the opportunity, and I shall prove myself worthier than any of my brothers."

"Enough," he said, frowning, "I have indulged you this far, and no further. Do not ask me to put you at the head of a war-band, or furnish you with ships and men that you might go sea-roving for a year."

The old chief's word was usually law, but he reckoned without his daughter's stubborn tenacity. All through the voyage to Britannia, through dangerous seas and ice-storms and every kind of foul weather, she asked the same favour, over and again. "Three keels," she begged, "let me take men north, to join our kinsman Wulfhere. Or further yet, to beyond the Wall. I can act as your envoy, and rouse the Picts to attack the British kingdoms in the north when you invade Cent."

Wulfhere was a distant cousin to Hengist and King of the Jutes, a people closely related to the Saxons, from the far north of Germania. Hengist had forged an alliance with Wulfhere, promising him dominion over the eastern half of Britannia, much of which was already in Saxon hands. Only the British territory immediately around Lindum, capital of the old Roman province of Flavia Caesariensis, remained to be conquered.

It was Wulfhere's task to storm Lindum and slay its native king, while Hengist and his brood overran the south. His men had already descended on the fenlands east of Lindum, daring the winter seas while the bulk of the Saxon host massed in southern Germania, waiting for the onset of spring.

"Why not stay with me," said Hengist, "and fight by my side in Cent? Once the fighting is done, I will give you your own hall, and some of the best land in the kingdom. Even a husband, if you consent to take one at last. You can choose whoever you like from my gesiths."

Aethelflaed shook her head. "No," she replied firmly, "I won't have Osla and Ebusa sneering at me, and insulting those warriors who choose to follow a woman into battle. I must follow the swan's path a while longer."

In the end Hengist relented, as she knew he would. Ever since infancy, she had been able to manipulate him, shamelessly exploiting his fond memories of her mother. He agreed to give her the three keels, the smallest vessels of the fleet he took over the northern seas to Britannia, and picked out thirty warriors to crew them.

The warriors were among the youngest in his war-band, some hardly more than beardless boys. Eager to win their share of glory and plunder, and suspecting their elders would claim most of it in Cent, they cheerfully swallowed their pride and accepted the leadership of a woman.

"Go, then," said Hengist when all was ready, folding his daughter in a last embrace, "make me, and your mother's shade, proud."

Aethelflaed went, her heart swelling with fierce joy as the burden of command settled on her shoulders for the first time. She had always known she was born to lead, to share the dangers of men, not linger at home in some smoky, fog-bound hut, tending fires and fretting over a pack of squealing children.

"To the deepest hells with Wulfhere," she informed Oswine, one of her warriors, when her father's ships were out of sight, "we go north, to the land of the Picts. I have a mind to see them for myself, and buy their friendship."

Hengist had given her a portion of his treasure, a chest full of golden torcs, arm-rings, brooches and other pieces of finely wrought jewellery, to help incite war and rebellion against the High King. Besides the Picts, there were plenty of northern tribes who could be tempted to attack British territory. Some of the British kings themselves were said to be chafing under Constantine's authority.

"The north of Britannia is a half-healed wound," Hengist had advised her, "Coel Hen kept order among the tribes, but his kind of peace was a fragile one. Now he is dead, and his sons are not their father. All we have to do is slip a knife into the wound, and it will bleed afresh."

I am the knife, thought Aethelflaed as her keel plunged through the choppy grey waters, *though a feeble one.*

The loss of ten of her warriors, snatched away by Thunor, had damaged her confidence more than she dared to admit.

Perhaps the gods themselves disapproved of her temerity.

She set her jaw. There was deceptive strength in her slender frame, and something of Hengist's iron will in her grey eyes and broad, plain features.

"If you wish to punish me, Thunor," she murmured, gazing up at the skies, where black clouds still lingered in the east, "then do your worst, but let my followers be. What kind of god dares not to strike at a woman? What a craven thing you are."

Her warriors would have been shocked to hear her insult such a powerful god. They were a credulous lot, the sons of minor gesiths, raised to fight and die, if necessary, in the service of their lords.

Like most of her folk, they were also hardy sailors, and steered their fragile, shallow-bottomed craft through the wintry seas with practised skill. They worked their way up the coast, past the fenlands where Wulfhere and his Jutes were supposed to be wreaking havoc, following the whale-road north and further north, to the untamed lands beyond the Wall.

At last, after an entire day and night spent labouring through sheeting rain and boiling seas, the gods smiled on them. The clouds parted, the rain suddenly ceased, and a new world revealed before them to the west, glorious in the morning sun.

"Gods be good," breathed Aethelflaed, shading her eyes. West lay a rugged coastline, buffeted by winds and tides, gradually curving away to the north. The landscape beyond was mostly deep forest, dominated by a monstrous spur of volcanic rock rising sheer above the trees a couple of miles inland.

There were people living there, on the high summit. She could make out faint traces of smoke, curling into the sky, and the outline of a palisade.

"Some great king must live there," remarked Oswine, his pale blue eyes fairly popping from their sockets as they drank in the awesome sight, "lording it over the local tribes. I wonder how many spears he commands?"

"We shall soon find out," said Aethelflaed, "row closer, and look for a safe place to land."

Oswine turned and gave the order to break out oars. The keels were single-mast vessels, and their shallow draughts meant they were able to sail far inland, following the course of streams and rivers. Aethelflaed intended to beach her ships and venture on foot towards the fortress on its enormous crag. She agreed with Oswine. The lord of such a place must wield great power, and be worth cultivating for an ally.

The thought passed through her mind that the king, or whatever he was, may not prove friendly. He might laugh at her offers of friendship, slaughter or enslave her and her pitifully small following, and take Hengist's treasure for himself.

Aethelflaed's instincts overwhelmed her doubts. She could not believe that her adventure would end in such a way. Fate had driven them here.

The keels rowed towards the cliffs, bobbing precariously on the churning sea. The sails of the vessels were furled, and they now relied entirely on the muscle and skill of the men plying the oars.

Aethelflaed picked out a beach, a thin strip of golden sand under the bluffs looming immediately to the west. When they were close enough, she and her men jumped into the waist-deep water and dragged the keels to shore. Gulls wheeled high above, filling the bright clean air with their cries.

Aethelflaed saw a cave, a deep hole chiselled out of the black rock of the cliffs. "Hide the boats in there," she ordered, "five of you will stay and guard the treasure. The rest come with me."

"If we are not back by dawn," she told Ceadda, the youth she left in charge of the five, "put to sea again, and return to my father. Whatever happens, keep the treasure safe."

Ceadda nodded, and swallowed, running a nervous tongue over his lips. He was barely fourteen, awkward and gangling and afflicted with spots. Aethelflaed judged him a weakling, more like to fall over his spear than stab anyone with it. Giving him a measure of responsibility would, she hoped, help to make a man of him.

With her remaining fifteen warriors, she climbed the narrow, grass-grown track leading up from the beach, and plunged into the forest that started a little way from the edge of the bluffs.

The track continued into the woods, and was clearly still in use, carving a more or less straight path through the wilderness. Aethelflaed hoped it would lead them straight to the fort.

She led the way, with Oswine to her left, the rest of her warriors in double file behind them. They moved quickly, clad in light tunics, each man carrying shield and spear, and a saex tucked into his belt. Only Aethelflaed wore mail, a shirt of glittering scales. Her father had ordered the shirt made especially for her, hiring one of the most skilled smiths in Germania to forge it, and the gold-hilted short sword she carried in a wooden sheath at her belt.

The forest reminded her of home, deep and ancient, with all kinds of dark secrets lurking in its depths. She had walked such places since childhood, and had no fear of them.

"I shall greet the lord of the fort in the name of Hengist," she breathlessly informed Oswine as they jogged along the beaten path, "he will surely have heard of my father. Once I have his measure, I will offer him gold in return for spears."

"How much gold?" cried a voice from the trees.

Aethelflaed stopped and looked around, trying to discover its source. She cursed her overconfidence. Instead of chattering, she should have kept a close eye on the trees, wary of ambush. How often had her father drilled that lesson into his children?

"Up here," said the voice. Aethelflaed looked up, and saw a man seated on one of the lower branches of a giant oak overhanging the path.

He was no warrior, but looked like some kind of priest, his tall, bony frame clad in a grubby brown habit reaching to his ankles. She spotted a wooden cross hanging from a length of sinew around his neck, confirming her first impression.

"The gold is not for you, shaveling," she said, recovering from her surprise, "though you will receive a length of sharp iron in your guts unless you come down from there and beg for your life."

She tapped her sword-hilt. "My father has killed more Christian priests than he can remember. They are like sheep, he says, ripe for the slaughter. I have a mind to follow his example."

The priest smiled sadly and folded his hands over his breast in mock fright. "*Mea culpa*," he said, "I should have known better than to challenge such doughty warriors. You would murder me, then, a defenceless man of God?"

"Like that," replied Aethelflaed, snapping her fingers. It was all show. She had never killed anyone, and disliked the thought of doing the deed in cold blood.

The priest shifted his uncomfortable position on the branch. He was an odd-looking man, his bulging eyes, sloping chin and little hooked nose giving him the appearance of a startled bird. His wiry, tangled reddish hair had long outgrown its tonsure and was clearly a stranger to the comb.

"Tut," he sniffed, "it is easy for Godless pagans to make such threats. Not so easy for me, who has sworn an oath on holy relics never to shed blood."

Aethelflaed was growing impatient. "Enough of your drivelling," she snarled, "come down, or one of my men will put a spear through you."

The priest raised a skinny finger. "I had not finished," he said in a tone of infuriating condescension, "I was about to say, that I may have sworn a sacred oath not to shed blood, but others in my company have not."

"Your company..." Aethelflaed heard a noise to her left, and looked around in time to see men emerge from the forest.

They appeared suddenly, levelling their short hunting bows at the Saxons. More came from the right, until Aethelflaed's little band was surrounded.

She forced down her panic and quickly took in the bowmen. Over two score lean figures clad in dark greens and browns. Forest brigands. Most were barefoot, and had a feral, savage look about them. Their pale arms and necks were covered in crude tattoos, dark swirling patterns that hurt the eye to focus on. Other than their bows and arrows, they carried no other weapon save little knives, good for gutting hares, but not much use in battle.

"The Lord has delivered these men into my keeping," said the monk, "but my control over them is limited, alas. I would suggest you put down your weapons at once. They require little encouragement to begin shooting."

Aethelflaed could see there was no help for it. She was outnumbered over two to one, and her father had taught her to value prudence over reckless valour. Her uncle Horsa would have charged the bowmen, and to hells with the consequences, but Horsa was long dead: slain, inevitably, in combat.

"Lay down your arms," she ordered her men, slowly kneeling to lay her sword and shield flat on the ground. After some hesitation, her warriors followed her example. Meanwhile the priest clumsily struggled down from his perch, showing a great deal of hairy white thigh.

"God bless you for your wisdom, noble lady," he said breathlessly after he had dropped the last few feet, "I have seen more than enough blood spilled in recent times. Most of it by those men around us, and their fellows."

He laid his hands flat against his breast again, and gave a little bow. "My name is Rhydderch. Might I beg the pleasure of knowing yours?"

"Aethelflaed, daughter of Hengist," she replied defiantly, expecting to see him flinch. Instead he cocked his head to one side.

"Indeed? Strange to see one of his whelps so far north. What is your purpose in coming to Gododdin?"

Gododdin, Aethelflaed knew, was the British name for a collection of native kingdoms immediately north of the Wall.

"To find allies," she replied, "spears, to take south and help our people fight the Britons."

He pulled at his lower lip, studying her closely with his protuberant eyes. There was something damp and clammy about Rhydderch, a sort of ingrained greasiness. Aethelflaed's skin crawled as he took a step closer.

"I shall take you to my lord," he said, "and let him decide. He may welcome you as friends, or torture you for your gold, or have you skinned alive and your pelts hung over the gates of his fort. He is difficult to predict."

His hand came up, long brown fingers gently dabbling at the side of her neck. Aethelflaed forced herself to remain perfectly still.

"Who is your lord?" she asked through clenched teeth, "we were on our way to the fort, mounted on the crag to the west."

"Then we are of like mind," murmured Rhydderch, taking his hand away with a sigh, "he dwells there. The fort is named Curia, and was once the home of the Votadini."

"And now?"

"Now it is the palace of Gwrgi Wyllt, Gwrgi the Manslayer, Gwrgi the Conqueror. To my knowledge, he has never set eyes on a Saxon before. For your sake, I shall pray he finds you interesting."

13.

The Dubglas River, Linnuis, April 473

The Jutes had rowed their keels along the main course of the river, leading directly inland from the North Sea, before turning to follow one of the many side-rivers cutting into the moors and fenlands. This was unknown country to them, though not dissimilar to the mud flats of their homeland in northern Germania.

Forty-seven warriors in five keels, come to explore and settle. They were one of the many smaller Jutish raiding parties pouring into Linnuis in the wake of the main war-band led by their King, Wulfhere.

It was early spring, and the fens drowsed in unaccustomed heat. The river steadily narrowed until it was little more than a muddy stream, forcing the Jutes to pull their boats onto the northern shore and pitch camp.

Dusk fell, bringing with it a light mist. A hush fell over the land, disturbed only by the distant call of marsh bitterns and the incessant croaking of frogs. The weary Jutes settled down to eat their rations of salt meat and hard rye bread. A few dozed in the warmth, lying just inside their rough hide tents, weapons ready by their sides.

The silence was shattered by the rising note of a bugle, piercing the mist in the north-east. Before the echoes had even died away, another answered it to the west.

"Spears!" bawled the Jutish chief, who had been sitting peacefully on the bank, gazing at the dark waters. He dropped his flask and raced back to his tent, where he had left his helmet and sword.

More cries of alarm flooded through the camp as horsemen exploded out of the mist, red-cloaked warriors on fast horses, their bright mail glinting in the poor light.

The horsemen came from the north, plunging recklessly at the tents. As the Jutes bravely rushed to meet them, they checked, hurled their light throwing javelins, and wheeled, galloping back into the mist.

War-shouts turned to howls of pain. Several Jutes went down screaming with the javelins stuck in their bodies. Others had caught the missiles on their shields, and blundered wildly after the horsemen.

"Come back, you fools!" roared their chief, "back to the boats!"

His men were slow to respond. Some turned back, others halted and looked around stupidly, frightened eyes searching for the enemy. The riders had vanished like wraiths.

The lull lasted no more than a few seconds. More horsemen surged from the west, crashing into the Jutish camp, bugles blowing and men shouting, horses neighing and long swords rising and stabbing as they galloped over the tents, scattering bowls and bits of food and war-gear.

They were led by a huge officer on a shining black mare, his face hidden under the ornate helm of a Saxon chief, complete with face-mask. His eyes behind the mask blazed with killing fury, and his sword whirled like liquid steel before the terrified Jutes.

The chief sprang to meet him. Their blades rang once, twice, and then the Jute buckled to his knees, blood spurting from the ragged slash in his throat.

"Kill them all!" shouted Artorius, turning Llamrei away from the dying man, "drive them into the water, kill them in the shallows! No mercy!"

The first troop of cavalry re-appeared, storming out of the mists to ride down the Jutes who had tried to give chase and cut off the escape of their comrades. Stranded between two fires, the remaining Jutes either threw down their weapons or fled for the river.

Those who surrendered were swiftly butchered: the Britons had no pity for these heathen plunderers, and Artorius had given the order to spare none. The screams of the Jutes echoed across the flat, dismal landscape of the fens, dying away among the peat bogs and trackless marshes.

The river offered no refuge. Just waist-deep, most of the Jutes who plunged into it were caught and slain before they had waded halfway across. Their bodies swirled gently downstream, blood oozing from their wounds and spreading out around them like crimson smoke, turning the blackish waters a dark shade of red.

Artorius had placed Llwch Llemineawg in command of the first troop, with orders to draw the Jutes out of their camp. He had succeeded, and his men slew the fugitives with methodical efficiency.

"Bastards," cursed the young officer as he sat his horse on the northern bank, the heavy blade of his spatha reeking with blood. Two of the Jutes had managed to escape the carnage and get across the river. His men were too busy destroying the last of their comrades to pursue.

Artorius reined in next to him. "Let them go," he said, his voice muffled behind the helm, "we always leave a few survivors, to spread word of their defeat."

"Yes, lord," replied Llwch, though with some reluctance. Not yet eighteen, he had aged in the past few months, having seen and done more killing than was good for one so young.

The brief slaughter was almost over. A few dying screams wafted over the fens, mingled with the piteous cries of wounded Jutes, begging for aid. Some of Artorius' men dismounted to finish them off and plunder the bodies.

Artorius untied the laces of his helm and lifted it off his head, gratefully sucking in lungfuls of air. He ran a gauntleted hand through his sweat-soaked hair, plastered to his skull and the nape of his neck.

He weighed the heavy Saxon helm he had taken to wearing in battle. It was meant to frighten and disorientate the Jutes. The gesith who once owned it was dead, his body mouldering in a bog near the River Glein, where Artorius had left him and thirty of his warriors.

The helmet was a thing of beauty. Artorius would have scarcely believed the Jutes were capable of such fine work. Made from a single vaulted shell of hammered iron, with a full face mask, a neck guard and long cheek-pieces, every panel was covered with protective symbols delicately traced into the metal: the face was a bird with outstretched wings, its body forming the warrior's nose, the tail his moustache and the wings his eyebrows. These facial features were picked out in bronze.

As the bird soared up to meet the crest of the helmet, it met the jaws of a dragon crashing down. The thick iron body of the dragon, inlaid with silver wire, flowed over the crest and ended in another snarling mouth, guarding the helmet's rear. There was a little hole near the top of the crest, into which Artorius had fitted a red plume.

The panels on the sides of the helmet were decorated with images of hunting and fighting. Artorius could well understand the imagery – warriors dancing in triumph after a victory, a vengeful horseman riding down his enemy.

Sometimes, in his darker moments, he wondered if the men he had committed his life to fighting and killing were so very different to him. Pagans they might be, red ravagers and sea-pirates, but they were brave, and Artorius felt an affinity for their rough, warlike culture. The Saxons and their ilk had far more in common with his own savage northern forebears than the Britons of the south, who had spent so long under Roman rule they had forgotten how to fight.

Fat, soft and coddled, he thought contemptuously, *without me to protect them, they would soon go down before pagan swords.*

"Lord," said Llwch, breaking into his thoughts, "we have slain forty-five of the enemy, for the loss of three of our own."

Artorius winced. Forty-five for three was a good tally, but every man in his war-band was a friend as well as a comrade. The ties between the men and their captain had grown ever closer in recent months, when it seemed the whole world was bent on destroying then. To Artorius, the loss of any of them was akin to losing a brother.

"Name our dead," he commanded, bracing himself.

There were tears in Llwch's eyes. "Pwyll Hanner Dyn, Sawyl Pen Uchel, and Medyr son of Methredydd."

"Methyr was my cousin on my mother's side," he said bleakly, "the finest thrower of a spear I ever saw."

"All three left sons," said Artorius, trying to comfort him, "even now the boys are growing up fast at Caerleon. In a year or two, they will be ready to replace their fathers."

Llwch nodded wordlessly, brushing away his tears. Artorius forced down his own sorrow and concentrated on practical matters.

His following had now dwindled to just over two hundred men, their numbers gradually whittled away by constant fighting. This bloody skirmish was the fourth in two months, all fought on the banks of the Glein and Dubglas rivers in Linnuis.

Artorius had brought his men here, far from Caerleon, to aid the local British garrisons in repelling the invasion of Wulfhere and his Jutes. His cavalry had proved indispensable, able to ride swift and hard, striking at enemy raiding parties as they tried to penetrate further inland.

For Artorius, coming here was a matter of both duty and necessity. He could not live at Caerleon. His sons never stopped screaming for their mother. Their anguished cries haunted the fort like the wailing of ghosts.

None of his men ever mentioned Ganhumara, at least not in his hearing.

Or what I did to her.

He turned quickly to Llwch. "Gather up the men," he said harshly, "we can't spend all day in this stinking wilderness, picking at corpses. Leave the Jutes to rot. They wanted our land so much. Let it consume them."

The Britons made their way back to camp, which lay inside a little wood some eight miles to the north, guarded by a ditch and a stockade. Artorius had chosen to make this hidden, easily defended place his headquarters, instead of stationing his troops inside the walled town of Lindum, another twenty miles north.

Cei met them at the gate. He had recovered from the head wound he suffered in Gaul, though Artorius feared it had caused lasting damage. Never the happiest or most light-hearted character, Cei often sunk into black moods, during which he refused to speak to any man, and lashed out savagely at any who came near him.

"News from the north," he said bluntly when Artorius hailed him, "Wulfhere is moving west in force. Our scouts report over a thousand warriors, all the men he can gather in haste."

"Is he advancing on Lindum?" Artorius asked.

"Of course. Where else? Seems he brought some engineers over with him from Germania, and they've built a few siege engines. Masgwid is holed up inside the town. Stupid bastard should have left a garrison to hold it while he rode back to his own kingdom for reinforcements, but he wants to play the hero."

Artorius thought quickly. Masgwid was the King of Elmet, a kingdom bordering Linnuis to the west. He was also a member of the Council of Britannia.

Before Constantine expelled him from the council, Artorius had known the man a little. Young, rash and proud, son of the King of Rheged and all too aware of his royal blood. Since the last King of Linnuis was killed by the Jutes, Constantine had given Masgwid what remained of British-held territory in the region. Defending it was his responsibility, and in theory Artorius was no more than a mercenary in the young king's service.

Masgwid had taken a spear-wound to his leg in his first skirmish. Astride a horse it didn't matter, but on foot he was obliged to walk with a crutch. His subjects called him Masgwid Gloff – Masgwid the Lame.

"Masgwid has no more than four hundred men inside Lindum," said Artorius, "has he got the citizens out? Their extra mouths will be nothing but a drain in a siege."

Cei shrugged. "Don't know. There were only a few people still living there anyway. Place is a shit-hole. Falling to bits. Not worth the defending, if you ask me."

"Fortunately, I'm not," snapped Artorius, "if Lindum falls, the Jutes will have a base from which to conquer the whole of the region. More of Wulfhere's foul kin land on our shores every week. Linnuis will soon be overrun. Curse Masgwid. If he gets himself killed, Elmet will be left without a leader. He has no sons. The Jutes will look west, and see his kingdom as easy meat."

Once again, he was aware of his men looking to him for leadership. For decision. The pressure was greater than ever before. If Linnuis and Elmet fell, Britannia would be cut in half. Cent was infested with Hengist's Saxons – who would have dreamed the old pirate would return! – while the whole of the eastern seaboard had been lost decades ago, conquered by the descendents of the foederati of the Saxon Shore forts.

"Where is the High King?" demanded Llwch, "where is the great warrior Constantine? He is no better than Vortigern. When Hengist slaughtered his men in Cent, he did nothing to avenge them or drive out the Saxons. While his kingdom falls to pagans and sea-vermin, he sits in Londinium, playing with his catamites."

There was a growl of agreement among the men. Artorius waited for their voices to die down. "The king will come to Lindum's aid," he said, privately cursing himself for a liar, "until he does, we must delay the Jutes as best we can."

He turned to Cei. "Give orders to break camp. We ride north with every man."

As ever, Cei seemed to regard it as his duty to question everything. "To Lindum?" he said doubtfully, "Wulfhere may have already laid siege to the place. We have barely two hundred men. Nowhere near enough to break his lines."

"No?" Artorius replied scornfully, "we slew almost fifty Jutes this morning, Cei, for just three of our own."

He raised his voice. "I rate any one of you as worth ten – no, twenty barbarians!" he cried, "we will ride to Lindum and glut our spears in Jutish blood. The bellies of the ravens will burst with the feasting we give them!"

His men raised their spears and cheered, especially the younger ones. The successful skirmishes of the past months had all but wiped out the memory of Gaul, if not the memory of the comrades they lost there.

Artorius avoided Cei's gaze. The other man was deaf to brave speeches. He knew the odds against them were great, and the chances of the High King galloping to their rescue slender at best.

Constantine is my enemy, thought Artorius, *but would he sacrifice two kingdoms just to see me dead?*

He could not second-guess the High King's intentions. All he could do was throw the dice high into the air and hope they landed in his favour.

14.

Morgana moved across the land like a ghost, flitting to and fro, seeing much and forgetting nothing. She was feared by all she encountered, respected by most, hated and persecuted by a few.

At times she had to flee for her life, pursued by those who would put a witch to death. Bands of peasants, usually, incited to murder by their local priest. At these times Morgana would fade into the landscape, becoming as one with the woods and fields.

The gods protected her and cast a veil over the eyes of her enemies.

This protection would only last, she knew, so long as she was useful. Compelled by the spirits of old, and her desire to see Artorius made High King, she made her way to Londinium and presented herself at the palace.

Constantine knew who she was, and had her ushered into his suite of private chambers. Morgana was escorted through the galleried corridors by a couple of trembling, white-faced guards. She could smell the fear rising off them. It gave her little joy to know how men feared her, the blind female seer, only child of Ambrosius Aurelianus, blessed as a child by the holy Saint Germanus.

It was only the saint's blessing that stopped the black-robed priests, who infested the palace like flies, from laying violent hands on her. Morgana sensed their hatred and contempt as she strode past, her staff clicking on the flagstones. They hid down side-passages, hissing at her and making the sign of the cross.

Cowards, she thought, *not one of them dares to confront me. How many of them truly believe in Christ, or chose to enter the church for the sake of an easier life?*

The central chamber of Constantine's suite was a large, vaulted hall. Morgana found the High King reclining at ease on a purple couch, surrounded by a twittering mob of lackeys and favourites.

They were in the latter stages of what appeared to be an orgy. Morgana wrinkled her nose. The stench of roasting meat and spices and stale wine filled the air, along with a hint of vomit. A number of bodies lay scattered about the tiled floor, sleeping off their excesses. The shutters on the high windows were locked, allowing not a hint of fresh air to penetrate the stuffy, cloying atmosphere. A rabble of drunken musicians sat in one corner, lute players and a harpist, murdering some tepid Greek melody.

"Noble lady," mumbled Constantine, wiping wine spillage from his mouth and attempting to sit upright, "you are welcome at court."

Constantine was a sight. His once-handsome features, now thickened with sloth and debauchery, were made hideous with rouge. The heat from the hypocaust had mixed with his own sweat, causing the cosmetics to run. Yellow and greenish paint trickled down his face, as though his flesh was melting.

She ran her gaze over his followers. Trash, most of them, prostitutes of both sexes sharing wine and their half-naked bodies with freemen and minor court functionaries. None of the Council of Britannia was present, save one.

"Pascent," she said, turning slightly to face Vortigern's youngest son, "you are much at court these days. Does not your kingdom of Brecon, which my father bestowed on you in good faith, have need of its king?"

Pascent scowled. Alone of the company, he was not the worse for drink, and had retained something of his youthful good looks.

She gave him a thin smile, while he glared back at her with fear and suspicion in his eyes. Morgana knew he had poisoned her father. The gods had revealed the secret to her, shortly after she left the monastery in Dumnonia. Someday, when her first duty was done, she would have her revenge on him.

"Lord king," she said, "I cannot stay long. I came merely to ask why you send no troops north, to aid King Masgwid and Artorius in the fight against the Jutes?"

"You have already lost much of Cent to Hengist," she added, "do not compound your folly."

Constantine's eyes gleamed dangerously at her tone. The pleasures of kingship had not entirely drowned the energetic, iron-willed young warrior he had once been. Batting aside the painted whore who kept snatching at his arms, he rose unsteadily, upending a flagon of wine lying on the floor beside his couch.

"Since when do you concern myself with my affairs?" he demanded, "do you think to instruct me how to rule? You may have power, Morgana, but your father is long dead. You have no authority over me."

She remained calm. "I am the Seer of Britannia. The welfare of the land is my responsibility, and the land cannot prosper under the rule of a High King who does nothing when she is threatened."

Morgana spread her arms. "Where are your armies, lord king? Why have you not sent out messengers to summon the lords of Britannia to Londinium? Hengist arrived in Cent with a handful of men at his back. They might have been dislodged long since and thrown back into the sea, if you had but tried."

Constantine lurched a step towards her. She tensed as he half-raised his right arm, fingers curling into a fist.

"Strike her down, sire," shouted Pascent, "and I'll have the guards whip the insolent bitch out of the city."

The king's brief effort of will didn't last long. Faced with Morgana's slender, indomitable figure, robed all in dark blue, his resolve cracked, and he dropped his arm.

"The lords won't come," he muttered, "even if I summoned them. There has been no council meeting for almost a year. They *disapprove*" – here he lashed out with his sandalled foot at a sleeping freeman, making him yelp – "of how I choose to live."

He scrubbed his melting face with his hands. "My own warriors are in Dumnonia, guarding the coasts against pirates," he moaned, "all I have here is the city garrison. If I send them north with Geraint to fight the Jutes, Londinium will be undefended against Hengist."

"I need more men, Morgana. There are none to be had. Hengist destroyed my only field army in the south. Thus I sit in my palace, and take comfort in music and wine and good friends."

Constantine referred to Hengist's shattering victory over the levies from Durovernum Cantiacorum, led by the magistrate, Natanleod. Ambushed in their camp by the Saxons, few had escaped. In his blind panic on hearing the news, Constantine had refused Hengist's ransom demands for Natanleod, condemning the luckless magistrate to death.

Neither the High King, nor any of his countrymen, knew how Morgana had helped the Saxons to win their unexpected victory She was a shadow, a mere tremor on the wind, detectable only when she chose to be.

He is making mistakes, Morgana thought, *too many. Now I shall persuade him to another.*

"You are a fool, lord king," she said, "not to see the opportunity before you. You have allowed your enemies to gain a foothold in your kingdom. What is done cannot be easily mended."

"How useful," sneered Pascent, "why not tell us if it rained yesterday, witch? Anyone can judge that which has already passed."

Morgana ignored him. "There is a way," she continued, "though it may hurt your pride. Forget pride, Constantine. The safety of the kingdom comes first."

Constantine swallowed, plucking at the hem of his gown, soiled with wine and meat grease. "Go on," he said.

"Cent is full of Saxons. Good fighting men. More will come, just as they did in Vortigern's day, braving the North Sea in their longboats. You must follow the example of Vortigern. Offer them gold. You have plenty of it. Hire them as soldiers. Use them against their kin in Linnuis."

Constantine's mouth fell open. "My father dug his own grave by hiring Saxons!"

Pascent said angrily, "would you lure our present king into making the same mistake?"

Yes, thought Morgana.

"I said follow Vortigern's example, not repeat his mistakes," she went on smoothly, "hire a limited number of Saxons and send them off to fight the Jutes. This will weaken Hengist's position in Cent, as well as reduce the number of barbarians in Linnuis. While they slay each other, you can send envoys to the kings and nobles of Britannia. Offer them anything. Lie to them, if need be. But persuade them to come to Londinium, with every fighting man they can raise."

"Then," she cried, striking the floor with her staff, "you may be king in deed as well as in fact. With such a mighty host behind you, you can sweep both Jutes and Saxons out of the land forever!"

After some further protest, mostly from Pascent, the king yielded to her ideas, and agreed to send envoys to treat with Hengist. Morgana stayed one night at the palace, and was gone before dawn, treading her own path back to the wild. She had done her work.

Artorius, she was certain, would not have been so easy to bend to her will. He was a cross-grained man, stubborn and independent. As High King, he would rule according to his own lights, and rely on no simpering court favourites. Nor would be turn to Morgana for guidance.

That was for the future. For now, Morgana followed secret paths into the forest, where she felt safest. Instinct guided her along ancient trackways to a small clearing.

Inside the clearing was a stone, a smaller version of one of the monoliths forming the henge near Mons Ambrius. It was the height of a man, and made of basalt, worn smooth by the passage of time and weather. Under the stone lay the remains of one of Morgana's predecessors, a druid of the old faith. His bones were centuries old, but she could still sense the echo of his spirit, pulsing up through the earth.

Here was a source of power she could tap into. She settled herself against the trunk of one of the gnarled beech trees surrounding the clearing and bowed her head, waiting.

Morgana remained perfectly still for hours. It was a painful discipline she had taught herself. Only with stillness, and the slowest beat of her heart, would visions come.

Finally, the mists parted. In her mind's eye she saw Constantine's envoys, riding south from Londinium to speak with Hengist. The Saxon chief still dwelled on the Isle of Tanatos, where he was busy rebuilding the fort Ambrosius had burned.

She saw the negotiations, held inside Hengist's half-finished hall. Hengist bawled and threatened the envoys, like the fine play-actor he was, and grinned when they went down on their knees and wept, begging him to spare them.

"Yes, beg, you worms," he laughed, throwing his mead-horn at them, "gods below, how have men such as these held onto this country for so long? Give me Cent, you gutless swine, and I may consider your request."

In the end, he agreed to send men to fight his own kin in Linnuis, as Morgana knew he would. The old wolf was utterly faithless, and happy to betray his allies for a pile of gold and a solemn promise from Constantine that Cent would belong to him and his heirs in perpetuity.

Morgana switched her Sight to the north, to the siege of Lindum. The Jutish army, some fifteen hundred strong, had surrounded the town, cutting off any hope of escape for the garrison inside.

A storm raged over the town, sparing it, for the moment, from almost certain destruction. Wulfhere's engineers had not yet pieced together his artillery. The war machines lay in orderly heaps of ropes and spars, covered by sheets to protect them from the foul weather. Meanwhile his warriors crouched inside their tents like frightened rats, waiting for the wrath of Thunor, as they called their thunder god, to pass.

Artorius will not come, thought Morgana, *even he would not risk battle in this maelstrom.*

She underestimated him. Come he did, he and his buccelari, charging out of the storm's black heart with the flash of lightning reflecting like green fire from their spear-heads.

To the Jutes on watch, huddled up miserably in their cloaks against the vile weather, it must have seemed as though a horde of mounted demons had burst out of the ground. They took to their heels, screeching in terror, even as the horsemen rode through and over them.

Bugles screeching, blades heavy with blood, the Britons carried their furious assault into the main Jutish camp. Shock and terror, Artorius' favourite weapons, made up for the massive disparity in numbers. Scores of Jutes died before they could even rise from their beds, trampled or speared to death.

Morgana saw Artorius riding through the chaos like some ferocious god of war, faceless under his stolen helmet, his spear Rhongymiad leaping in his hand. Few tried to stand before this terrifying apparition. As the Jutes ran, so he slaughtered them, until his mail was as red as his cloak.

There was no connection of blood between Morgana and Artorius. Her father Ambrosius had formally adopted him as a child, but they saw little of each other in their youth, and had even less in common as people.

Despite all this, Morgana thrilled to her adopted brother's martial skill, the way he turned the enemy's weight of numbers against them. Artorius deliberately singled out the high-ranking Jutes for death, their chiefs and gesiths, leaving the ceorls without leadership.

Only in one place did the Jutes make a stand. Wulfhere himself, a giant from British nightmares, colossal and red-bearded, gathered his hearth guards before his pavilion.

These men had sworn solemn oaths to give their lives in defence of their lord. Few had had time to wrestle on their mail when the Britons attacked, and stood in plain tunics and bracae, hurriedly forming a ring of shields around Wulfhere.

They had barely locked shields before a tide of horsemen burst among them, led by Bedwyr. The fury and speed of his attack was enough to shatter the ragged line.

Morgana grimaced at the carnage, the screaming horses and scrape of steel, the wet thud of spears in flesh, war-cries, curses, whimpers of pain.

Amid the rain and thunder and spurting gore, Bedwyr leaped from his horse to face Wulfhere. Bedwyr was a dwarf next to the Jutish warlord, who howled as he swung his long-axe. There must have been ten pounds of iron in the head of the dreadful weapon, enough to cut any man clean in half.

The axe sliced through thin air as Bedwyr rolled under it, and was up again, stabbing at Wulfhere's belly. The Jute wore no mail, and the sweep of his axe had thrown him off-balance.

The sword punched clean into his abdomen, up into his heart. Even as Bedwyr tugged the blade free, blinded by blood showering from the wound, Wulfhere was dead, the fierce vitality fading from his eyes.

With the loss of their chief, the Jutes were done. Save a few gesiths who chose to stay and join Wulfhere in death, they scattered in bloody, headlong rout, their army reduced to a frightened rabble in little more than half an hour.

Even as they fled the field, horns sounded from inside the town. The southern gates swung open, and King Masgwid, glorious in his finely wrought mail, led his warriors out to complete the victory.

Morgana smiled wryly. *A victory already won. Perhaps Masgwid is not such a fool after all.*

She slowly released her hold on the Sight, allowing it to cloud over and dissipate. To hold onto it for so long required a mighty effort. Morgana was sweating profusely, her muscles aching with more than cramp.

As the vision left her, she leaned her head against the tree.

For now, she was content. Constantine's Saxon mercenaries would reach Lindum too late to share in the victory over their kin. All they could do was help mop up the survivors.

The lords of Britannia will see that Artorius won the battle, and saved Linnuis. They will see that the High King did nothing until the fighting was over. Even then he hired the enemies of our race, the hated Saxons, to his duty for him.

They will see that only Artorius can lead them.

Slowly, Morgana was shaping the course of events. Gritting her teeth against the pain in her muscles, she rose, and turned her face north.

It was time she spoke with her brother.

15.

Lindum

Artorius was reluctantly impressed by Geraint, the man Constantine had chosen to replace him as Magister Militum. A practical, quietly-spoken officer, about forty years old, he had served Cadeyrn, the High King's father, as captain of the royal bodyguard before the Treachery of the Long Knives robbed him of his old master.

"Constantine never lets me forget my failure to defend his father," Geraint told Artorius as they shared a jug of wine, "he uses my guilt as a weapon, holding it like a sword over my neck."

He sipped frugally. A tall, rangy man, most of the hair rubbed from his scalp, his only affectation was a pair of long black moustaches.

They were sitting together in Artorius' quarters at Lindum, inside the barracks of the old Roman legionary fort. The barracks, along with the rest of the town, was derelict and slowly falling to pieces, but served well enough as temporary accommodation for Artorius and his soldiers.

"Cadeyrn's death was not your fault, surely," said Artorius, "as I remember it, Vortigern summoned his councillors to that meeting with orders that none was allowed to come armed, and with just one servant each."

"Yes," said Geraint, nodding, "I pleaded with Caderyn to let me accompany him, but he thought taking a soldier would look wrong. He took his groom instead. Otherwise I would not be here, idly drinking Masgwid's wine."

Artorius smiled and reached for the jug to pour Geraint a fresh cup. There was little need for either to voice what happened at the stone circle, all those years ago. Hengist's Saxons had arrived at the assembly carrying hidden knives. On a signal from their chief, they set about the astonished councillors and slaughtered them almost to a man, including their servants.

He gently swirled the ruby-red contents of his own cup. It was a hot May afternoon. Shouts, and the tramp of marching feet, filtered through the room's single lattice window. Masgwid's infantry were drilling on the yard outside.

The room he had taken for himself was sparse enough. There was no furniture save his camp bed, a small chest and a couple of stools. Either the barracks had been looted, or the Roman officer who once occupied it had taken all his belongings with him. The tessarae on the floor were coated in a thick layering of dust, now disturbed by the footprints of Artorius and his guest.

"Are you close to the High King?" he asked, "does he ever confide in you?"

Geraint shrugged away the question. "He is the king. The oath I swore to his father naturally passed to him when Cadeyrn was killed. I cannot say we are great friends."

"Does he ever speak of me? If so, what does he say?"

"He does. Usually when in his cups. I can't repeat most of it. Let's just say he has no liking for you, distrusts you, and suspects you of wanting his crown."

Artorius stood up, almost upsetting his stool. "Suspects me?" he cried, striding angrily about the room, "if I wanted his wretched crown, I could have challenged him for it after Ambrosius died. Instead I stood aside. I let him have it all – crown, kingdom, council, all wrapped up and presented on a golden platter for him!"

"I know," said Geraint, unmoved by this outburst, "he knows it too, but gratitude does not come easily to the great. He thinks you are playing some kind of long game."

In his rage, Artorius forgot the need for caution. "Constantine tried to have me killed in Gaul, didn't he?" he shouted, "me and all my men. That's why he sent us off on that fool's errand. He lacked the courage to wield the assassin's knife himself, so hoped the Visigoths would do the job for him."

Geraint took a long swallow of wine before responding. "That I cannot say," he answered, wiping his moustache, "all I know he was closeted for hours with Pascent and the envoys from Amorica. I, a mere bone-headed soldier, was not made privy to their secrets."

Pascent. Mention of his name was enough to confirm Artorius' suspicions.

"How can you serve such a man?" he asked, resuming his seat, "can't you see how he dishonours you?"

Geraint didn't answer, though Artorius' meaning was clear enough. As Magister Militum in command of the High King's armed forces, he had been dispatched from the capital with orders to relieve Lindum. Most of his troops, save for a single unit of British horse, were Saxon mercenaries: two hundred mailed axe-men led by Hengist's eldest son, Osla Big-Knife.

The appearance of Saxons outside the walls of Lindum had caused panic and consternation inside, and very nearly another battle. Only the sight of Geraint's men, riding under the golden stag banner of the High King, dissuaded the hot-blooded Masgwid from charging out at the head of his guards.

Now an uneasy peace ruled Lindum. Osla's Saxons were permitted to camp outside, and employed in small bands to hunt down the surviving Jutes, many of whom had gone into hiding in the deep fens. They were never mixed with British troops. The tension between Briton and Saxon was already taut as a bowstring. Just one mistake on either side, one word out of place, and the string would part.

"I carry out my king's orders," said Geraint, "if there is any dishonour in making allies of the sea-wolves, it lies with him, and he shall answer for it before God. Not I."

Artorius gave up. It was clear he had extracted all the information he was going to get out of Geraint. Whatever the Magister Militum's reservations about his master, he had been in the service of Constantine's family too long to even think of betraying him.

"You're a loyal man," he said, draining the last of his wine, "deserving of a better lord."

So are we all, he added silently, *Constantine is my lord too. I swore an oath to serve him. Why has he made peace with the Saxons in Cent? Has he bribed Osla to put a knife in me one dark night?*

His answers were not long in coming, and came from an unexpected source. Mid-May brought light winds, blowing in from the sea and disturbing the still air of the fens.

It also brought Morgana.

"That damned pagan witch you call sister is at the gates," Cei informed him, "she wants to talk to you. Let me turn her away. Her presence is bad for morale."

"No," said Artorius, "I will speak with Morgana, but not here."

He had not seen her for over three years, since their meeting at the stones. She looked thinner than he remembered, and older than her years. Something about Morgana put him in mind of a raven, though a rather shabby one, her dark blue robe soiled and dusty from her travels.

She was standing patiently outside the southern gate, apparently oblivious to the nervous glances and whispers of the sentries.

"Sister," said Artorius, "you cannot enter Lindum. Walk with me."

Neither wasted breath on formalities. Morgana gave a little nod, and followed Artorius when he strode out of the gateway, towards a thin cluster of trees beside the road.

He turned and leaned his back against one of the withered trunks. "Well?" he said, folding his arms, "you have sought me out for some reason. What is it?"

Artorius gave an involuntary shiver, aware of being in the presence of dark magic. He knew her eyes under the silk covering were useless, destroyed by a childhood illness. Morgana had no need of them. The power that had called his sister away from her remote Dumnonian convent also lent her the Sight.

"I would know your intentions," she said abruptly, "all Britannia resounds with the news of your victory over the Jutes. What use will you make of it?"

"Use?" he replied, "Wulfhere is dead, and his remaining followers scattered to the winds. Even now my men are hunting them down in the fens. Others have returned to their ships and disappeared back to Germania, where they belong. Linnuis is safe. I will remain here until the last Jute is accounted for."

"And then?"

"Then I will go wherever I am needed. Some part of our shores are always being threatened. I will never lack for work."

He noticed her knuckles whiten as she clenched her staff. "So you mean to spend the rest of your days as a sort of roving watchman. Britannia's guard dog, fighting and killing her enemies until one day you are unlucky, or too slow, and die in some chance skirmish."

Artorius grinned. "Britannia's guard dog," he said, "I like that. Ambrosius raised me to fight. To defend our borders. I am merely following his instruction."

Morgana took a step towards him. "He raised you to *rule*," she hissed, "you were destined to be his successor. To govern as well as fight."

"I am a captain of horse," Artorius said heavily, staring at the ground between them, "nothing more."

"No. You are also a coward, who turned away from his destiny because he lacked the stomach to embrace it. A coward and a traitor. What else should I call one who freely gives up the land to a man like Constantine? Under him, Britannia shall go back into the darkness our father rescued it from."

She pointed the end of her staff at his breast. "Only you can stop this. Britannia's kings are little men, concerned with nothing save their own glory and petty squabbles. Even they are starting to wake up to Constantine's inadequacy. Tell me, what does Masgwid think of his Saxon auxiliaries?"

Artorius bore her insults with difficulty. "He would rather accept the Devil for an ally," he said, swallowing his irritation, "but they are good fighters, and seem content to butcher their own kinsmen in return for gold and land. Set barbarians to fight barbarians. It is an old Roman strategy. Perhaps Constantine is shrewder than you think."

"Joke if you will," she said quietly, "but you will one day accept the crown. At the point of a spear, if need be. The old gods…"

Artorius held up his hand. "I will hear none of your old gods. My people set them aside long before I was born. Those voices you hear are sent from the Devil."

"You know nothing of them, and you have never paid any more than lip-service to Christ. I know you, brother, better than you know yourself."

"A storm is coming," she added, turning her head to the north, "it will either sweep us away, or sweep you to power. You will have to choose. This time, choose wisely."

"I have had my fill of prophecies," said Artorius, "they can mean everything and nothing, and are too easily twisted."

He moved away from the tree and stepped past her. "Forgive me if I don't invite you to dinner. The men would not tolerate your presence. They think you are the Devil's get. Perhaps they are right."

"Beware the storm, Artorius," she called after him as he walked back to the gate, "the storm, and the shadow in the north."

He heard no more of Morgana after that. She simply vanished back into the forests, like the wild thing she was. In the following weeks Artorius did his best to put her out of his mind.

At the beginning of June, when the lingering threat of the Jutes was all but extinguished, a messenger arrived from Eburucum, coated in sweat and dust from the road and riding a near-foundered horse. He gasped out his news before Artorius, Geraint and Masgwid.

"King Peredur sends you greetings, lords, and begs your help. He has sent envoys to all the kings of the north, summoning them to arms."

Artorius and Masgwid exchanged glances. Peredur was the eldest son of Coel Hen, and had succeeded the old tyrant as King in Eburucum. Like his father, he was responsible for the defence of a large section of the Wall.

"A raid on his land, I presume," said Masgwid, "it is the season."

"No mere raid, lord king," replied the envoy, "the barbarians are pouring over the Wall in force. A great coalition of northern tribes. They are led by Rhitta, King of the Damnonii. He spent the winter months forging this unholy alliance, and hired Picts and Scotti as auxiliaries."

Artorius cursed. The Damnonii were supposed to protect the northern frontier of Britannia. Now it seemed they had sensed the weakness of Constantine's rule and broken the age-old treaty.

The envoy wrung his hands. "My lord dares not meet them in the field. We barely have enough men to defend the walls of Eburucum, let alone risk a battle against such a horde. They cover the land like locusts, devouring everything in their path!"

The storm, thought Artorius, *Morgana's prophecy has already come true, curse her. She sees and knows all.*

For the present, he could do nothing to avoid the path Morgana seemed determined to set him on. The north country, Britannia Secunda, had to be defended.

"Rhitta must be driven back," Masgwid said briskly, his eyes shining with the prospect of another war, "our work is all but done here. We can leave a garrison in place and take the rest of our forces north."

He paused, glancing uncertainly at Artorius. "You will be fighting fellow northerners. Maybe your own kin."

"The Selgovae mean nothing to me," Artorius said shortly, "Ambrosius made me a southerner."

He lied. At heart Artorius was still proud of his northern roots, but his personal feelings had to be set aside. Even if Rhitta was his own brother, he would march to stop him ravaging Britannia. Duty was all.

"What of Osla and his Saxons?" asked Geraint.

"We take them with us, of course," said Masgwid, "we left them here, they would only start pillaging the countryside.."

He chuckled, and rubbed his hands. "They can fight in the front line. With luck, they shall be wiped out to a man, and take a heavy toll of Picts before they die. Let pagans kill pagans."

Artorius laughed at the young king's cheerful ruthlessness. Still, he could not forget the last words of Morgana's prophecy.

The shadow in the north.

16.

Curia, August 473

The lord of Curia was fond of playing gwyddbwyll in the evenings. It was one of his few refinements. Ignorant, unlettered and superstitious, he was a mere peasant, with no royal or noble blood in his veins. Somehow he had clawed his way to power, seizing the mighty hill-fort of Curia and making it his home.

Aethelflaed suspected him of even humbler origins. During their frequent games of gwyddbwll – he insisted on choosing her for an opponent – she would study the faded tattoo-marks on his wrists, and the unmistakable mark of a branding iron on his upper left shoulder, and wonder.

A criminal, she would think, *an outlaw, guilty of the most evil crimes.*

Gwrgi's attention was usually fixed on the board, but once he looked up and caught her studying him.

"They caught me once," he said, tapping the mark on his arm, "I was still very young, and stole bread to survive. The headman of the village was a kind man. He might have hanged me. Instead he gave me a good scar and let me go."

His yellow teeth flashed in a grin. "I was more careful after that. They never caught me again. Your move, yellow-hair."

Aethelflaed hurriedly looked down at the board. She loathed being called 'yellow-hair', but had learned better than to protest.

She was quite alone in Curia. All her followers, Oswine and Ceadda and the rest, were dead. Gwrgi had lingered over their deaths. Flaying and slow slicing were just two of his preferred methods. The mildest. She preferred not to dwell on the others. Aethelflaed's hand hovered over one of her pieces. As always, she had been ordered to play the aggressor. Her pieces, sixteen flat circles made of pewter, were arranged around the edge of the square wooden board, which was divided into forty-nine equal squares.

She had already lost four of her pieces. Not once, in over four months of captivity, had she come close to winning a game. Gwrgi was a talented player, and she dared not try too hard to beat him. It might prove the end of her.

He, as the defender, started the game with half her number of pieces. So far Aethelflaed had failed to take a single one. They were made of bronze, and arranged in a cross-section in the centre of the board. Their task was to defend the 'king', which occupied the central square. He won if the king managed to reach the border of the game board. Her aim was to get the king in a position where he could not move at all.

In place of a king was the figure of a man with a dog's head. The body was carved from a piece of bone, and the head cast in iron. Aethelflaed thought the body and the head must have been made by different craftsmen, since the latter was of far superior quality. Its flattened eyes, slitted eyes, long snout and rows of serrated teeth figured largely in her nightmares, whenever she did manage to sleep.

Aethelflaed's hand shook as it moved one of her three remaining pieces on the edge of the board closest to her. It shuffled forward two squares.

Gwrgi struck, sliding one of his pieces five squares across the board in a diagonal line. Her piece lay now lay directly between two of his. Any piece caught between two opposing forces was removed from the game.

"Another for the pot," he cackled, snatching up his opponent's dead piece and adding it to the pile of slain on his side of the table.

Aethelflaed nervously brushed back a loose strand of hair. She preferred to bind up her long fair tresses, but Gwrgi insisted otherwise.

His interest in her appearance was purely aesthetic. So far as she knew, Gwrgi never lay with any woman – or man, for that matter. He had an almost monkish disapproval of sex, and forbade his warriors from bringing their women inside the walls of the fort. Curia was like some nightmarish monastery perched on the roof of the world, swept by powerful winds billowing in from the sea.

"I...I don't know why you keep playing me, lord," she stammered, "I am no fit opponent for you. Why not challenge Rhydderch to a game? He has far more skill at it."

Rhydderch, the Christian priest who had brought her to this place, was not present. He preferred to spend his time in a cave at the foot of the great lump of rock Curia was built on, or wandering alone in the forest.

"Rhydderch is not so pleasant to look at," said Gwrgi, "and he stinks of shit. He has some problem with his bowels. Can't keep his food down."

Because he is frightened, thought Aethelflaed, *we all are. This monster holds us in thrall.*

Her father held the loyalty of his warriors through a mixture of fear and respect. Gwrgi was different. His followers walked in terror of him, but there was something else: he exerted a strange, overpowering charisma, almost hypnotic, to which lesser men always succumbed.

He wasn't much to look at. A small man, even shorter than Aethelflaed, he had a meek, almost childlike face, with large blue eyes framed by long lashes. The childlike effect was completed by his lack of a beard. Unlike almost every other man she had known, Gwrgi went clean-shaven.

She wondered whether he could even grown a beard. His fair hair was fine as silk, and rapidly receding from his scalp. There was very little hair on his long white arms. Altogether there was something incomplete or half-grown about Gwrgi, as though God had neglected to shape him like other men.

"Rhydderch was my favourite," he said, running a finger down his smooth cheek, "until you came. He is clever, I will give him that. Useful, too. Without his advice, I would not have thought of taking this place."

Aethelflaed knew the story. He had repeated it to her many times. Having gathered a band of outlaws and broken men around him, the very dregs of humanity, Gwrgi found Rhydderch by sheer chance. The priest had been cast out by his village, for some crime or other he refused to speak of.

She had her suspicions. Rhydderch had a marked fondness for little children. Whenever Gwrgi returned from a raid on some neighbouring chief's territory, he always brought back a few human captives as well as stolen goods and livestock. Most of the captives were employed as slaves. The youngest were sent down the hill to Rhydderch's cave and never seen again.

Gwrgi looked at her knowingly. "You don't like my tame priest, do you?" he said, "I can tell. You have no art at hiding your thoughts."

"No," Aethelflaed admitted, sensing it was what he wanted to hear.

Gwrgi gave a little half-smile, and promptly changed the subject. "Curia was empty when we found it," he remarked, gazing mildly around the hall, "I was destined to come here."

Had she wished to die horribly, Aethelflaed might have laughed at him. His mead-hall was a wreck, with the shadows of damp creeping up the walls and great holes in the thatched roof. For some reason he forbade any effort at repairing it, even when the frequent rains poured through the gaps. The water had soaked into the packed dirt of the floor, and in places formed puddles of fetid water.

She duly lost the game, and was permitted to return to her chamber. This was a dilapidated outbuilding, once a storehouse for grain. Aethelflaed spent the rest of the night there, in fear and trembling, and much of the following day. It was cold, with just a pile of old straw and a thin woollen blanket for a bed, but at least offered refuge. Gwrgi permitted no-one to disturb her, except the slave who brought her meals and summoned her for the nightly game of gwyddbwyll.

Every night she prayed to her gods for forgiveness, even though she knew they would not listen. Sometimes, when exhaustion, fear and cold had reduced her to the most wretched and miserable of creatures, she prayed to the shades of her murdered followers.

"Forgive me," she would beg, rocking back and forth on her knees, "I should have died with you. I could not. I was found wanting. Please, forgive me..."

In this, her first trial, Aethelflaed had failed. The knowledge of that failure was almost as bad as the fear and biting cold. Alone and defenceless (Gwrgi had taken her sword and shield, and fine shirt of mail) she could do nothing to retrieve her honour or avenge her men.

The long day slowly drew to a close. She waited in the shadows of her tiny, cramped chamber, waiting for the dreaded knock on the door.

At last it came. "Lady," said the cowed voice of the slave, "please, my lady, Lord Gwrgi summons you."

Aethelflaed composed herself, and lifted the bar on the door. It swung open, and for a moment she stood blinking in the light, heart hammering. Would Gwrgi choose this night to drop the mask of courtesy, and send her to the long house? Part of her hoped so, but she could not bear the thought of being subjected to his tortures. She would go mad. Madness would be the only escape from the pain.

He was waiting for her in the usual place. Tonight, however, there was something different. The gwyddbwyll pieces were laid out in neat rows either side of the board, and on the board rested a wicker basket.

"Welcome, yellow-hair," he said, "I have a gift for you."

She walked towards the table, trying to hide her terror and walk straight, as a daughter of her warlike race should. Without looking at Gwrgi, she flipped open the lid of the basket.

Rhydderch's dead eyes stared up at her. His neatly severed head lay inside. The gods knew what Gwrgi had done with the rest of him. Aethelflaed didn't care to speculate.

"You said you didn't like my priest," said Gwrgi, "and I agreed. He was boring me. You shall be my new advisor."

He lifted the basket off the board, carefully setting it on the ground, and beckoned at her to sit. Aethelflaed obeyed without thinking. She was numb, broken, entirely his creature.

"The god is still waiting," he said with one of his sweet smiles, tapping the dog-head as he laid the pieces out on the board, "he is very patient. You are yet to pose any kind of threat to him."

She braved a smile in return. "Nor will I tonight, lord," she replied, tentatively moving a piece.

"We shall see," he remarked, folding his slender hands together as he studied the board. They ended in long, curving nails, like the talons of some wild beast. Aethelflaed had watched him run them down the skins of his helpless victims.

Oswine was one such victim. He had taken longer to die than most, his stubborn soul clinging to its steadily eroding cage of flesh and bone. Aethelflaed trembled at the memory.

Gwrgi placed his finger and thumb on the dog-head, and swivelled the figure around until its little dead eyes were staring directly at her.

"The god is safe from you," he said in his quiet, insistent voice, "and now he wants your advice. Should we join Rhitta?"

By the god, he meant himself. Gwrgi told her he had found the figurine in some underground cave, and believed his soul resided inside it. The dog-head, so he liked to claim, gave him ambition where before there was none.

"I was a beast," he would say, his pale eyes shining with deep internal fires, "a mere beast in the forest. Then my eyes were opened. My fellow gods wanted me to find that cave and realise my destiny. I will hold dominion over men. All men, in time, shall call me master. Those who refuse shall die."

Aethelflaed tried to bend her terrified and exhausted mind to his question.

Rhitta, known as Rhitta of the Beards thanks to the cloak of beards he wore, stitched together from the facial hair of his defeated enemies. A savage and effective warrior, he had defeated most of the major tribes and seized the fortress of Din Eidyn, an even more impregnable stronghold than Curia.

Hungry for land and riches, Rhitta then led his hordes south, overrunning the weakly defended Wall. Now his army was howling around the walls of Eburucum. King Peredur's beleagured garrison had so far managed to keep the Picts at bay. Unless relieved, the city would not hold out much longer.

Perhaps wisely, Rhitta had made no attempt to take Curia before marching south, even though the fort lay just a few miles east of Din Eidyn. Instead he sent an envoy respectfully requesting Gwrgi's help in the assault on Eburucum.

"Well?" said Gwrgi, "the god is waiting. Speak your mind. Have no fear. I would not harm you."

As yet he had not laid a finger on her. Something about Aethelflaed seemed to fascinate him: especially her hair, which he was fond of describing as a flowing river of gold.

The real gold, Hengist's gold, lay in a covered pit in his bedchamber. She had given up the secret of its whereabouts to him, as a doomed attempt to halt the torture of her followers.

Yes, join Rhitta, she thought, *take your band of thieves and rapists and murderers to him. If the gods are kind, the Britons will slay you all.*

Aethelflaed hesitated. Gwrgi had spies in the south, following Rhitta's progress. One had recently returned with news that King Masgwid of Elmet was on his way to relieve Eburucum.

With him rode Artorius. Aethelflaed hated
that name, even more than she hated the
name of Gwrgi Wyllt. During her youth in
Germania, defeated Saxon warriors had
come home bearing tales of Artorius, a
British cavalry commander of genius,
unbeatable in the field. He and his accursed
horsemen had slain many of her kin. Her
father made Aethelflaed and her brothers
swear a solemn oath, on the bones of their
ancestors, not to rest until this bane of their
race was dead.

She glanced up at Gwrgi. The shades of
her murdered followers also demanded
revenge. They would have to wait. An older
score had to be settled first.

"I've seen your northern warriors," she
replied slowly, "they have little in the way
of cavalry. A few chariots and spearmen on
ponies, nothing like the mailed riders
Artorius commands."

"Rhitta's host is said to be vast," said
Gwrgi, "an ocean of men. How can this
Artorius and his little band of horse-soldiers
hope to turn them back?"

"You have not seen them fight, lord,"
Aethelflaed said, with a flicker of her old
courage, "nor have I, but my people have.
He has put many of my kin in the long
house. Every one of his soldiers is protected
by heavy armour, and expert at fighting

from horseback with lance, sword and javelin. The horses themselves are trained to kick and bite, and respond at a touch of the reins from their riders. They can wheel and charge, withdraw, re-form and charge again with a skill and discipline to match the Romans."

"If Rhitta plans to match his half-naked savages against Artorius in open battle," she went on, "then he may as well save himself the trouble and fall on his own sword. No, lord, I would advise you not to join him."

It was hard to tell if Gwrgi was impressed. His face seldom expressed any emotion, save when contorted in the ecstasy of inflicting pain on others.

He picked up one of his lesser pieces. "Artorius," he said, rolling the name around his mouth, even as he held the bronze disc before his eyes and rolled it between finger and thumb, "I know his name, but little else. Tell me what you know of him, yellow-hair."

Aethelflaed obeyed, and darkness gradually claimed much of the dimly-lit hall as she spoke of Artorius.

Gwrgi sent no spears to aid Rhitta. Instead he sat in Curia and waited, as summer slowly died in the north, for news from south of the Wall.

He continued to treat Aethelflaed as a kind of honoured guest, permitted to do and go where she willed inside the walls of the fort.

"But no further," he smilingly informed her, "my little Saxon bird must remain caged. If you set foot outside the gates, I will have no choice but to add your skin to my collection."

The mere threat was enough to kill any thoughts of escape. She had seen the skins of her followers, flayed from their bodies and draped over the outer walls of the fort. Their skulls were stuck on spears over the battlements of the timber gatehouse. The rest of the bones were flung into the ditch, where Gwrgi's slaves emptied the night-soil.

As the chill of autumn settled over the land, Aethelfled's nightmares gave way to dreams of rescue. She thought her wits would desert her if she had to spend any longer on top of this hellish rock, playing gwyddbwyll every night with an evil madman.

I would welcome Artorius himself, she thought one evening as she stood on the walkway and gazed longingly at the forests to the south, *if he and his cavalry came to save me now.*

She started to regret advising Gwrgi not to join Rhitta, until his spies finally returned with news from Eburucum.

The tale they had to tell was a sorry one, though not unexpected. "All is over, lord," reported their captain, cringing on his knees before Gwrgi's chair, "Rhitta is utterly defeated, and fled to Din Eidyn with what is left of his host."

Gwrgi took the news calmly. "How?" he asked, folding one leg over the other and resting his chin on his fist.

"There has been weeks of fighting, lord. When Rhitta heard of British reinforcements coming up from the south, he abandoned the siege of Eburucum and withdrew back over the Wall, hoping to lure the enemy into his own country."

Gwrgi and his assembled followers listened in silence as he babbled out his story. Rain drummed on the roof. Some found its way through the gaps and dripped onto the floor.

"His retreat was disorderly, the stragglers harassed by British cavalry. Whenever the northerners tried to turn and fight, Artorius fell upon them like a ravening lion. Hundreds died before ever they reached the Wall."

Gwrgi looked knowingly at Aethelflaed. "So Rhitta's host was destroyed, a piece at a time," he said. The spy shook his head.

"Not so, lord. Rhitta continued to fall back until he reached the shores of the River

249

Bassas. There he turned at bay and offered battle. Artorius attacked at dawn without waiting for his allies."

"And then?"

The spy threw up his hands. "He had Saxons fighting with him. Giant warriors, clothed in iron from head to toe, wielding great axes that carved holes in the northern ranks. They smashed Rhitta's spearmen, even as Artorius and his riders fell upon them, flank and rear."

Aethelflaed could not imagine why her people were fighting alongside Artorius. Still, she felt a glow of pride, and held herself a little straighter.

"Even then, Rhitta was not done," the spy continued, "he got away from the field of slaughter with enough men to fight another day, and took shelter in the deep forest of Celidon, a few miles north of the Bassas."

"Artorius allowed him no respite. He attacked again, this time under a full moon, sending in his Saxons to drive the northerners from the wood. There was much hard fighting, but at last Rhitta had to flee."

"The British cavalry were waiting for him in open country," he finished in a hollow voice, "this time Rhitta was taken prisoner, while the flower of the north's fighting men were slaughtered on the field."

"But he is still alive?" Gwrgi asked, surprised.

"Yes, lord. Artorius chose to mock him rather than take his head. They shaved his beard and added it to his cloak. Then Artorius took the cloak and burned it, and allowed Rhitta and his servants to depart."

Laughter rippled around the hall, quickly stilled when Gwrgi failed to join in.

"What of Artorius and his allies?" he asked sharply, "do they lay siege to Din Eidyn?"

Aethelflaed understood his concern. Curia was just a day's march from Din Eidyn, and might be threatened if the latter fell.

"No, lord. They seem content with breaking Rhitta's power, and have returned south."

Gwrgi said nothing for a while. He seemed lost in thought, his index finger tap-tapping against the arm of his chair.

At last he rose, stretching like a cat until his joints clicked.

"It seems Rhitta of the Beards is suddenly in need of friends," he said, "let us go to Din Eidyn."

"What can you offer him?" asked Aethelflaed, whose pride in the battlefield exploits of her kin had made her bold, "a few spears, and a damp stronghold?"

His thin lips split into a grin. "Much more than that, yellow-hair. I will offer him Hengist's gold, and Hengist's daughter to go with it."

17.

Cent, 475

The snows and ice of deepest winter lay
heavy on Hengist's kingdom when death
came for him. In the last days of the
previous summer a fever had entered his
lungs. As the nights grew longer, so his
sickness worsened, until he could hardly
breathe, and frequently coughed up blood.

When the darkest time of year came,
Hengist took to his bed, knowing he would
never rise from it again. The pain was like
nothing he had ever known, only held at bay
by the foul-smelling potions and cordials
mixed by the elderly wise woman who
served him for a physician.

His father, he knew, would have despised
such a lingering, drawn-out death. "To die
peacefully, like a cow in the straw," the old
tyrant used to say, "is for women and slaves,
not true-born warriors. We go to meet our
gods like honourable men, sword in hand."

Old fool, Hengist thought, *murdered by his
own hearth guards. Where was the honour
in that, father? Perhaps you can tell me
when we meet again. Soon.*

Since retaking his kingdom, Hengist had
built strongholds all over it. Never again
would his people be driven out and again
reduced to wandering the seas as mere

pirates, landless and despised. He chose to die in one of the largest of these new forts, built near one of the Roman towns the Britons had left to fall into ruin. The town lay in the north of Cent and was called Durobrivae.

Now his last days had come, Hengist had leisure to reflect on his long life, and the people who had shaped it. Most had long since gone into shadow. His warlike father. His mother, whom he dimly recalled as a sad-eyed woman, clever and wise and gentle with her children, deserving of a better mate than her brutish husband.

His brother Horsa. Hengist was eager to see him again. They would drink each other to death – so to speak - in the halls of Valhalla, and roar and feast and fight for eternity in the company of all their slain comrades.

No, dying was not to be feared. When the time came, the pain would abate, and his shade would be permitted to glide free of its withered shell.

Hengist's work on earth was not quite done. He sent for Cerdic, his third son, summoning him from the marshes and forests of the southern coast of Britannia, where he was busy carving out a petty kingdom for himself.

He doubted the young man would come, and was surprised when the lean, red-haired figure ducked under the lintel of his bedchamber.

"Father," said Cerdic, halting at a respectful distance from the sickbed, "I must say, you have looked better."

Through the haze of pain and narcotics, Hengist peered up at his youngest son. The loose muscles in his face worked as he tried to smile. It was like Cerdic to jest at a time like this. Smaller and weaker than his brothers, he relied on guile rather than brute strength.

Hengist remembered him as a little boy, struggling to keep up with his siblings. They quickly sniffed out his weakness, as children tend to do, and made him suffer endless taunts and beatings. His survival to adulthood was a minor miracle, as the Christians might term it.

What was his mother's name? Some British woman, taken as a slave during a raid. Hengist could barely even remember her face. She must have been pretty, he supposed. Otherwise he would not have raped her.

"Come closer, boy," Hengist rasped, wincing at the stabbing pains in his chest when he spoke, "too cursed dark in here. I can hardly see you."

"You should have more lamps," said Cerdic, moving closer to the bed, "and get the slaves to douse the fire a little. The heat in here is like an oven. Do you mean to bake rather than die?"

Hengist coughed out a feeble laugh. Dark blood spattered his chin. He would have wiped it away, but Cerdic leaned down and gently removed it with a fold of his cloak.

Coming from him, such a tender gesture was slightly unnerving. Cerdic was not one to show affection. He was cold and self-contained, a schemer and a watcher, with a lump of iron in place of a heart. The type of man who carefully weighed every word in the balance before allowing it to trip off his tongue.

"I summoned you," breathed Hengist, while his son's face drifted hazily before him, "for a purpose. Not just to say farewell."

"Nor to make me any parting gifts, I'll wager," replied Cerdic, "you have never given me anything. Why begin now?"

His tone was sardonic, and laced with bitterness. It was true Hengist had never given his youngest son any land, or arranged any favourable marriages. Not, the dying man liked to think, through lack of affection – though Cerdic hardly encouraged it – but his elder brothers had to come first.

Hengist intended Osla to succeed him as King of Cent, which was only right. He had arranged for Ebusa to marry the daughter of Raedwald, a King of the East Saxons. Raedwald's territory lay near Branadunum, one of the old Saxon Shore forts on the eastern coast of Britannia. When the girl's father died, Ebusa would inherit a large chunk of the kingdom.

It was a good legacy, he reflected, the fruit of long years of struggle. The east and south-east of the island were now firmly under Saxon control. Little victories won by British captains like Artorius, however galling, did nothing to dislodge them.

The real threat to the Saxon hegemony came from within. From dissatisfied spare princes like Cerdic. Hengist meant to nullify the threat before he died.

"My son," he whispered, "you must do me justice. I have given you nothing because there was nothing to give. All the land had to go to your brothers. But you have no need of gifts. You are the wisest of my sons. In time, you can be the greatest of them, if you step carefully."

He made an effort, and lifted his yellow hand to place it over Cerdic's white one. Heavy gold rings, encrusted with gems, adorned his son's middle and index fingers.

"Even now, you are hardly a beggar," said Hengist, glancing significantly at the rings, "you and your cousin Aelle shall carve out grand kingdoms of your own in the south."

"My grand kingdom," spat Cerdic, "is currently no more than a few miles of bog and waterlogged forest. My mead-hall is a sty. I have few warriors, and those who choose to follow me are the worst of men, the scrapings my brothers had no use for."

"Patience," said Hengist, "you are still young, and can wait. I had to."

He looked past Cerdic, to the doorway, where two of his gesiths had taken up position. Their bright ring-mail glinted through the smoke curling up from the hearth.

"You will swear an oath," he went on, "a solemn oath, on the bones of your forebears."

One of the spearmen stepped forward. He carried a long wooden box in his hands. In it resided the skull of Hengist's father, mixed with the bones of more distant ancestors.

Cerdic heard the movement behind him and spun around, hand flying to his saex. He relaxed slightly when he saw the box.

"Ah, dear grandfather," he said, "it is many years since you dug him out. What words would you have me mumble over his dusty old bones?"

"No jests, lad," hissed Hengist, struggling to prop himself up against the wool-stuffed bolster supporting his head, "such an oath is not taken lightly."

"You will swear never to make war against your brothers after I am gone. Break your word, and your shade will never reach Valhalla. It will be cast into darkness, beyond the realm of the gods, never to find its way back."

Cerdic's narrow face etched into a frown. He was meant to stretch out his right hand, place it on the rough wooden lid of the box, and repeat the words of the oath as Hengist dictated them.

"I have been through this ritual before," he said, "when I was a child. You made us swear to kill Artorius. Yet he still lives, and has Osla for an ally."

"Osla is merely doing what I told him," replied Hengist, "the High King must be disposed of before Artorius, who is not the threat he once was. A mere irritant, stripped of all rank and authority. His own king saw to that. The gods blessed us when they placed that fool Constantine on the throne."

"You have it all planned, I see," said Cerdic with one of his lopsided smiles, "even after death you mean to move us all, like pieces on a board. Not me, father. I am no man's pawn. And I am already oath-sworn."

Hengist closed his eyes for a moment, trying to muster his strength. Arguing with Cerdic was exhausting. No-one else would defy him to his face.

No-one save Aethelflaed.

A pang of guilt sliced through Hengist, sharp as any knife. There had been no word from his daughter since she vanished into the frozen north, almost two years gone. How he regretted letting her go!

"She was another like you," he said aloud, "strong as a fortress, stubborn as an ass. Where is she now? Where is my girl, my joy, my sweetling?"

His eyes cracked open, to see Cerdic standing over him.

"Who, father?" the young man asked, "your speech is wandering. Do you mean Aethelflaed?"

Hengist waved it aside. "No time," he wheezed, "no time to linger over regrets. Mistakes. You said you were already oath-sworn."

"Yes. I cannot take the oath you ask of me. It goes against the one I have already sworn."

Hengist failed to understand. "Someone…made you swear an oath to fight your brothers?"

"No, father. Not quite."

Cerdic suddenly leaned down to whisper in his father's ear. "What was my mother's name?" he hissed.

"Your mother…"

"Her *name*. Tell me!"

Surprised, Hengist found himself searching his fading memories. No name presented itself. Only the vague silhouette of a pleasing figure, and the futile screams of a woman who didn't want him.

"Conna," said Cerdic when the dying man failed to respond, "her name was Conna."

Conna. The name stirred up no more vivid memory of her. Hengist had bedded countless women in his time, with their consent or without.

"She made me swear an oath," Cerdic went on, "shortly before she died. That was three winters ago. You didn't know she was dead? No, why should you. A chill took her. I buried her myself, within sight of the sea. She always loved the sea. It offered the promise of escape. Poor, deluded woman. Only death could free her."

"As she lay dying, she called me to her side, just as you have now. Isn't it strange, how the gods work their will on us?"

Hengist said nothing. He was waiting for Cerdic to kill him. His spearmen hovered close by, poised, ready to strike the moment

Cerdic tried anything. Who would prove the quickest?

"She wanted revenge on you," said his son, still in the same conspiratorial whisper, "that's what she said. *Avenge me on your father. He enslaved me, raped me, and cast me aside. Avenge me.* And I swore to do it."

Breathing quickly, he straightened and moved away from the bed. "Sadly, I waited too long," he added with a rueful smile, "and now it is too late. What revenge can I take on a dying man? You are already eaten up with pain and guilt. What would putting a knife in you achieve?"

"Only your death," muttered Hengist. The spears of his guards were levelled at Cerdic's breast. At a word or a nod from their lord, they would run him through.

Cerdic didn't even spare them a glance. "You see my problem, father. I can do nothing to you. My brothers, however, are a different matter. Stags before the wolf."

He tapped his chest. "I am the wolf. You have given Osla and Ebusa much power. Gold and land, and good fighting men to hold them. I tell you they shall not hold them. Osla shall not rule in Cent for long. Ebusa may enjoy his fair young bride for a while, but shall not live to inherit her fat acres."

"This is my revenge. Conna's revenge on you. I believe the Christians call it fratricide. The sin of Cain and Abel, or some such nonsense."

His soft voice rose to a shout. "*My* sons shall have their lands. My sons, and their sons, and so on until the breaking of the world. The fruits of my seed, not theirs, shall inherit Britannia."

Cerdic went, cloak swirling around him as he stalked towards the door. Hengist's spearmen looked to their lord, but he was beyond speech.

"Be comforted, father," cried Cerdic, turning to stand framed in the doorway, "look not so sad. You always dreamed of founding a dynasty!"

Then he was gone. The sound of his footsteps died away, replaced by the crackle of the fire and the painful scraping of Hengist's windpipe as he fought for breath.

18.

In the years following his victory over Rhitta, the fame of Artorius grew. He and his men roved about the land, offering their military services to the Kings of Britannia in return for food, shelter and a share of any plunder.

Thankfully, he was not required to fight alongside Saxons any longer. Osla Big-Knife had gone back to Cent, though some of his warriors now served as part of Constantine's personal guard in Londinium. Artorius was loath to admit it, but he had rather liked Osla, a blunt, plain-spoken man with a certain wit. It had been the Saxon's idea to shave Rhitta and add his beard to the famous cloak. Artorius had almost befriended Osla during the northern campaign, and would be sorry to kill him when the time came.

He hardly ever went home. Caerleon was polluted by the memory of Ganhumara. His captains often remonstrated with him, arguing he would be a stranger to his sons, but Artorius could not be moved.

"My sons can know me when they are men," he would say, "I have little use for children. Let my slaves and freemen raise them."

Bedwyr looked pityingly at him. "I placed my son's first wooden practice sword in his hand," he said, "and lifted him onto his first pony. No father should miss such pleasures."

"There are other boys at Caerleon," Cei put in, "the sons of your warriors. They will fight for you one day. It is folly not to let them see your face more often. Else you will be a stranger to them as well as your boys, with little claim on their love or loyalty."

Artorius refused to yield. "We have battles to fight," he said stubbornly, "what should happen to Britannia, if I vanished into the west and spent my days dandling babies on my knee? The men who rule this land can't defend it by themselves. Most of them can barely lace up their own bracae without slaves to help them."

Cei exchanged weary glances with the other two. "Pride," he said, "pig-headed pride. It will prove your undoing."

Artorius was right in one sense. There was no end of work for them to do. The ranks of the war-band swelled as they galloped up and down the country, using the old system of Roman roads, driving back the pagans wherever they found them.

Men flocked to serve under the dragon banner, drawn by the rapidly spreading fame of Artorius and his supposedly invincible cavalry. Most of these eager volunteers were turned away, since Artorius only took the best. Even so, the number of his following swelled to over five hundred. Hoping to retain the close ties of friendship that gave them an edge over other mercenary companies, he named them the Companions, sword-brothers in body and spirit.

Two years of endless fighting followed, bloody skirmishes, raids on Saxon settlements, pitched battles against heavy odds. The greatest of these was fought on the plains outside Deva, the City of the Legion. Here Artorius replicated his adoptive father's victory over a host of invading Picts and Scotti, leaving great heaps of their slain as a feast for crows.

This victory was gained with the help of Cadwallon Lawhir, son and successor of Cunedda, King of Venedotia, now better known under the British name of Gwynedd. All over the former province, Roman names and customs were fast disappearing as the memory of imperial rule slipped under the tides of history.

Artorius was not sorry to see them go. The Roman betrayal of Rigotomos in Gaul was still raw in his memory, and it was high time Britannia cut her last ties with the diseased hulk of the Western Empire. He drew some consolation from the knowledge that

Anthemius was dead, murdered in Rome by his Magister Militium, Ricimer, who made and broke emperors as he pleased.

Ricimer himself was dead now, and the city of Rome herself fallen, taken over by the barbarian general Odoacer. The last emperor, a mere boy named Romulus Augustus, had been packed off into exile, and the imperial regalia sent to Constantinople. Nothing remained of the Western Empire save a few scattered territories, and the memory of eagles.

Artorius found he didn't care overmuch. The time of imperial glory was long past, and the Caesars had become a tawdry and short-lived parade of figureheads, rising and falling in meaningless succession.

He often thought of Ambrosius, and wondered if his shade was looking down in disapproval. The last of the Roman rulers of Britannia had tried to mould Artorius in his image, forgetting that blood always told.

In his few moments of privacy, Artorius would speak with his predecessor's shade, devoting his prayers to him rather than Christ.

"If I have failed, then I am sorry," he said, "but you must accept your share of the failure. You chose me, plucked me at random from the wilderness. My blood-father was a mere warrior, like his fathers before him. One spear among many. My kinsmen were farmers and cattle thieves. How can I wear a crown? What right do I have to rule over a kingdom? I don't know how. I cannot do it. Dare not."

Silence followed. Artorius desperately waited for a sign, anything, to hint at forgiveness. There was nothing. The soul of Ambrosius hung in limbo, disappointed and unavenged.

"I will find your assassin," Artorius vowed, "and consign his soul to Hell. When we have peace in the land again, I shall root him out."

For the time being, his vow was impossible to fulfil. The Companions were much in demand, riding from one trouble-spot to another, helping to shore up Britannia's creaking defences. They moved as swiftly as bad roads and good horses would allow, but could not be everywhere at once.

Artorius was still in Gwynedd, staying as Cadwallon's guest, when word reached him of disaster in the south. Aelle, son of Horsa, had landed on the southern coast and attacked Anderidum, the last of the Saxon Shore forts still in British hands.

"The fort is lost," reported the exhausted and travel-stained messenger, "Aelle spared no one inside. He butchered soldiers and civilians alike. In mockery of the Crucifixion, he had the commander of the fort nailed to a great cross and set it up over the gate."

The mead-benches of Cadwallon's hall were packed with warriors. Their angry voices rose like a storm as they listened to the dreadful tale. Cadwallon raised his hand to still them and let the messenger finish.

"Even as Aelle stormed Anderidum, his kinsman Cerdic struck inland at the head of another war-band. They are ravaging the countryside around Caer Guinnion. The town may have fallen by now."

Caer Guinnion lay some sixty miles south-west of Londinium. By rights, the High King should have marched to deal with the twin threat of Aelle and Cerdic, but Artorius doubted he had done anything half so decisive. Constantine's reign was now almost six years old, and every year had seen him sink further into sloth and debauchery, like the worst of Roman emperors.

A fit king, thought Artorius, *for a kingdom slowly falling to pieces.*

"We can be at Caer Guinnion inside four days," he said, rising from his seat, "maybe three, if the weather holds."

"Wait," said Cadwallon, laying a hand on his arm, "it is the High King's duty to defend his land. If you wish to win his trust, let him win a battle or two."

The young King of Gwynedd was much like his father, pale and red-haired, with a taste for finery. Hammered torcs of dark red gold gleamed at his wrists and throat, and a circlet of the same metal adorned his brow.

"Wait for Constantine to remember his duty?" Artorius replied scornfully, "we may as well yield up all our land to the Saxons and have done with it."

He led the Companions out of Gwynedd at a furious pace, tearing down the dust-dry roads as though he wished to kill his horses, using up two sets of remounts before they came within twenty miles of Caer Guinnion. Artorius prayed the good spring weather would hold, and Christ saw fit to answer, holding off the rainclouds threatening to burst in the east.

Artorius' scouts discovered the main body of the Saxon war-band in the act of crossing a ford, laden with slaves and plunder from some luckless town. Three of their wagons had got stuck, the wheels bogged down in thick river mud, and they were still trying to haul them clear when the Companions attacked.

The battle was brief, more of a series of bloody skirmishes as the Saxons tried to flee to safety in the surrounding woods. Artorius allowed no respite. Soon the shallow waters of the river were rank with Saxon blood, corpses bobbing in the water beside their overturned wagons.

Cerdic was discovered hiding under a bush, and made no resistance as he was dragged out, bound, and brought before Artorius.

"You have given me a deal of trouble in the past," said Artorius, glaring down from Llamrei's back at the defeated Saxon chief, "this is the end of it. Have you anything to say before you die?"

The two had never met before, though Artorius had occasionally glimpsed Hengist's youngest son across various battlefields. Cerdic was like an eel, slippery and evasive. Now the eel was netted at last.

He didn't seem worried by his impending execution. Bruised and bloodied from the skirmish, Cerdic yet had the nerve to smile up at his conqueror.

"Just this," he replied with easy confidence, "my brother Osla is now the King of Cent, and a friend and ally of your High King. My second brother, Ebusa, can summon a thousand spears in the east. Kill me, and your own death will soon follow."

He cleared his throat and looked around triumphantly at the Companions. "You will all hang," he cried, raising his voice, "every one of you. Constantine will stretch all your necks, or face the wrath of my kin."

"Not before I stretch yours," growled Cei, starting towards the prisoner. Bedwyr held him back.

The Companions looked to Artorius. Usually so quick and certain in his decisions, now he hesitated. The stench of Saxon blood was still in his nostrils, sorely tempting him to act, to strike down Cerdic with his own sword.

Hengist had died the previous winter. The news of the old wolf's death caused little rejoicing among the Britons, who feared the onslaught of his whelps. So far Osla and Ebusa had kept to the fragile peace, staying inside the borders of their lands and conducting no raids against British territory.

Are they conniving with Cerdic? he pondered, *were the attacks on Anderidum and Caer Guinnion merely the beginning of some grand co-ordinated assault? Or did he act without their approval or knowledge?*

It mattered little. Cerdic was untouchable. Whatever his relations with Osla and Ebusa, his brothers would not stand by and do nothing if Artorius put him in the ground. They would demand the blood-price for Cerdic, and Artorius' head on a platter would be the only payment to satisfy them.

Constantine would serve it up to them. This grinning red-headed devil standing before him was right. The High King no longer knew who his true friends or enemies were, and might relish the chance to do away with Artorius once and for all. Especially with Pascent goading him on, and the brooding threat of Osla and Ebusa to consider.

Artorius gestured wearily at Gwalchmei. "Loose his bonds," he ordered, "and let him go."

Cries of protest erupted among the Companions, but their discipline was iron, and none dared to lay a finger on Cerdic as Gwalchmei reluctantly cut through the binding on his wrists.

"It is a long walk back to my kingdom," the Saxon remarked, rubbing his wrists to get the blood flowing again, "might I borrow a horse?"

"Perhaps not," he added with a grin, catching Artorius' expression.

"Go, Cerdic," Artorius snarled, "before I stick your head on the end of a spear and send it as a gift to one of your brothers."

The ranks of the Companions shuffled aside to let Cerdic through. Many hissed insults as he sauntered past. He laughed off their hatred, and walked off with an unhurried step into the woods.

19.

There was just one mirror in Caerleon. Mirrors were a luxury made of bronze and copper, or mercury behind glass, and owned only by the wealthiest.

Medraut held up the mirror, a circle of polished bronze, and turned it this way and that, trying to get a clear image of his face. His reflection in the metal was murky and indistinct, which was perhaps for the best.

The mirror had belonged to his mother. She had gone away when he was still very young, and there had never been any clear explanation of her fate. The slaves at Caerleon pretended not to know, though many of them had served at the fort for years.

His eldest brother, Cydfan, advised him not to ask. "God will tell us, in time," Cydfan would say, seven years old and already a bishop in the making, "if He doesn't want us to know, there is nothing we can do."

Medraut pretended to agree. Even at his tender age, he was learning how to lie. How to hide his true thoughts. Sometimes his thoughts frightened him. They were full of darkness and violence. He preferred others not to know them.

He turned the left side of his face to the mirror. This was his bad side. His evil side, as his nurse called it when he misbehaved. He had no memory of it, but sometime in his infancy he had suffered a terrible injury. It had broken his jaw in two places, crushed his cheekbone and almost taken his eye. Only the skill of Elias, the Frankish doctor, had saved him from being rendered half-blind. The vision in his left eye was slightly blurry, and he often suffered from headaches.

Elias was dead now, having finally succeeded in drowning his liver in strong hot wine. Medraut missed him. He had been friendly enough, at least in the mornings when he was relatively sober, and liked to enthral Medraut and his brothers with tales of his wandering life. Most of the tales were doubtless exaggerated, but there was a suggestion of truth to his accounts of Gaul and Germania and distant Constantinople, jewelled capital of the Eastern Empire. Elias claimed to have travelled even further, to Jerusalem itself, the heart of the world, and worshipped at the Holy Sepulchre.

The old drunk's stories lit a fire in Medraut's imagination. A quiet boy, fond of his own company, he loved to daydream of exotic people and places, far removed from the dull, grubby reality of everyday life at

Caerleon: glittering palaces and domed temples, dark-skinned emperors swathed in purple and cloth of gold, barbarian tribesmen marching under the banners of imperial Rome, epic battles fought across the sweep of desert plains, lives full of glorious endeavour.

Medraut peered closer at the distorted lines of his face. The bad side had a disjointed, flattened look, and his damaged eye was permanently half-closed. He was very ugly. His twin brother Llacheu, who lacked Cydfan's pious restraint, liked to tell him so.

A familiar sadness burned through him. He put down the mirror and waited for the tears to come. His eyes stung, but nothing flowed from them.

So far as he could remember, Medraut had never wept.

His daydreams were seldom uninterrupted. There were only so many places to hide in the fort, and his nurse knew them all. Her name was Gwawr, a sweet-natured girl who had been a surrogate mother to Medraut and his brothers since their real one vanished.

One late autumn afternoon, with frost in the air and brown leaves thick on the ground, she found him in the forge, quietly watching the smith, a silent, broad-beamed giant of a man, hammering out spearheads.

Medraut liked it here. It was always warm, and there was something comforting about the presence of so much iron. The smith, who had lost his only son to a fever several years back, seemed to welcome his presence.

"Out," snapped Gwawr, storming in and taking Medraut by the ear, "you are late for your lessons, and Caedmon has been whining at me ever since he arrived. I have better things to do than listen to the drivellings of some foul-tempered old man."

Caedmon was their tutor, a toothless, wizened priest, hired to teach the boys their letters as well as give them a grounding in Greek and Latin and mathematics. He rode up to the fort from his church in the town twice a week, plodding along on an old donkey that smelled almost as bad as its owner.

"I hate Caedmon," protested Medraut as he was dragged outside, "he stinks, and lisps, and is too free with his whip."

"Be thankful your father thinks of your education," said Gwawr, "you could be like the sons of other warriors, and grow up ignorant as the day you were born. Mere brutes, good for nothing but killing and being killed."

She wagged a finger at him. "Now, a man who can read and write as well as fight is different from his fellows. He wields a special kind of power."

Mention of his father cowed Medraut into silence, as it always did. He saw precious little of Artorius, who had only visited Caerleon once in the previous year. To his sons he was an occasional, terrifying presence, a frowning giant who stood over them and asked stilted questions about their progress before riding back to his wars.

Medraut remained silent until he was delivered to Caedmon. The priest was impatiently waiting for him in his mother's old bedchamber, which now served for a schoolroom. Cydfan and Llacheu were already present, sitting at a desk and poring miserably over a series of histories in Latin.

"Late," moaned Caedmon when he saw Medraut, "you are always late, or absent altogether. I ought to beat you, but it hurts my arm, and you take little notice. You have the hide of a bull-calf."

He confined himself to rapping Medraut's knuckles with his stylus, and ordering him to sit. The rest of the afternoon was spent in weary rote chanting of Latin and Greek forms and times tables, until Medraut's jaw ached and his head pounded.

Artorius had left the running of Caerleon to his chief servant, Cacamwri. Loyal and able, Cacamwri was also easily to manipulate, and could refuse his master's sons little. At the end of most days, unless the weather was foul, they were permitted to venture outside the fort (under guard) and exercise their ponies in the meadows beside the glittering waters of the Wysg.

At the end of this autumn day, the same routine was observed. As soon as they were released from Caedmon's clutches, the boys rushed to the stables, eager to enjoy a few hours of freedom before the sun went down. Too young to handle their ponies themselves, they persuaded a couple of grooms to fetch the beasts and lead them down to the river.

The spearmen who escorted the boys were young, and didn't pay as much heed to their charges as they should have. While they laughed and joked among themselves, Medraut eyed the edges of the forest bordering the meadow.

"Llacheu," he said, handing his twin the reins of his pony, "look after her for me. I am going away."

Llacheu looked confused. The boys weren't identical, and he was slightly taller and heavier than Medraut. He was also slower on the uptake.

"Away?" he said, "what do you mean? Where to? You can't go into the forest. It's getting dark."

"Just away. I want to see the world Elias told us about."

Medraut put a finger to his lips and stole away, knowing Llacheu wouldn't betray him. Though they had often quarrelled, and were very different in some respects, the bond between the twins was a powerful one.

He moved quickly and silently through the long grass, running on the balls of his feet. The guards had fallen to arguing over whether they could make the ponies race, and which animal would win. Cydfan was standing on the edge of the river, gazing up at the darkening sky in his dreamy way, lost to the antics of mere mortals.

It was even darker under the trees. Medraut had seldom entered the forest after nightfall, and always in company. Breathing hard with fear and exertion, he screwed up his courage and forced himself to go further, crawling through the damp undergrowth like a wild animal.

He heard a shout behind him. The spearmen had finally noticed his absence. Whimpering, Medraut rose and broke into a run, careless of the uneven ground or the thorns and branches whipping at his flesh.

If they caught him, he would be whipped. For all their kindness, Cacamwri and Gwawr would have to punish him.

Perhaps they will beat me so badly, I will even weep.

A shadow detached itself from the trees ahead of him. Medraut skidded to a halt.

The shadow had substance. A slender but powerful hand closed on his arm and held him in an iron grip.

"Let me go," he panted, "or they will catch me. I will scream if you don't , and they will punish you for daring to lay hands on me."

"Catch you or punish me," said an amused female voice, "which shall they do first, little prince?"

Medraut quit struggling, and squinted up at his captor. He saw a thin woman of average height, lost somewhere in middle age, her sallow features scored with deep lines. She wore a soiled blue robe and her greying hair was scraped ruthlessly back and twisted into a single plait. Unlike Caedmon, and his stench of old dog, she had a pleasant, earthy smell, like the woods after heavy rain.

Strangest of all, her eyes were hidden under a white silk cloth. The cloth was spotless. In her left hand she held a long staff of shining black wood.

The woman smiled down at him. "I promise they won't catch you, little prince," she said, "if you come with me."

He swallowed. "I'm not a prince. Why do you call me that? My father is no king. I was bastard-born."

More shouts drifted through the trees, and the sound of a hunting horn. The spearmen were getting closer. They would be desperate to find Medraut while the light lasted.

The woman didn't seem worried. "I call you a prince because so you are," she said in her calm, unhurried way, "your father may not be a king, but you could be. If you come with me."

Medraut's instincts screamed at him to cry out, to get away from her. His overwhelming curiosity stifled them.

"How could I be a king?" he asked, "tell me."

Smiling, she let go of his arm and gently took his hand. "I will tell you more than that, if you come with me."

He allowed her to lead him away, deeper into the shadows of the forest.

"We shall begin," she said, "with the fate of your mother."

20.

Din Eidyn, 477

The fortress of Rhitta of the Beards, self-styled King of the Northlands, had chosen to make his own was every bit as impressive as Curia. Built atop the basalt core of an extinct volcano, the slopes of the fort rose sheer above low-lying plains, guarded to south and west by natural cliffs. To the east, it was defended by a lake, and the only gate lay to the north. The outer wall, running all the way around the base of the mighty hill, was made of timber. Further up, a drystone wall offered a second line of defence on the hill's eastern flank, and the settlement itself on the summit was protected by a drystone ring-wall.

Here, inside his draughty hall, Rhitta sat and brooded over his defeats. Four years had passed since Artorius shattered his host in two swift battles, fought on the shores of the Bassas and inside the forest of Celidon. His best fighting men were dead, and Rhitta himself was fortunate to be alive.

The memory of those terrible defeats had remained fresh, haunting his nights. The faces of his slaughtered warriors hovered before him in his sleep. Barely a night passed when he didn't wake up screaming and drenched in sweat.

Aethelflaed knew of his torment, because she was obliged to share it. She had been his concubine for a year and his wife for three, though more of a nurse than either. Rhitta was barely forty, yet looked and behaved like a man twenty years older. Wizened and grey-haired, his nerves shattered beyond repair, he was a broken vessel, good for nothing save an outward show of authority.

On this night, like so many other nights, she sat beside him at high table and tried to coax him to eat.

"Have some of the broth, lord," she said, gesturing at a slave to fill his bowl, "your men killed a calf this morning. It is full of shredded beef, and will fill your belly."

"Slop," he muttered, pushing the bowl away. Lacking most of his teeth, he could eat little save broth and mash.

Aethelflaed regarded him with pity. Her husband was slowly wasting away, his flesh hanging loose from his brittle bones. Once a big, well-muscled man, in recent months his appetite had dwindled alarmingly.

She glanced at the shadows at the rear of the hall, where she knew Gwrgi Wyllt was lurking. Despite his unofficial status as the king's chief counsellor, he refused to take a seat at high table, or even break bread with Rhitta's warriors. No-one ever saw him eat.

Rhitta's power, such as it was, had long since passed to Gwrgi. The king might sit on his throne and bully his slaves, but any important decisions were taken by his counsellor. The lord of Curia had become King of the Northlands in all but name, first oiling his way into Rhitta's favour, and then gradually taking more and responsibility on his shoulders. Now he was indispensable.

For all her loathing of him, Aethelflaed could only admire Gwrgi's shrewdness and determination. But for him, Rhitta's remaining warriors would have long since deserted their feeble master. There was no honour or profit in serving the man who had led the north to disaster. Thanks to Gwrgi's potent mix of threats, bribes and promises, a good number of the king's men stayed, hoping for better days. The gold Gwrgi had stolen from Aethelflaed went a long way to retaining their loyalty.

Rhitta showed little gratitude. "Look at those curs," he whined, flicking a finger at the warriors on the mead-benches, "I mind the old days, when the best spears in the north were proud to call me lord. Now I must feed a pack of outlaws and thieves, robbers and broken men of all kinds. Crow's bait, fit for nothing save a good hanging."

Aethelflaed looked pityingly at him. Try as he might, the beard Artorius shaved off had never grown back properly. Tufts of coarse reddish hair, streaked with grey, sprouted from his pointed chin, failing to cover the unsightly wattle dangling from his neck. His popping eyes and red beak of a nose, forever with a drip on the end, completed the unfortunate effect.

He looks like a startled chicken, she thought, putting a hand to her mouth to cover a smile. The last time Rhitta caught her laughing at him, he had burst into tears. She thanked the gods they were alone in their bedchamber at the time. A king who wept so openly could not expect to hold onto the loyalty of the meanest slave.

It was true his warriors were a rough set, drawn from the very worst or most desperate to be found north of the Wall. Gwrgi had brought his own followers from Curia to swell the decimated ranks of Rhitta's war-band. These were the ones the king described as broken men, whom any self-respecting chieftain would hang rather than employ.

"My lord," she said in a low voice, "do not speak so loud. Your warriors may take offence."

"Let them," he snorted, "I am sick of giving shelter, and the best of my meat and drink, to such vermin."

Aethelflaed was patient with him. She had developed vast reserves of patience in the past four years, from the moment Rhitta's eyes first saw her and immediately filled with longing.

"These vermin, as you call them, are your followers," she said, "if you insult them, they will leave your hall and take service with another lord. Where will you be then? You cannot be King of the Northlands without men to fight for you."

He pursed his lips, sucking on the single remaining tooth on his lower gum. It was an irritating and unpleasant habit, one that had caused Aethelflaed to commit murder in her mind on countless occasions.

"King of the Northlands," he said bitterly, "a nothing title. I drape myself in an empty coat. My allies are dust, slaughtered at Bassas and Celidon. Their sons laugh at me and scorn my offers of friendship."

"Not all, lord. Gwrgi has forged new alliances for you. The kings of Aeron and Calchfynydd are your friends, and send gifts of gold and cattle in your honour."

Rhitta grimaced at the mention of these, two of the smallest kingdoms in the north.

"Their kings are beardless youths," he muttered, "else I might insist on taking their beards for a new cloak. I defeated their fathers in battle, and shaved the hair off their chins with my own knife. Grand days."

Aethelflaed patted his withered arm. "Soon you shall be able to weave a new cloak," she said encouragingly, "you shall know those grand days again, and the men of the south shall learn to fear your name."

To her relief, his raddled features broke into a smile. "You are such a comfort to me, my love," he murmured, leaning over to plant a dry kiss on her cheek, "is it time, then, to send messengers to your father?"

Gods, let me not strangle the fool, she thought. Rhitta would not let go of the notion that Hengist would one day come to his aid at the head of a mighty war-fleet, crammed with Saxon warriors. Gwrgi had put the idea in his head in order to persuade him to finally marry Aethelflaed, and make an ally of her renowned father.

Aethelflaed was still very much Gwrgi's creature. She hated and despised him, but feared him more, and never dared to refuse his wishes. Marrying her to Rhitta had been a way of increasing his influence over the king. Through her, Gwrgi knew Rhitta's most intimate secrets.

"Lord," she said, "my father is dead. My brother Osla rules in Cent now. I have not seen him for many years, and we were never close. He is unlikely to send any warriors to help your cause."

Rhitta frowned. His memory was beginning to fail him, as well as his appetite.

"Hengist dead?" he said peevishly, drawing his brows together, "I thought the old sea-wolf would live forever. All the great ones are departing from the world."

"Not all, dread king," cried a voice from the darkness beyond the mead-benches. The murmur of conversation died away as Gwrgi stepped forward.

He had aged little in four years, his round, pleasant face as smooth and beardless as ever. The folds of his fur-trimmed red cloak pooled behind him as he advanced slowly towards the dais. Gwrgi had developed a taste in fine clothing. Gone were his patched cloak and rough woollens. In their place was a silver-linked belt, a tunic of yellow silk, buskins of soft brown leather, and a golden brooch in the shape of a stag's head fastening his cloak. The eyes of the stag were tiny green gemstones, sparkling in the smoky darkness of the hall.

One aspect of his appearance remained constant. The icon of the dog-headed god still hung from his neck on its leather strap, mouth gaping in a perpetual snarl.

Aethelflaed quailed. Under Gwrgi's silks and furs dwelled a monster of unspeakable cruelty. She knew. She had seen his claws.

"Not all, dread king," he repeated, stopping and bowing gracefully before the dais, "your greatness lives on. A torch, lighting the world."

Rhitta preened. He loved flattery, and was either unable or unwilling to see through Gwrgi's heavy-handed compliments. Even in private he spoke highly of his advisor, and never breathed a word of criticism against him.

"I thank you," he said, beckoning at a slave to serve Gwrgi wine, "you have always been the most loyal and capable of men. You were the first to rally to my banner after Celidon. I shall never forget it."

Gwrgi waved away the slave. He drank little save watered ale, and Aethelflaed had never seen him the worse for drink.

"Night comes on quickly," he said, mounting the first step of the dais, "winter is here again, shrouding the land in her foul cloak."

He gestured at the windows of the hall. The heavy wooden shutters were fastened against the pounding of the elements. Din Eidyn was regularly battered by storms in the winter months, and tonight was no different.

"Indeed, yes," said Rhitta, wiping the drip on the end of his nose with a cloth, "we must lie low, and pray the gods spare us until the spring."

He smiled weakly. "I fear my light may sputter out before then. I grow old, my dears."

"No, lord king," said Gwrgi, "you shall never grow old."

Something gleamed in his hand. He moved quickly, too quickly for Aethelflaed's eye to follow.

The blur of sharp steel was followed by a wet gurgle, issuing from Rhitta's lips, and a torrent of blood spouting from the neat line in his throat.

His mouth trembled, eyes bulging up at his assassin, full of confusion. As their light faded, his grey head slumped forward and landed face-down in the discarded bowl of broth.

Another woman, upon witnessing the bloody murder of her husband, might have screamed or fainted. Aethelflaed was made of stronger stuff. She pushed back her chair and stood up, dabbing at the drops of wet blood on her robe.

Rhitta's murder was greeted with silence. None of the assembled warriors lifted a finger to avenge him. Athelflaed wasn't surprised. Most were Gwrgi's men, and the few who weren't possessed enough sense to stay quiet. Rhitta was not a man to throw away your life for.

Aethelflaed looked sadly at him as he twitched and choked his last. For all the boredom and irritation of the past few years, she had grown fond of her husband.

No. Not fond. I pitied him, that was all.

She glanced up at Gwrgi, who was wiping his knife on Rhitta's cloak.

"It was his time," he said curtly in response to her unasked question. She had known he would kill Rhitta, one day, and take his place.

He turned to face the assembled warriors. In response every man rose to his feet, a mark of respect they had seldom shown their old master.

"The King of the Northlands is dead," he announced, "a great man in his day, but every day ends. Now we must look to the future."

Gwrgi raised his knife high. "To a bright dawn!" he shouted, his voice echoing in the dusty rafters, "and a red sunrise!"

The warriors echoed his words, their fierce shouts sending tremors through Aethelflaed's soul.

"A bright dawn! And a red sunrise!"

21.

Anderidum

Cerdic's boats made their way around the southern coast of his kingdom, carved out of part of the greater British kingdom called Gwent, and through the wetlands surrounding the fort of Anderidum.

He stood in the prow of his keel, squinting at the squat towers of the fort as they rose through the fog to the north. Anderidum was an impressive piece of Roman military architecture, a double ring of stone walls and towers, protected on three sides by the sea washing over the coastal marshes. The fort was built on a peninsula, and had formed part of the chain of Saxon Shore forts built by the Romans during the latter years of their occupation.

"So much wasted effort," he murmured, wiping the rain from his eyes. A fine, insidious drizzle hung in the air, seeping through his woollen cloak and layers of mail and leather. The waves of the Narrow Sea boomed in the distance behind him.

Anderidum's double layer of fortifications, so grim and forbidding to look at, had failed to keep out Aelle. Two summers gone, Cerdic's cousin had sailed his keels up this same marshy inlet and stormed the fort at night. The British garrison had largely consisted of old men and civilians. Their resistance was brief, though the killing went on, so the scops sang, for over three days and nights.

Once the corpses were thrown into the marsh and the blood washed away, Aelle had turned Anderidum into his palace. The brute styled himself a king now. His war-bands roved up and down the old Roman roads, extracting tribute and oaths of allegiance from local British settlements.

"King," Cerdic said, spitting the word into the black waters, "king of mud and reeds, and a patch of waterlogged forest."

My own kingdom is little more than that, he reminded himself, *we are rats, building our nests among the ruins left by giants.*

Cerdic possessed an able, questing mind. Unlike most of his kinsmen, he was not content to live in ignorance. The slowly decaying ruins of Roman civilisation, dotted all over Britannia, fascinated him. He occasionally liked to explore the ruins of their abandoned villas and houses, gazing at the peeling frescos and wondering at the lives of the people who created them.

They were an infinitely more sophisticated race than his own. The Saxons and their ilk had little use for Roman dwellings, failing to understand the workings of the hypocaust and the simple beauty and efficiency of

Roman architecture. Sometimes a war-band would camp among the ruins of a town, but more often avoided them altogether, leaving them to nature and the slow decay of time.

Cerdic was different. He knew something of the glory of the Caesars, how they had come to this island with their legions and stamped their mark all over it. Britannia had been a mere outpost of the unimaginably vast Roman Empire, now split into two, the Western half all but crushed under waves of barbarian invasions.

He had gleaned his knowledge from speaking with captured British priests, who were the keepers and writers of history. The more learned ones he kept as slaves. They were teaching him to read a little, an excruciatingly slow and frustrating process, but Cerdic persevered.

His late father's words came back to him. *You are still young, and can wait. I had to.*

Hengist had given little to his youngest son. One of his few gifts was the gift of patience. No-one could wait like Cerdic. Now twenty-five, he had spent much of his life in the background, watching and studying the world around him. Learning. Waiting for his moment.

He sensed the moment was near. Aelle had summoned him, and the other Saxon kings of note, to a great assembly at Anderidum.

Cerdic, who commanded no more than eighty spears in his war-band, would be one of the lesser voices at the assembly. He had lost over two hundred men during his ill-advised raid into British territory, two summers gone, when Artorius came tearing down from the north with impossible speed and fallen on Cerdic's unsuspecting war-band like a hawk on a pigeon.

Cerdic grimaced at the memory. Never again would he underestimate Artorius and his cavalry. It was his one great mistake. There would not be another. The next time he faced the man on the battlefield, it would be on his terms.

He had brought thirty of his surviving warriors for an escort, leaving the rest to guard his hall. Thirty men was a pitiful retinue, especially when compared to the great Saxon war-chiefs.

Even so, my voice shall be heard. I am Hengist's son. That counts for something. I may be a half-breed, but I have twice the brains of my kin.

The outer wall of the fort gradually appeared before him, a grey monster looming through the mist. A sentry hailed him, and ordered the gate to be opened. The gate was flanked by two solid round towers, huge buttressed piles of stone with semi-circular fronts. As the timber doors swung inwards, Cerdic vaulted over the side of his keel and waded through the murky, knee-deep waters of the quay, towards the bridge over the ditch.

He was grateful to be admitted. Sea-mist lay heavy over the fens surrounding the fort, imbuing them with added mystery and danger. To the Saxons, such marshy regions were the den of monsters such as the firedrake: a hideous, fire-breathing beast, half bat, half reptile, with teeth longer than a man's arm.

Though an educated man by the crude standards of his race, Cerdic was no less superstitious. He shivered and hurried inside, wrapping his sodden cloak tight around him. His warriors followed close behind, casting frightened glances at the dank wilderness before the gates slammed shut.

"This way, lord," said one of the guards. He held a torch, lighting their way through the drifting tendrils of mist to the inner gate.

Cerdic's warriors stayed close to their lord, casting suspicious glances at the spearmen and archers lining the walls. He had warned his men to guard against treachery. Aelle was his cousin, but such blood ties had counted for little among the Saxons before now. Cerdic kept in mind the ruthless example of his own father, who happily betrayed his kinsman Wulfhere in return for gold and land.

A small forest of tents had sprung up in the outer court. More warriors sat outside, singly or in groups around their supper fires. Cerdic exchanged wary greetings as he walked past.

These men were the followers of the other kings invited to the assembly. Cerdic could almost smell their fear. Every man was armed. It would take precious little to have them flying at each other's throats.

What a pit of snakes, he thought, *and yet they are my own people. My allies. It would be safer to make common cause with a pack of wild dogs.*

"Your men must remain outside, lord," said the guard when they reached the gate, "Aelle commands it."

"Does he, now?" Cerdic replied doubtfully, "I recall my father playing a similar trick, many years ago. The Britons remember it as The Treachery of the Long Knives."

The guard's face was pale but determined. "No treachery here, lord. Aelle is your own blood."

"And perhaps he means to spill mine," Cerdic retorted. However, seeing there was no use in argument, he gave the order for his men to wait outside.

Within the inner gate lay the main part of the fort, containing the residence of the Roman officer who once commanded the garrison, a hall with a timbered roof, and the barracks. Cerdic's sharp eyes also picked out a two-storey house next to a walled garden. Lights streamed from the windows of the hall and the barracks. The rest of the buildings lay in darkness.

The guard led him to the steps leading up to the entrance of the hall. Judging from the noise coming from inside, a muted feast was in progress. Instead of the usual raucous singing and laughter, Cerdic heard the steady drone of conversation, with a harpist plucking out a slight melody in the background.

"You can go in, lord," said the guard, pushing the door open and standing to one side. Hand resting lightly on the hilt of his saex, Cerdic stepped through.

The hall was warm, thanks to a fire burning in a hearth at one end, and well-lit by torches in sconces on the walls. Aelle stood at the head of a large, rough-hewn oak table placed in the middle of the room. He was a giant, his father Horsa come again, huge and broad-shouldered and barrel-chested, with long, silvery fair hair parted in the middle and a beard flowing down to his waist.

"Welcome, cousin," he rumbled, his icy blue eyes fixing on Cerdic, "there is a place at the table for you."

Cerdic gave a bob of his head in reply, and briefly looked over Aelle's companions before taking his seat.

There were twelve of them. He knew most of their names and faces. Osla and Ebusa sat flanking Aelle, showing a distinct lack of fraternal joy at Cerdic's arrival. The rest were lesser kings, though even the meanest of them outranked him.

I will not be intimidated.

"A cold night," he remarked as he sat down, reaching for the nearest pot of ale, "I would much rather be snug in bed with a woman or two. As would we all, I suspect."

One or two of the other men smirked, but his brothers might as well have been carved in stone. They gazed disapprovingly at their little brother as he helped himself to meat and drink.

Blood or no blood, he thought, *they are not my friends. I have always been an embarrassment. They think me tainted, a half-British mongrel with the blood of slaves in my veins. And yet they must call me brother. How they must wish I would die, or crawl away somewhere, never to be heard of again!*

"You are lucky to be anywhere, Cerdic," said Cissa, one of the sub-kings of Cent, "the scops still sing of your little raid. You took two hundred men to Caer Guinnion, and only you came back again."

A ripple of laughter followed. Cerdic shrugged it off.

"I was caught off-guard by Artorius," he admitted, "you know how quickly his riders can move. It won't happen again."

"No, it won't," said Aelle, "for Artorius will soon be dead, as will the High King, and all the other British kings."

Cerdic sipped at his ale. It was spiced, and helped to draw some of the chill from his bones.

"Is that why you summoned us all here?" he asked brightly, "to discuss a slaughter? I doubt our father's feat can be repeated. It will be a long time before the rulers of Britannia accept another invitation to a Saxon conference. They know better than to trust us."

"You would know what the Britons think," said Ebusa, glowering at him, "since you are one."

"Sweet brother," replied Cerdic with a warm smile, "you know what I am. Our father's son."

Aelle placed his huge hand flat on the table between them. "There will be no bickering," he growled, "we finally have it in our power to destroy the Britons and claim much of their isle for our own. I will not let the chance slip away."

His hand was bigger than Cerdic's skull. It was callused, scarred and swollen, and Cerdic recalled his fondness for snapping necks. Unarmed, Aelle was said to be twice as dangerous as with a sword.

Even Ebusa knew better than to challenge their massive kinsman. He fell silent, and confined himself to shooting evil looks at Cerdic from under his heavy brows.

"Yes, a slaughter," Aelle resumed, "but on the field of battle. Enough of our folk live on this island now. More come every year. Together, we shall raise a host large enough to conquer this land from Londinium to the Wall. I have two thousand spears. The rest of you can well raise twice that number."

Six thousand warriors. Cerdic could well believe it. During his nine-year reign, the High King had made only token efforts to stop the flow of Saxons coming over the North Sea to settle on his lands. His alliance with Osla made halting the influx all but impossible.

"What's your plan?" he asked, "to break the treaty with Constantine and attack Londinium?"

"No," said Osla, speaking for the first time, "Londinium has strong walls, and is well-stocked for a siege. Even Constantine is not fool enough to neglect his greatest city. Instead we shall amass a fleet and sail west, around the coast to Dumnonia. Constantine's heartlands. Invade his territory, burn his crops, kill his warriors. Dumnonia is the bread basket for the entire kingdom. All the best land is there. Once we have it, the Britons will starve."

A seaborne invasion, thought Cerdic with a flicker of excitement, *up through the guts of Constantine's ancestral kingdom. A sword into his heart.*

"Ambrosius built his strongholds there," he said, nodding slowly, "and that great defensive dyke cutting off the road to the east. Take the forts, and Constantine will be left with nowhere to run."

It all sounded too easy. "What of Artorius?" he reminded them, "he must be crushed, if you wish to break native hearts."

"He and his Companions are devils," said Cissa, making the sign against evil, "no mortal men should be able to move that fast, even on the swiftest horses."

"He's just a man," replied Osla, "I fought alongside him in the north against Rhitta. A good soldier, yes. Probably the best the Britons have. But his men are few, and there is some feud between him and Constantine. It has never been patched up."

"A man doesn't have to like his king to serve him," said Aelle, "if we attack Dumnonia, will Artorius ride to its aid?"

"Maybe. I think it worth the risk. His skill lies in the sudden ambush, a swift strike, and then withdraw again before his enemy can recover. In the open, his cavalry would struggle to break our shields."

"What if Constantine sends Geraint against us?" asked the greybeard Raedwald, father to Ebusa's wife, "or comes in person at the head of his troops?"

A roar of laughter greeted this. The High King's garrison in Londinium numbered no more than a thousand men. Enough to defend the city, but no more. Constantine's own high reputation as a warrior was a distant memory. These days he rarely left the palace, and was said to have become a bloated, hopelessly debauched hulk, immersed in wine and barely capable of walking unaided from one end of a room to the other.

More discussion followed. Eventually, after some minor protests from the lesser men, Aelle's plan was agreed upon.

"Every spear is vital," he said, nodding at Cerdic, "so you will bring all the warriors you can find.."

Cerdic sat back in his chair. "No," he said after some consideration, "no, I don't think so."

His brothers goggled at him. "What's this?" said Aelle, frowning, "either my hearing is effected, or you have swallowed too much ale."

"Not at all," replied Cerdic, who had been careful to drink in moderation, "I merely wish to have no part in this war."

A shocked murmur ran around the table. His brothers sprang to their feet, while Aelle's broad face filled with angry blood. The giant seemed to swell until his huge form dominated the room.

"No part?" he shouted, making the rafters shake, "no part? What in hells do you mean?"

The force of his rage was almost physical. Steeling himself against it, Cerdic slowly pushed back his stool and stood up.

"You don't need me," he said, "my eighty spears will make little difference. I will, of course, pray to the gods to give you victory."

He gazed defiantly at his brothers. If they were going to kill him, now was the time. Fortunately Osla looked more baffled than angry, and Ebusa, though his eyes promised murder, would do nothing by himself.

"Our father always said you were clever," said Osla, while Aelle spluttered and rubbed his head like a confused bear, "where is your cleverness now? Surely you can see the profit for yourself, even if you care nothing for your kin. Once the land is ours, we can share it out as we like. Fight with us, and you will get your fair portion."

"Desert us," growled Ebusa, "and you get nothing. Nothing! Do you hear me, brother?"

He spat out the last word as though it was poison. "No lands," he cried, "no gold, no slaves, no cattle – you will be left to rot in your few acres of bog and marsh!"

"You misunderstand me," said Cerdic, "I am quite happy with my little kingdom. My mother, as you never tire of reminding me, was a slave. With such tainted blood, I should be grateful to hold any lands at all."

"I also have no desire to rob you," he went on in his most reasonable tone, spreading his hands, "how could I demand a share of the lands you win? A man who leads five hundred spears in battle will surely resent having to give up good land to one who leads eighty. For your sake, my kinsfold, I will take no part in this war."

His false humility was persuasive. Cerdic had inherited his father's skill at play-acting. Realising what he was saying – or rather, totally misinterpreting it – Aelle and Ebusa subsided a little.

"A king with no ambition is a strange creature," said Osla. Cerdic feared him most, knowing he was slightly shrewder than the others.

"I have ambition, brother," Cerdic replied blandly, "but it is not personal. My ambition is to see our people ruling this island, in peace and prosperity, and a man of our race as High King."

"And the Britons? You would be happy to see them defeated and enslaved? Your mother's people?"

Cerdic poured all his effort into sounding indifferent. "Some men are made to rule, others to be ruled. It is the way of things."

This was enough to convince them of his good faith. It helped, he knew, that they wanted to be convinced. Their natural greed overrode any doubts. If a man was fool enough to throw away his chance of winning riches and glory, and gaining more lands for his sons to inherit – well, that was his affair.

"Go then, cousin," said Aelle, with something like awe in his voice, "back to your little realm. Perhaps, in time, the scops will sing of Cerdic the Selfless."

Cerdic bowed gracefully, and walked out of the hall. Silence followed him out.

Cerdic the Selfless, he thought with a smile, *no, cousin. They will sing of Cerdic the Wise.*

22.

Caerleon

The five young men knelt in terror before Artorius, heads bowed, quivering as they waited for him to pass sentence. He sat alone at high table, hands folded before him, glaring down at the offenders.

One, the eldest, screwed up the courage to meet his eyes. "Mercy, lord," he begged, "spare us, and let us join the search for your son."

Artorius' face might have been carved in marble. Then he seemed to sag, all the cold anger seeping out of him.

"You are forgiven," he said wearily, "by rights I should dismiss you from my service, but I need every man to look for Medraut. Go."

The youth's eyes widened in surprise. He and his companions rose and hurried gratefully out of the hall.

"That was lenient," said Cei, "I expected you to make an example of them. A couple of hangings, at least."

Artorius rubbed his eyes. His head ached. He hadn't slept properly for weeks, ever since word reached him in Gwynedd, where he had spent the past few months hunting Scotti pirates, of Medraut's disappearance.

Leaving his friend Cadwallon Lawhir to the bloody sport of pirate-hunting, he sped south to Caerleon. He and his followers – warriors, freemen, slaves, all who were fit and able– had spent every day and night since combing the town and the surrounding countryside. Consumed by fear for his son, Artorius had led the search with relentless fury, only resting when he reached the verge of collapse.

He had deliberately put off the punishment of the six young warriors who allowed Medraut to slip away. Enough guilt lay on his conscience.

"I am not hypocrite enough, Cei," he said, kneading his brow, "to punish others for my own mistakes. It is my fault Medraut fled."

"Or was taken," said Bedwyr, "perhaps by some enemy. We don't lack for them."

"He ran," Artorius insisted, "if he was taken, why have we received no demands for his ransom?"

The unspoken answer hung in the air, too terrible to be voiced. Artorius refused to even contemplate it. One of the first things he did after arriving at Caerleon was speak with Llacheu, who told him Medraut ran away of his own accord.

"He wanted to see the world, father," Llacheu had said, white-faced with terror of his sire, "the world described to us by Elias."

Something broke inside Artorius. He knelt and scooped both Llacheu and Cydfan up in his arms, holding them close for the first time since they were born.

"My boys," he said, closing his eyes and resting his head against theirs, "my poor boys."

They have nothing of me in them, he thought sadly as they clung to his neck, *because I have given them nothing of myself.*

He could scarcely believe Cydfan was even his. Soft, plump, mild-mannered Cydfan, a little priest in the making. Llacheu was made of harder stuff, but entirely his mother's creation: his raven-black hair and pale good looks were all too painful reminders of Ganhumara, and what Artorius had done to her.

Neither was allowed to leave the fort until Medraut was found, or even venture far beyond the hall. Six spearmen – trusted veterans this time, not callow boys – guarded them as they slept. Artorius had already lost half his family. He was determined to cling on to what was left.

"What now, then?" asked Cei, back in the present, "most of your people are still out in the woods, even the women and children. They have to rest sometime."

Through his fug of exhaustion and worry, Artorius tried to think . The countryside for miles around had been searched, to no avail.

He had sent a message to Caradog Freichfras, the King of Gwent, asking for men to help with the search. It was difficult to believe Medraut could have gone beyond the borders of the kingdom. How could a young boy, travelling on foot, with no food or water, get so far by himself?

Unless he is dead in a ditch somewhere. The woods are full of dangers. Maybe he was gored by a wild boar, or killed by wolves, or fell in with outlaws, or...

He thrust these evil thoughts aside. "The search has to be widened," he said forcefully, "I will send messages to Maridunum, and Eidol Cadarn at Glevum. Maybe to Powys and Viroconium and Gwynedd as well. We shall scour this island from end to end, if necessary"

Too tired to speak further, he dismissed his captains, and they quietly filed out of the hall.

Artorius was grateful for the privacy. He had scarcely enjoyed a moment to himself since returning to Caerleon.

Think, he raged at himself, *where can he have gone? Who might have snatched him?*

Ganhumara's face rose before him. Her face as he had last seen it, pale and frightened and and pleading for mercy.

"Be gone," he whispered. He refused to be haunted by Ganhumara, if indeed she was dead.

He still considered his punishment to be just. After killing Melwas he had taken her west, out of the benighted Summer Country, to a fishing village on the coast of Dumnonia. There he hired a boat with no oars and a single sail, and put Ganhumara aboard. Alone, with just enough food and water to last her three days. Shutting his ears to her pleas, Artorius commanded a fishing vessel to tow the boat far out to sea, and then cut it adrift.

"God and the elements shall judge you," he cried, "drown or live, sink or swim, I care not."

He watched as the boats dwindled until they were mere specks on the wind-tossed seas. The fishermen returned, but Ganhumara's fragile craft vanished from view.

Could she have come back? Snatched Medraut as revenge?

No. It was impossible. Was it? Artorius cudgelled his wits, struggling for answers. There were none.

He trudged to bed. The same bed he had shared with Ganhumara, as well as his other concubines. He had got rid of the others, paying them off or offering them as wives to his followers. Lisanor, his old favourite, had married his servant Cacamwri. They were wed in the church in Caerleon, and she was already heavy with his child.

Artorius had lost his taste for women. The Melwas-Ganhumara affair had killed that part of him. All he wanted was his son back.

Before sleep enfolded him, he pictured Medraut, the dark little boy with the ruined face. A quiet and self-absorbed child, from all accounts, fond of his own company.

I was the same, at his age. Medraut is the son I understood most. And I lost him.

Artorius cursed Elias for filling the boy's head with idiotic stories, and himself for not being at Caerleon often enough. Things would be different, he vowed, when Medraut was found.

His fading hopes turned to despair in the following weeks. His allies sent the men he requested to help with the search, and promised to look for Medraut in their own lands, but all was for nothing. The boy was gone, apparently vanished into thin air.

Artorius would not give up. Weeks turned into months, until the futile search had taken up most of the summer.

At last, in the dying days of August, a group of riders came to Caerleon.

"You have news of Medraut?" Artorius asked with pathetic eagerness when Cei admitted them to the hall.

They looked pityingly at the red-eyed, hollow-cheeked, emaciated figure before them. Artorius had lost an alarming amount of weight over the summer. He slept little, and what sleep he got was plagued by nightmarish images, most of them involving Medraut's death.

"No, lord," said one of the newcomers, "though we know of your loss, and are sorry for it. We come from the north, from the court of King Masgwid."

Masgwid Gloff, King of Elmet. Artorius had heard nothing from him since they campaigned together against Rhitta.

"Honour to him," he said, remembering his duty as a host, "be seated, and I will have a slave fetch wine. It is a long ride from your country. Has Masgwid sent you to help find my son?"

"I fear not," the other man replied, "my king sympathises with your plight, but needs every man to defend his borders. The Wall is overrun."

"Again?" exclaimed Cei, "it may as well be made of parchment. I suppose Masgwid wants us to ride north to rescue him. Can't these kings fight their own battles?"

"Peace," Artorius said, frowning at him, "these are our guests, and it shames you to speak ill of their lord. If he seeks our aid, then we must give it."

"By the hand of my friend," spat Cei, "if you were to take my advice, you would not go north again on any account."

"You are wrong to say so, Cei. Remember, we are noble men only so long as others seek us out."

Artorius turned back to the envoys. "Please, deliver your message," he said courteously as the wine was brought.

"It is a grim one," replied their leader, shooting an evil look at Cei, "an army of northerners have invaded in force, just as they did four years ago."

He gulped down his wine. "This time they have come to destroy, not conquer. They are committing horrible acts. Sins against man and God and nature. Villages burned, whole populations put to the sword rather than enslaved. None are spared. Our scouts talk of children tossed onto spears, even as the mothers are raped and butchered before their eyes."

His eyes filled with tears. "That is just a taste of the evil sweeping the north," he said, "my lord is mustering all the fighting men in

Elmet. His father, the King of Rheged, marches to join him. King Peredur has also pledged his support. There is no word of the kingdoms beyond the Wall. We think they have either thrown in their lot with the enemy, or perished."

Artorius struggled to absorb this new and horrifying reality. "Is it Rhitta, come again?" he asked, "if so, he has run mad. His troops committed none of these atrocities in the last war."

"We don't know. There was a rumour last winter that Rhitta was dead, murdered in his own hall. It was never confirmed. The man leading this new invasion also calls himself King of the Northlands. What manner of king massacres the people he means to rule? Crucifies them, flays them, burns them alive as he laughs and warms his hands over the fires?"

Artorius rubbed his face. "No king at all," he said, "but a mad dog. One we have a duty to put down."

"Three kings," yelled Cei, "are they not enough to deal with this marauding rabble?"

"They are much more than a rabble," said the messenger, "they lured the garrison at Vercovicium into a trap and slaughtered every man. The enemy we face may be savages, but they know how to fight. My lord fears this may be a long war."

He looked keenly at Artorius. "He begs your aid, general. You have never been defeated in battle. There are no soldiers in Britannia like the Companions. With you at our side, even this unholy terror can be overcome."

Never been defeated, Artorius thought sourly, *except in Gaul. How soon men forget.*

He found himself torn between his duty to the people he had sworn to protect, and his duty to Medraut. The dilemma was almost too much to bear. For a moment Artorius swayed on his feet, fearing his mind would split in two.

"Go north," said Bedwyr, touching his arm, "and leave me here with fifty Companions. I will carry on the search."

Artorius looked at him with gratitude. Bedwyr was his rock. So was Cei, albeit one he tended to trip over.

The prospect of war caused his energy to return in a flood. Within two days the Companions were ready to move north. Some of the men of Gwent and Gwynedd went with him, risking the anger of their lords for the honour of riding with Artorius.

He left Caerleon at the head of over seven hundred men, leaving the faithful Bedwyr in charge of his household, and the search for his son. The Companions rode out on a cold,

still day in early autumn, and thundered up
the Roman roads, past the depopulated ruins
of Ratae and Lindum, on their way to
Eburucum.

Masgwid's envoy claimed that the allied
kings were gathering their host at
Eburucum, while the wild northerners
ravaged the lands between the city and the
Walls. Artorius hoped to reach the allies
before they marched.

His Companions moved as swiftly as ever.
They covered the two hundred miles
between Caerleon and Eburucum inside five
days. More horsemen joined them on the
way, led by loyal magistrates and sub-kings
who had heard of the atrocities in the north.

They were no more than an hour's ride
from Eburucum when the first casualties
appeared. Artorius called a halt when he
spotted them limping down the highway.

"Christ have mercy," breathed Cei, whom
almost nothing could sicken.

From a distance, the little group of men
heading towards them were a pitiful sight.
Close to, they were enough to turn the
hardest veteran's stomach.

They had been soldiers, once. A few used
their spears as crutches, or still wore mail.
All were horribly mutilated. The wounds
were almost too frightful to look upon.
Castrated men, blood still dripping from

their groins, led comrades who had been blinded, their eyes gouged out with hot knives. Others carried severed hands on strings around their necks.

Artorius fought down the bile in his throat and spurred forward. "You men," he cried, "are you of Elmet, or Rheged? Where are your lords? Do they still live?"

It was hopeless. The horrors inflicted on the crippled men had broken them. None were capable of answering, or seemed to even hear him.

"What can do we do for them?" asked Gwalchmei, his broad, freckled face drained of colour. He had to raise his voice to be heard above the mindless wailing of the human wrecks as they limped past.

"Nothing," said Artorius, "this was done deliberately to slow our advance and wear away our morale. Most of these poor wretches are beyond our help."

He gave the order to move on, forcing the wounded off the road. Artorius closed his ears to their piteous cries. *Whoever did this,* he vowed, *will soon pay in kind for their crimes.*

The Britons encountered more survivors as they neared Eburucum, some staggering along in little groups, others lying by the roadside, calling feebly on Christ and their mothers as they bled to death. There was no sign of the enemy, save ominous trails of smoke rising into the sky from the direction of the city.

Artorius expected the worst. The horribly wounded men could only be the survivors of the British army mustered at Eburucum. A battle had been fought, and the allies smashed by the forces of the King of the Northlands.

"He cannot be Rhitta," he said to Cei and Gwalchmei, who rode at his side, "Rhitta was a hard man, but never indulged in such cruelties."

"I don't care who he is," snarled Cei, "he will soon be dead. By my hand, if God is good."

"What of the kings?" said Gwalchmei, "if they were beaten in open battle, Masgwid and his father may have retreated to their own lands. Perudur would take refuge in Eburucum."

He soon had his answer. The stench from Eburucum hit them first, a foul odour of death and burning. Artorius led his men on in grim silence, knowing what awaited them.

The greatest city in the north, one-time Roman capital of Britannia Secunda, had been sacked. Its destruction was recent, and occasional flames still leaped from the gory, reeking shambles. Plumes of black smoke drifted into the sky from the barracks and the grand palace in the heart of the city where Coel Hen had once held court.

The top of the outer palisade was decorated with the heads of British soldiers and civilians. Their flayed bodies were nailed to the wall itself like so many skinned rabbits, while the skins lay in ghastly heaps below. Crows picked at the latter, dispersing in a flurry of midnight wings as they sensed the approach of humans.

Clapping a hand over his face against the obscene smell, Artorius reined in before the gatehouse. The gate hung awry, smashed in by a ram, and the arrow-riddled bodies of the men who tried to defend it were piled under the entrance.

He looked up at the heads of Masgwid Gloff, Masgwid's father Cadell, and Peredur, impaled on spears above the gate. The three kings had suffered the same fate as most of the populace. Their naked bodies, flayed like the others, were nailed upside down to the outer rampart.

"It isn't Rhitta," said Cei, breaking the deathly silence, "their beards are intact."

Only Cei would notice such a detail in the midst of such horror. However, he was right: all three men still wore their beards.

Followed by ten of his Companions, Artorius ventured a little way into the city. What he saw soon drove him out again. He had been a soldier since he was young, and often seen men at their worst. War never failed to unleash the dark side of their nature.

He had never encountered anything like this. The monster who destroyed Eburucum had done so with no thought of conquest or plunder in mind. He came to kill, to satisfy his own depraved appetites, ripping apart living bodies with no more qualms than a child picking the legs off a spider.

"When we come back," he said to Cei, "we will burn Eburucum."

"Much of it is burned already," the other man pointed out. Artorius shook his head.

"No. I mean raze it to the ground. Leave nothing but stone. We must wipe out the memory of what happened here."

"First," he added, staring at the fires burning among the hills north of the city, "we will hunt down the one who has done this."

The hunt was brief. Artorius led the Companions along the road leading from Eburucum to the Wall. The range of hills were full of smoke and fire, hanging like a gauze over the fertile, low-lying lands immediately north of Eburucum.

The shadow in the north, he thought, *Morgana warned me of it, all those years ago. I thought Rhitta was the shadow, but this is the true darkness.*

"On!" he shouted, drawing Caledfwlch. Seconds later the air was filled with the squall of bugles and the thunder of hoofs.

The Companions advanced.

23.

From her vantage point on a ridge overlooking the flat lands to the south, dominated by the fire-ravaged ruins of Eburucum, Aethelflaed watched the long lines of horsemen gallop towards her.

"Artorius," she whispered.

At their head was the famous dragon banner. The wind streamed through its gaping jaws and the long tube attached to its head, making the dragon seem alive.

Under it rode Artorius. At this distance he was a tiny figure, but Aethelflaed caught the light glinting from his golden helm. He was pushing his black mare at a furious pace, outstripping the riders behind him.

She chewed her lip. Was he taking the bait? His reputation suggested a man who never lost his head in battle. Perhaps Gwrgi's murderous strategy had worked. The destruction of Eburucum, and the cruelties inflicted on British warriors taken captive in the recent battle, may have driven Artorius into an unthinking rage.

The Companions and their allies were tearing along the north road. Hundreds of men, perhaps as many as a thousand.

Her view was slightly obscured by smoke drifting from the trees below her. At her suggestion, Gwrgi had ordered the edge of the forest to be set alight. The fires were meant to lure Artorius into the trap she had devised.

"Come," she said, tapping her companion on the shoulder. He was a scout, a lean, black-bearded man of the Novantae, one of the northern tribes who had joined Gwrgi's host.

They ran back to their horses, tough, shaggy little hill ponies, and urged them down the slope on the northern side of the ridge.

Here the land undulated, rising and falling in a series of gentle ridges, much of it bleak moor and hillside. There was plenty of open ground among the patches of forest. Aethelflaed and her companion rode down into a little valley and followed it to the bare flanks of another incline. Another of Gwrgi's fire smouldered at the summit, this time a beacon made from piles of timber cut from the forests.

As she rode, she calculated. Artorius would come this way. It was the easiest route, and the fires marked out his path.

He will surely smell the trap, and slow his advance. Artorius is not the kind of man to ride headlong into a pit.

Aethelflaed had carefully studied his way of fighting. She knew his tactics well, from listening to the accounts brought back to Germania by her kinsmen. The tales of his battles against Rhitta were the same. Artorius relied on speed of horse and the ability to manoeuvre quickly, outpacing and outwitting his enemies before they had time to react. Slow-moving infantry were his particular targets.

Hengist's daughter had worked him out. Long years of playing gwyddbywll – Gwgi had insisted on the nightly ritual, even at Din Eidyn – had sharpened her strategic instincts. She could now beat Gwrgi two games out of three, and lost much of her fear of him. No matter what atrocities he inflicted on others, he would never hurt her. She was too valuable.

She reached the summit of the hill overlooking Gwrgi's host. Aethelflaed had chosen the position.

"You have set your pieces well, yellow-hair," Gwrgi had remarked when they came here, "Artorius himself could do no better."

His words filled her with an odd sort of pride, even though she loathed him with undimmed intensity.

Below her the hill led down to a stream, winding east-west across the moor into the dark forests bordering it in either direction.

The stream was shallow enough for men to cross on foot, though treacherous and almost waist-deep in places.

Gwrgi's army was drawn up on some stony ground north of the stream. It was not as large as the massive host Rhitta had led south, four years previously. Y Hen Ogledd had barely recovered from the slaughter of its menfolk at Bassas and Celidon, and Gwrgi had been obliged to stiffen his ranks with Pictish and Scotti auxiliaries. The last dregs of Hengist's gold had proved enough to buy their services, as well as the promise of riches to be plundered in the southlands.

Not as large, perhaps, thought Aethelflaed, *but better-led, and governed by no rules of war.*

Her pride battled with shame at fighting alongside such beasts in human shape as Gwrgi had assembled. They were cast in his own image, the very worst the north could offer, brigands and outlaws and scum of all kinds. Beside them were a few men of honour, petty kings who had allowed themselves to be persuaded of the rightness of Gwrgi's cause.

In her mind she replayed one of the fiery speeches Gwrgi had made when he toured the kingdoms of Gododdin and Alt Clut, summoning men to his banner. The little man was a surprisingly brilliant orator, capable of holding the roughest of warriors in thrall with his passionate delivery.

"There was a time," he howled before an audience of Novantae and Damnonii warriors, "when Britannia stood alone, self-governing and proudly independent, a torch lit by the gods to brighten the world of man. Then the Romans came, a stream of robbers sallying forth from the degenerate lands far to the south, across the Narrow Sea, burning, murdering and looting their way across the West until they reached the shores of our fair island. A true scourge, sent by the gods to punish us for forgetting them, and allowing their temples to fall into ruin. After centuries of slavery, our people threw off the Roman yoke and drove our oppressors back to the Wall, that mighty bastion they threw up to hide behind, a refuge, not a defence, for their arrogant and cowardly race."

He paused to draw breath. "The people who dwell now in the heartlands of this island," he went on, his voice dropping with venomous contempt, "call themselves Britons, yet they still observe Roman laws and Roman customs. They live in the shattered ruins of Roman towns, too afraid to embrace the lands of their forefathers. They hire foreign mercenaries, pirates from distant Germania, to do their fighting for them. Unlike us, they allowed themselves to grow soft under Roman dominion – fat, coddled and weak, ripe to be conquered and enslaved by stronger men. Nothing is rightfully theirs. The gods despise those who cannot fight for themselves!"

Though Gwrgi's notion of history was blurred, and his continued harping on the old pagan gods took no account of the many Christians living north of the Wall, his speeches never failed to whip up storms of approval. Over the summer his host gradually swelled until he had over three thousand men. While their bloodlust was still fresh, Gwrgi took them south, overrunning the Wall at night and flooding over the hills beyond.

They met the army of the three kings on the high moors, near the source of the river called Tribruit. Casualties on both sides were severe, but after two days of rain-soaked battle the allies fled, closely pursued all the way to the gates of Eburucum. So close, they failed to shut the gates in time.

Aethelflaed had blotted out the memory of what followed. While his troops pillaged the city and massacred the populace, Gwrgi personally executed King Peredur. Using a heated knife, he removed his shrieking victim's skin, inch by bloody inch, while his followers laughed and pressed flaming torches against Peredur's raw flesh. The other kings, Masgwid Gloff and his father Cadell, wisely chose to die fighting rather than surrender.

"Artorius," Gwrgi declared when he was done, holding up his filthy knife and licking it clean, "will soon go the same way."

Afterwards he drank a horn full to the brim with Peredur's hot blood, claiming it gave him strength. Aethelflaed had concealed her revulsion under a mask of indifference. Inside her guts were churning. To see honourable men, even her enemies, butchered in such a fashion disgusted her beyond measure.

When this battle is won, she vowed,, *and Artorius has paid for slaying my kin, Gwrgi shall follow him to the long house.*

It would be easy enough. She had played the broken, submissive slave so long Gwrgi thought she was harmless. Soon he would learn his mistake. Aethelflaed would slit his throat and leave him to bleed, making good her escape across the moors while his mead-sodden followers were still celebrating their victory.

She gave her reins a twitch, urging her pony down the slope. The open ground before her led down to the stream, with more woodland on either side. The trees formed a corridor, down which she hoped the Companions would pour to attack their enemy drawn up on the northern bank.

Screams and war-chants filled the air as she and her companion guided their ponies through the icy water. The Picts and Scotti and the wildest of the northern tribesmen were working themselves up into a battle-frenzy. Already awash with strong mead, some of them danced on the water's edge, tearing off their plaids and daubing their pale, tattooed bodies with river mud. When the time for battle came, they would hurl themselves shrieking at the enemy with no thought for their own safety, stark naked and baying for blood.

Aethelflaed gave them a wide berth, making her way towards Gwrgi's battle-standard to the rear of the northern host. This was made of a single sheet of human skin, ripped from the corpse of her late husband Rhitta, cured and stretched over a wooden cross-piece. Even in death, Gwrgi allowed his victims no dignity.

Gwrgi himself stood under the dreadful totem, dressed for war in Rhitta's coat of ring-mail, Rhitta's sword and Rhitta's helmet. Both men were of a size, so the gear fitted him perfectly. He wore his favourite red cloak over his mail, fastened at the shoulder with the stag's head brooch. As ever, the little god containing his soul hung from his neck, though by a light silver chain these days in place of a leather strap.

"Welcome, yellow-hair," he said cheerfully, "is Artorius coming, then?"

He was in high spirits, Aethelflaed noticed, and had already drunk more mead than was wise. A slave lurked at his elbow with a jug, replenishing his master's drinking horn with a sweet yellow flow whenever it threatened to run low.

"He is, lord king," she replied, "I saw him riding north from Eburucum at the head of his Companions. They will have reached the foothills by now."

Gwrgi's eyes, visible through the slits in his helm, gazed shrewdly at her. "How many men has he got?" he asked before taking another long swallow of mead.

"A thousand or so," she replied, "all cavalry."

His eyes shone. Even after his recent losses, Gwrgi had over twice that number.

As Gwrgi said, Aethelflaed had indeed set out her pieces well. The front of the northern host was protected by the stream, and their flanks by the forest. She had placed archers and Picts armed with crossbows in the woods beyond the stream. When Artorius' men advanced down the corridor towards the stream, they would be exposed to a rain of missiles from both sides.

Aethelflaed placed great faith in the Pictish crossbows. They were clumsy one-shot weapons, awkward to reload, but more powerful than the hunting bow. Powerful enough to punch through light mail and bring down a horse.

"If we can stop the Companions crossing the river," she said, "they will have to fight on three sides at once. He has no archers, and our bowmen have been told to aim for the horses. His strength lies in his cavalry. Kill the animals, deny the Companions room to manoeuvre, and Artorius will be forced to retreat."

"I don't want him to retreat," Gwrgi snarled, "I want him to come at us like a wild boar. Beating him isn't enough. He must not escape."

Aethelflaed smiled confidently. "Artorius has tasted nothing but victory for years. Maybe his pride won't allow him to run away. If so, we shall have him."

Then it is your turn, she added silently. Her fingers stroked the hilt of her saex, eager to draw the serrated blade across his throat.

"Look there," he said, pointing to the south, "there, on the ridge. He is coming."

Aethelflaed wheeled her pony. Her pulse skipped a little faster as she beheld dust rising over the slope on the far side of the stream, and the snarling head of the dragon banner.

24.

Cei's skull was bursting. It had never been right since the wound he suffered in Gaul. The bone had healed over the cut, but the pain inside never truly went away. On good days it was a dull ache, persistent but bearable. On bad days – growing increasingly frequent of late – it felt as though his head was splitting in two.

It effected his moods. Never the most even-tempered of men, he swung unpredictably between inconsolable melancholy and fuming rage.

The destruction of Eburucum, and the mindless slaughter of its people, had brought on the worst bout of pain he could remember. When the Companions rode north, in search of the King of the Northlands and his army, he could barely keep his seat in the saddle.

Now the enemy lay before them. An army, if it could be called such, of pirates and northern tribesmen, drawn up in ragged lines beside a stream. The air was full of their frenzied chanting, the rumble of drums and the blowing of horns. Cei struggled to endure the noise. It made him feel as though wild horses were galloping through his head.

Artorius had followed the trail of fires, careful to slow his advance as the Companions entered the hills, sending out troops of light horse to scout the land ahead. His patience and caution threatened to make Cei's seething temper boil over.

"For God's sake, let us have at them!" he shouted, ramming his sword in and out of its scabbard in frustration, "there they are, and here we are, and nothing happens. Give the order to advance, Artorius – that rabble down there won't stand up to a single charge."

Artorius didn't seem to hear. He turned his Saxon helmet over and over in his hands, eyes narrowed as he stared down at the northern host.

"Their lines are too deep," he said, "one charge won't do it. We need to lure them out. Break them up. "

While Cei sat and suffered, Artorius carefully arranged his cavalry into five companies. There was no room to deploy them in line abreast on the slope before the stream, so he kept three in reserve and sent two forward.

The first company, led by Gwalchmei, was made up of light horse. Nothing more deadly than catcalls and abuse greeted them as they trotted down the slope.

"They have no bowmen," observed Artorius. Cei, now virtually bend double and seeing with difficulty through a blur of pain, cared little. All he wanted was to charge in among the enemy and lay about him, hoping it would help to appease the devils in his head.

Gwalchmei's troop spurred into a canter. They splashed into the stream, riding full-tilt at the enemy line. The King of the Northlands had sensibly placed his worst troops at the front: naked, howling fanatics and half-naked Pictish infantry armed with crude stone axes and bone-tipped spears.

The British cavalry charged close enough to hurl their javelins among the packed enemy ranks, and then turned smartly and galloped back the way they had come.

Their javelins took a lethal toll. Scores of men fell, pierced by the missiles, and the stony ground beyond the stream was quickly strewn with dead and dying. A handful of warriors broke ranks and splashed across the stream, lured into giving chase. The Companions rallied and butchered these men as soon as they reached the southern bank.

"Not enough," said Artorius, "nowhere near enough. The northerners hold their line well. They have a measure of discipline."

He turned his head, about to give further orders, when screams erupted from the cavalry drawn up immediately below.

Cei winced at this fresh noise. His own mount shied at it, and he had to fight to bring her back under control.

When she had calmed a little, he looked down, and was struck dumb by the sight of horses and riders falling like autumn leaves. Arrows and evil-looking stubby darts fell among them, pouring from the woods on either flank.

He twisted his head to the left and saw men among the trees, archers and Picts armed with crossbows.

Cei swore. For once Artorius had not thought to guard his flanks, and it seemed the King of the Northlands was something of a general as well as a bloody-handed savage.

Artorius was already roaring at the men of his own company to dismount.

"Flush those bastards out!" he cried, stabbing Caledfwlch at the enemy in the woods on either flank. Led by their officers, his men split into two groups and stormed towards the enemy. Savage fighting broke out among the trees.

Horns sounded, echoed by shrill, exultant cries from thousands of northern throats. Cei looked down in horror, his aching head briefly forgotten, as the mass of the enemy host burst into life and charged across the stream.

Gwalchmei's company, distracted by the archers in the woods, were taken by surprise. His bugler sounded the retreat, and they turned and galloped back up the slope, pursued by a horde of screaming warriors.

They blundered straight into the company drawn up behind them. The ordered British ranks dissolved into a tangled chaos of men and horses, striving desperately to get out of each other's way.

Then the northerners struck, spearing and dragging men from their saddles, beating them to death on the ground. The screaming, rearing horses were pitilessly butchered, their hamstrings cut by men crawling under their bellies with great knives.

The Companions fought bravely, but as leaderless individuals, the shouts of their officers drowned by the triumphant baying of the northerners as they whetted their spears in British blood. For a moment the iron discipline of Artorius' men threatened to crumble.

Time seemed to slow for Cei as he watched the slaughter. His hearing ebbed, replaced by the pounding of angry blood. His heart beat too quickly. Artorius was shouting something nearby, but his voice was indistinct, a meaningless buzzing in Cei's ears.

Rage, a black, all-consuming rage like he had never known, flooded him. A red curtain fell over his eyes. He started to shake uncontrollably. Blood started from his nose. Spittle flecked at the corners of his mouth.

Cei's mouth opened in a silent scream. He grasped a handful of his horse's mane and cruelly dug in his spurs, forcing her into a breakneck plunge down the slope. Then he was in among the heaving throng of bodies, sword whirling, veins pounding in the side of his neck.

He lashed out at the men on foot, carving skulls and hacking off limbs with joyful abandon, laughing as they died, glorying in the stench of spilled blood and entrails. The exultant cries of the northerners turned to howls of fear as they retreated before this unstoppable swordsman, whose battle-fury and lust for killing outmatched even theirs.

As Cei slew, he sang:

"An army is but vanity
Compared with me in battle.
My sword in battle is
Not to be averted
Prince of the plunder,
The tall man in my wrath;
Heavy am I in my vengeance;

Terrible in my fighting,
When into battle I come
I slay as would a hundred.
Unless God should accomplish it,
My death will be unachieved."

Inspired by his example, the Companions rallied. The shattered ranks of horsemen re-formed and turned on the northerners, who in turn refused to yield another step. Fighting became general, spilling into the woods and the stream, men tearing at each other with spear, sword and dagger.

Cei stalked through the carnage with blood in his eyes and murder in his heart, looking for the King of the Northlands. His horse was dead, brought down by a spear in her guts. He chopped down one warrior after another, careless of his own wounds, his sword shearing bloody holes in the enemy ranks. The red mist spun before him, even as the thunder in his head rose to a howling storm.

"Nine-and-thirty I have slain," he growled, counting the men he killed, "I do not think it too many."

The tides of battle parted for an instant, and he spotted his quarry. The King of the Northlands was unmistakable. He stood among his personal guards on the edge of the stream, a royal figure in gleaming silver ring-mail, his face concealed under a helmet similar to the one Artorius wore, though not quite so ornate.

Cei put down his head and charged, roaring like a bull, smashing aside anyone who stood in his path.

The king's guards saw him coming. They sprang to defend their master, presenting a wall of spears and shields to the blood-slathered madman bearing down on them.

In his red rage, Cei would have happily leaped on their spears. He was saved by Gwalchmei, who led a troop of horse into the flank of the shieldwall. The guards were scattered and ridden down, leaving their master exposed to the wrath of Cei.

The King of the Northlands seemed unafraid. He drew his sword, a gold-hilted thing of beauty, and stood ready to meet his attacker.

Cei was fearsomely strong, and had learned to add speed and guile to his bearish strength in combat. Fuelled by the battle-rage coursing through his veins, he smashed aside the king's sword and cut at his head.

The king was a clumsy swordsman. He flinched under the barrage of savage blows, tripped on his cloak, and almost fell backwards into the stream.

"Coward! Butcher! Murderer!" Cei bellowed, striking again and again at his foe, swinging his sword double-handed.

Lurid images of what he had seen at Eburucum surfaced in his memory. This man was responsible for that slaughterhouse, the wanton rape and massacre of so many thousands of innocents. He had ordered it, presided over it, no doubt revelled in it. Laughed, as his warriors hacked up defenceless men like so many pieces of meat and raped the women before slicing their throats and adding their violated, bloody carcases to the steaming piles of dead.

Cei had had friends at Eburucum, as well as some distant kin. Sobbing, he drove his already beaten opponent to his knees, breaking his shield to splinters, knocking the sword from his grasp.

The king tried to reach for his blade as it lay in the mud. Cei stamped on his hand, relishing the muffled scream of pain inside the gilded helmet.

Bugles sounded all around him, signalling the charge. The noise of galloping hoofs rose above the din of battle. Dimly aware that Artorius must have launched a counter-attack, Cei thrust the edge of his bloody sword under the king's helmet and sawed through the chin-strap. When the strap parted, he jerked his sword upwards. The helmet came off, dropping with a splash into the water.

A frightened, beardless, almost childlike face gazed up at him. Cei's fury ebbed. He had expected some hard-faced warlord. Not this bland, pale, almost angelic visage.

"Mercy," pleaded the King of the Northlands, his mild blue eyes yearning up at Cei, "I am in your hands."

Cei made a supreme effort to rein himself in. He knew Artorius would want to interrogate this man. They knew nothing about him: his origins, his motives, even his name.

The beast inside Cei demanded more blood. In spite of all the men he had killed, it was not yet sated.

He raised his sword in both hands. Groaning at the conflict in his head, he struck down with the hilt.

25.

Artorius knew he had never been so close to defeat. Shame and anger washed through him as he stood on the high ridge overlooking the battlefield, watching his men search for wounded comrades.

The evening sun cast a spectral crimson glow over the place of slaughter. Groans and pleas for aid drifted over the field, a chorus of the damned. Carrion birds fluttered among the bodies scattered over the field. Soon, when night had fallen, the wolves would emerge for their share of the feast.

Gwalchmei limped up the slope. He had suffered a spear-wound to his thigh, and blood oozed sluggishly from the bandage.

"Well?" said Artorius, fearing the worst. Gwalchmei had been entrusted with counting the British dead.

"Over a hundred so far, lord," he replied, "maybe twice that number of wounded."

Artorius winced. Three hundred casualties, including scores of his precious horses, bred from the original stock imported (at great expense) by Ambroisius from Gaul and Hispania. They would take years to replace. He couldn't afford such losses.

The fault lies with me, he told himself, *I misjudged the King of the Northlands. Thought him a mere savage. I walked like a blind man, straight into his trap.*

If not for Cei, the damage could have been far worse. Cei's actions, plunging alone into the thick of the fight with selfless courage, had inspired the Britons to rally at a crucial moment. His defeat of the enemy leader in single combat broke the morale of the northerners, allowing Artorius to lead a counter-attack at the head of his reserves.

He had been found lying next to the defeated king. Both were unconscious, Cei from loss of blood. Anxious not to lose the difficult, quarrelsome man who had nevertheless saved his army, Artorius had him taken up and carried away for treatment. His wounds were said to be ugly, but not fatal. With Christ's favour, he would live.

"They should have revived the prisoner by now," said Artorius, turning to Llwch, "bring him to me."

The young man, who had survived the battle unhurt, hurried away. Artorius was left alone. A line of stretcher-bearers trudged past. The men they carried were all horribly maimed.

Most of them will be dead by morning.

One of the wounded men saw him, and feebly lifted a hand in greeting. Both his legs were missing below the knee. Artorius raised his own hand in salute.

His self-disgust threatened to choke him. Casualties were inevitable in battle, but there was no excuse for losing men through incompetence or arrogance. Artorius had always despised commanders who played with the lives of their soldiers, treating them as disposable.

Unable to cope with the guilt, he turned it on his enemy. The King of the Northlands was responsible for all this death and misery. How many lives had he taken? They all cried out for vengeance. Justice. It was Artorius' duty to provide both.

Llwch and a troop of spearmen brought the culprit before him. The so-called king had been stripped of his armour, and his hands tied behind his back. There was a lump on his brow, just above the left eye, where Cei had hit him.

Artorius was surprised to find the king was a short, nondescript-looking man, clean-shaven and with wispy blonde hair. He might have been a priest, until you looked into his eyes.

These were large, almost too large for his face, and a limpid blue. Artorius saw through them, clear to the depths of the man's soul. What he saw made him recoil.

"Tell us your name," he demanded as the prisoner was forced to kneel before him, "and what became of Rhitta."

The other man didn't reply at first. His blue eyes searched Artorius up and down, taking him in. Absorbing him.

Llwch raised his fist. "Answer the general, you carrion," he growled, "or I'll beat some manners into you."

"My apologies," the prisoner said in a soft, fluting voice, "I am Gwrgi. My predecessor is dead. I cut his throat while he sat at meat, and took his pelt for a banner."

"His *pelt*?" Artorius exclaimed, "Rhitta was a man, not a beast. He deserved a man's death."

"Death is death, General Artorius. It matters not how we die. The reaper comes for us all, and cares not for our notions of honour. You know that."

Artorius sensed this monstrous, unsettling little man was trying to goad him. "Your own death is coming soon," he said, "what if I chose to give you some of your own justice? Have you tortured to death, just as you tortured those poor wretches at Eburucum? Would you be so careless then?"

Gwrgi gave a little shrug. "Do as you wish. My time is over. How I end matters little. I have lived, Artorius. Gods above, the things I have seen and done! I won great victories. Drank the blood of kings. Tasted the despair of my enemies. It is enough."

Artorius saw it was useless to remonstrate. The man was quite mad, though his madness hadn't prevented him from raising an army and leading it with no little skill.

"You are an animal," he said flatly, "a mad dog. Mad dogs are put down."

He spied the pendant hanging from Gwrgi's neck, and reached down to grasp it.

For the first time a spark of fear showed in the prisoner's eyes. He tried to pull away, but Llwch's spearmen held his arms in a tight grip.

Intrigued, Artorius held the pendant up to examine it. A crudely shaped thing of bone and metal, possibly meant to represent some long-forgotten pagan god.

Fittingly, considering its owner, it had the head of a dog.

Artorius gave it a wrench, snapping the thin silver chain the pendant was attached to. As he stepped back, Gwrgi screamed. It was the scream of a terrified child, not a man.

"You!" he wailed, tears coursing down his face, "I know you, Artúir of the Selgovae. Oh, yes. You think to judge me, do you, and rob me of my essence? Look to yourself first!"

He looked up at one of the men holding his arms. "Cut away my sleeve," he ordered, the soft quality in his voice quite gone.

His tone of command was such the spearman actually reached for his knife. He stopped, looking up guiltily at Llwch.

"Do it," said Artorius, "let the condemned man have his last wish."

It was done, and the sleeve of Gwrgi's tunic on his left arm cut away and rolled back to the elbow, revealing a slender, almost womanly forearm.

His wrist was encircled with tattoos, faded with time, but still visible. The pattern was in the form of a double-headed blue serpent, with the heads meeting in the centre of the top of his wrist.

Artorius' breath caught in his throat. Exactly the same faded pattern adorned his own wrists. His father Uthyr had put them there, decades ago, when he was still a child. The double-headed snake was one of the symbols of his people, the Selgovae.

"See, Artorius?" Gwrgi cried, holding up his arm, "we are of the same tribe. I was there, when the Painted Ones came at night and fell on our people like wolves. I remember the blood, and the fires, and the spears in the dark. And I remember you, and your parents. Strong, warlike Uthyr and fair Ygraine. Your family were kin to mine.

Cousins. When the Painted Ones came, my father stood with yours and tried to fight them. They died together, spear-brothers to the end. You were taken for a slave, but I ran away and hid. Were it not for the raid, we might have been playmates. Friends. *Cousin.*"

Artorius was shaken. This man, who had committed the most appalling crimes, was his kin. He thought the Selgovae had been wiped out by the massacre that claimed his father's life. Artorius was just a child when it happened, and had no memory of the rest of his tribe.

The notion of there being any ties of blood between himself and this creature was revolting. Foul. Not be thought of.

And yet....they shared the same tribal marks. As for the man's brutal nature, did not Artorius display equal savagery when he slew Melwas outside the walls of Caer Thannoc? He gave his foe no honourable death in combat. Rather, a slow, cruel execution, taking him apart a piece at a time.

"We may be barbarians, you and I," he said slowly, mastering himself, "yet I take no pride in it. There lies the difference."

He nodded at Llwch. "Kill him. He started in blood. Let him end in hemp."

Gwrgi's eyes remained fixed on the dog-head pendant as they took him to a stout oak on the edge of the woods.

"This is not the end, Artorius," he called out, "my shade will wait for you in Annwn."

Artorius glanced down at the thing nestled in the palm of his hand.

His shade, he thought, *his essence...*

Not far off, a group of Companions had lit a fire. They sat around it, cooking supper.

While Llwch threw one end of the rope over a stout branch above Gwrgi's head, Artorius walked over to the fire. The Companions saw him coming and shuffled aside.

"No!" shrieked Gwrgi, "please!"

Artorius turned to face him. Llwch gave the signal to four of his men, who took hold of the loose end of the rope and heaved Gwrgi into the air.

As the dying man's legs kicked wildly under him, his eyes bulging in pain and terror, Artorius held the pendant high and let it drop into the flames.

*

A good number of Gwrgi's followers had escaped the field. Artorius' men were too battered and exhausted to pursue, so he allowed them a few days' rest. In the meantime he sent Llwch ahead with some light horse to look for the enemy.

"Most have taken refuge on Din Eidyn," he reported on his return, three days later, "I've never seen a fortress like it, stuck high up on a rock. Nothing can prise them out of there."

Artorius sighed. "Starvation will," he said, "we'll have to lay siege to the place. There can be no respite this time. The power of the north must be broken for good."

He didn't relish the prospect of a siege. Autumn was not far off, and winters north of the Wall were especially severe. Sitting outside Din Eidyn for months on end in the cold and wet, waiting for the men inside to surrender, promised to be sheer hell.

His captains groaned, but Artorius' mind was set. "I will not be satisfied," he declared, "until the last rebel has laid his spear at my feet."

The remnant of his army trudged north, through ever-worsening conditions, until the rock of Din Eidyn rose into view on the horizon.

Artorius peered through the rain at it, rising like a swollen black tumour from the surrounding plains.

He twisted in the saddle to look back at his Companions, strung out on the road behind him. Barely six hundred fit men were left to him. How many would sicken and die over the winter, while the garrison inside Din Eidyn lived off their stores?

For once, he compromised. He would show the garrison the body of their king, carried behind the army in a covered wagon, and if that failed to break their morale, withdraw south for reinforcements. Perhaps some fresh men could be taken from the scattered garrisons on the Wall.

He sent Llwch and his scouts ahead to reconnoitre the fort. They discovered the only approach was from the north, since the other three sides were defended by sheer sides and high walls. Artorius swung east, leaving the road, and took his men around the eastern flank of the rock.

He kept a wary eye on the fort, in case the garrison should sally out. There was no knowing how many of Gwrgi's men were holed up on the summit.

Nothing stirred, and the Companions were able to work their way around the difficult terrain until they were facing the northern gateway. This provided the only access to Din Eidyn, a path leading straight up the steep flank of the rock to the inner palisade.

Artorius' spirits plummeted as he studied the defences. The gate was defended by a ditch, itself protected by rows of sharpened stakes. There was a fighting platform above the gateway, from which the defenders could drop rocks on anyone foolish enough to try and take their home by storm.

The wall itself was timber, mounted on a base of dressed stone. Further up the slope was a drystone wall, with ramparts for more archers to shoot down from. Behind that was yet another drystone wall, this time protecting the fort itself.

"Three layers of defences," he said to himself, rubbing his beard, "and only one way in. Fifty men could hold this place against five thousand."

"If we can't get in, they can't get out," Cei said stoutly. He was recovering well from his wounds, or claimed he was, and had refused to be left behind with the other casualties.

Artorius leaned forward in the saddle a little, straining his eyes through the murk to get a better look at the outer wall. A few banners flapped limply on the battlements, but there was no sign of any men.

"Let us approach the gate," he said, "and show them their king."

A dozen Companions, including Cei and Gwalchmei, accompanied him. The wagon carrying Gwrgi's body, drawn by a team of six horses, creaked along in their wake.

Artorius went forward slowly, keeping low behind his shield. It was a risk, placing himself within bow-shot of the walls, but he wanted the defenders to see who was coming for them. Perhaps his fame, which he generally had little use for, would compel them to surrender.

"Men of Din Eidyn," he shouted when they had gone close enough, "I am General Artorius. Know that your king is dead, and his cause with him."

As he spoke, three of the Companions dismounted and lifted Gwrgi from the back of the covered wagon. The dead man had been stripped naked, and the rope-burn around his neck was clearly visible, a livid purple line cutting deep into his white flesh.

They laid the body on the grass, in full view of anyone inside the fort.

Nothing happened. All was silent, save for the lash of the wind and the patter of rain.

Artorius' suspicions were confirmed when the gates creaked open and a one-legged spearman limped out. He was old for a warrior, with a bald pate and a ragged grey beard, and used a stave to support himself.

The old man wrapped his thin plaid tighter around himself. "God help us, it's cold," he lisped, "I have lived on this rock most of my life, and it never gets any warmer."

"They've all gone," he added, grinning toothlessly at Artorius, "run off. Some to their own homes, others with the yellow-hair."

Artorius was relieved, even though the rump of Gwrgi's army had escaped him.

"The yellow-hair?" he asked, "who's that, old one?"

The spearman leaned his aged back against the gateway. "A woman," he replied, "and a Saxon. Hengist's daughter, or so she claimed. A great favourite of Gwrgi's, she was. I see he's dead."

He spoke carelessly, as though the death of his king meant little or nothing. Artorius suspected this one had seen as many kings come and go as he had winters.

Hengist's daughter, he thought, *the sea-vermin get everywhere.*

"The yellow-hair, as you call her, will have gone to sea," he said, "where we cannot follow."

The old man shrugged. "They went east," he replied, "her, and those who cared to go with her. That's all I know. I am too old and crippled to run, so they left me and a few slaves to hold Din Eidyn."

"It's yours," he added, throwing down his spear, "take my head, too, if you wish. My old bones ache with the rheumatics, and I'm ready to die."

"Keep your head," smiled Artorius, turning Llamrei about, "and get your old bones to a warm fire."

"Take that," he ordered his men, pointing at the body of Gwrgi, "into the forest, and leave it for the wolves. Let the beast return to the wild."

It was done, and he never spoke of Gwrgi Wyllt after, though the man often haunted his thoughts.

He and the Companions entered the fort, which was as empty as the old man claimed. The few slaves who remained met him outside the mead-hall on the windblown summit. Artorius dismissed all save the cooks, who he instructed to find meat and drink for his men.

After taking Llamrei to the stables and rubbing her down, Artorius walked alone into the hall. There were signs of it being abandoned in a hurry: platters of half-eaten food on the tables, charred logs and cold ash in the hearth, overturned flagons of mead.

He approached the dais at the further end of the hall. The king's chair, inevitably larger the others, loomed above him.

More people entered. Slaves, carrying fresh kindling to relight the fire, and hungry Companions, laughing and stamping their feet as they shook the rain from their cloaks.

Artorius mounted the steps, walked around the table and pulled back the royal chair. The scraping of wood on wood sounded unnaturally loud in the cavernous hall.

Rhitta and Gwrgi had sat here. King of the Northlands, they called themselves. A false title, for the sake of which thousands had died, all in terrible pain and suffering.

The chatter of his warriors died away as Artorius lowered himself into the chair. He picked up one of the overturned flagons and inspected the dregs inside.

"Stale," he said, tossing the flagon away, "someone fetch me some fresh mead. I have a thirst."

No-one moved. The assembled Companions, his chief officers, were all on their feet, watching him.

"What's this?" he demanded, "sit, all of you. The slaves will soon have a fire going. With luck those northern pigs won't have devoured all the rations."

Still there was no movement among his men. A chill of fear crawled up his spine. The old tale of Julius Caesar came back to him. Stabbed to death by people he counted as friends.

Artorius carried Caesar's sword. His fingers brushed the hilt. Was he about to share the fate of its previous owner?

He searched the faces of his officers. Every scarred and battered visage was familiar. These men had ridden and fought alongside him for nine long years. Some for even longer, stretching back to the time of Ambrosius. They would never turn on him.

Cei stepped forward. "Lord," he said, "we have spoken together, and come to an agreement."

This did nothing to quell Artorius' nerves. Cei almost never referred to him by his title.

"Spoken?" he said harshly, "not to me, you haven't. What agreement?"

Now Gwalchmei came forward. "We are your loyal men, lord," he said, "oath-sworn until death. We keep our oaths."

He coughed, as if uncertain how to go on. "None of us are young, lord. We have served with you for many years, leaving behind our homes and families for your sake. It is time we found a home."

"Your wife and bairns are at Caerleon," said Artorius, "you are free to visit them if you wish, though it will be a long journey in bad weather. Leave it until the spring."

Cei butted in. "Caerleon is no more our home than it is yours. Ever since Melwas abducted your woman, you have kept away from the place, and us from our kin."

"Be warned, Cei," said Artorius, "I won't talk of Melwas or Ganhumara."

"I meant no insult," replied the other man, "but we are plain men, and should be able to speak plainly to each other."

He stabbed his finger downwards. "*This* should be our home," he cried, "here, in Din Eidyn. The strongest fort in Britannia. Where you sit now, Artorius, should be your seat for the rest of your days. Bring your sons north, and our families with them."

There was a murmur from the men clustered behind him. Encouraged, Cei went on, allowing Artorius no time to respond.

"For years we have fought other men's wars. What have we gained from it? Nothing save a high reputation and a little plunder. Yet without us, the kings of Britannia would have lost their lands to the barbarians years ago. Are we to go on riding up and down the country, like common sell-swords, until we drop of old age or meet an enemy we cannot overcome? Gwrgi almost proved the end of us."

"We want something for ourselves," shouted Henbeddestyr, one of the longest-serving Companions, "and something for you, lord. No more than is your due."

Artorius sat back in his chair. "You think I should take Din Eidyn for myself?" he said, folding his arms, "sit on this freezing rock until I die? To what end?"

"You and I are northerners," said Cei, "bred in this hard land, of a hard people. Why should you not take a crown at last, and call yourself King of the Northlands?"

Artorius' laughter rang the length of the hall. Far from coming to slay Caesar, his men wanted to make him one.

His laughter fell on stony ground. "God love you all," he said, "can you not see how absurd it is? I have fought two campaigns in the north. Slaughtered the menfolk. You think all those widows and orphans would accept me as king? The people would rise up in furious anger, small blame to them, and burn this place about our ears."

"No," said Cei, "it is because you have beaten them that they will accept you. The people of the north only respect strength. You have shown strength, and have the blood of the Selgovae in your veins. They will happily take a man like you for their king, over some debauched southerner who has never even set foot beyond the Wall."

He meant Constantine. Artorius could only imagine the High King's reaction upon being informed that yet another pretender had risen to usurp his authority in the north.

When he discovered who that pretender was, the fat fool would most likely have a seizure.

Artorius put aside this appealing thought. "You have all forgotten one thing," he said, bracing himself against the hard wood of his chair, "I have no desire for a crown. The High Kingship could have been mine. I refused it. I am not the stuff kings are made of."

"True," cried Henbeddestyr, "I have seen the stuff kings are made of. Usually in the contents of a privy."

"Why do worthy men refuse crowns?" said Cei, "leaving the scum to inherit? Ambrosius should have been High King. Instead he hid behind some old Roman title. As for Constantine, I care not a straw for him. I renounce my fealty."

Artorius stood up. This was going too far. "We all swore an oath," he cried when the shouts of approval had died down, "an oath before God, to serve the High King as his loyal subjects. Break it, and you put your souls at risk."

He tried to reason with them. "You think I have any love for Constantine? He is corrupted, and neglects his duties, and has done his best in the past to destroy me. Nevertheless he is the king, chosen in formal council to rule over us."

"To hell with him," bawled Gwalchmei, "to hell with our oaths, and to hell with the council. Let him rule in the south until his swollen guts burst. We will have you for our king, and the north for our kingdom."

In the end, Artorius could only divert them, promising he would think on the matter. Something like calm descended, and all talk of kings was put aside when the slaves came to his rescue, carrying in platters of salt pork and skewers loaded with hot peppered chops.

The feast was at its height, with rain battering at the eaves of the hall and Artorius lost in contemplation, when the doors were flung open.

Two luckless spearmen entered, having lost at dice for the dubious honour of guarding the gate in vile weather. A third man, soaked through and splattered with wet mud, traipsed in behind them.

The noise and drunken mirth died down as the newcomer pushed back his hood, revealing a face pale as death.

"General Artorius," he rasped, swaying with fatigue, "I come from the south. The High King is defeated, and all his soldiers slain. The west is lost to the Saxons. Britannia is lost. Lost, lost, lost..."

He folded, crumpling to his knees even as the Companions rose and looked to their chief.

26.

Mount Badon, Aquae Sulis

"Jesu, have pity," the dying man whispered, "forgive me my sins, for they are many...God, God forgive me!"

His hand tightened on Bedwyr's. Since there were no priests available to act as confessor, Bedwyr had agreed to sit by the deathbed and listen to its occupant pour out his soul.

Pascent had suffered an axe-wound to his shoulder during the fighting on the wall the previous day. The wound had festered quickly, and now the room was filled with the stench of gangrene.

Bedwyr did his best to comfort him. "Peace," he said, laying Pascent's hand on his chest, "your sins, whatever they may be,

are no blacker than any other man's. Christ
will forgive all."

Privately he doubted it. Pascent had
already blurted out the truth of his affair
with the High King. The church taught that
sodomy was a terrible crime in the eyes of
God, though Bedwyr failed to see why love
of any sort was a crime.

Pascent had stopped short of describing
his other sins. Bedwyr thought he knew
why. "Tell me," he said, in as kind a voice
as possible, "did you plot with Constantine
against Artorius? Was the expedition to
Gaul all a sham?"

Another spasm of pain passed through
Pascent. He groaned, his entire body tensed
against it. "It...it was the Prefect," he
muttered when he could speak again, "the
Prefect of Gaul...Arvandus...he sent us
letters...it was all...his plan..."

Bedwyr grimaced. He loathed deceit, and
could tell when a man was lying through his
teeth. He was about to ask why the Prefect
of Gaul should care whether Artorius lived
or died, but stopped himself.

It does no good, he thought, *Pascent's soul
will soon be judged in the balance. I cannot
influence the verdict.*

He straightened on his stool, ignoring the
delirious mutterings of the man in the bed.
The room was tiny, a dim alcove hidden

behind a curtain, with a single arrow-slit window. Through it a half-moon shone, adding its wan light to the few guttering candles.

Bedwyr judged it to be almost midnight, yet the Saxons pressed the siege with undimmed ferocity. From outside he could hear the hiss and thump of their catapults, hurling flaming missiles over the walls of Aquae Sulis; the pounding of their iron-tipped rams at the gates; the mocking chants of their warriors, daring the terrified citizens to come out and fight.

God save me. If only I could sleep. Just for a little while.

He yawned, and pressed his knuckles to his eyes. This was the second night he and his men had spent, holed up in the ancient hill-fort of Mount Badon. Outside the Saxons raged, though most of their efforts were concentrated on the town.

The fort lay north-east of Aquae Sulis, perched on a small flat-topped hill that gave dramatic views of the town, nestled in its vale below, and the surrounding country.

In his heart Bedwyr knew he had made a mistake. Soon he would pay for it with his life. When he had come here, fleeing the slaughter of Llongborth with what remained of Constantine's cavalry, he had divided his command between the town and the fort.

A more ruthless man would have left Aquae Sulis to its fate. Bedwyr was incapable of such a decision. Left to themselves, the populace could not defend their walls for long against the Saxon onslaught. He gave them eighty men, keeping almost as many for the fort, hoping they could hold out until help arrived.

He found it impossible to think clearly. Exhaustion took its toll, and the horrors of Llongborth were still raw in his memory.

Bedwyr was still at Caerleon, overseeing the hopeless search for Medraut, when the summons arrived: Osla Big-Knife had broken his treaty with the High King, and an enormous Saxon fleet had been spotted, sailing west around the coast of Dumnonia. All loyal men were to join the High King's host as it marched from Londinium to deal with the threat.

"I could scarce believe it," Bedwyr murmured, though he knew Pascent was probably beyond hearing now, "at last, after nine years, Constantine had shaken off his lethargy and taken the field. I was almost proud to call him my king."

Bedwyr had responded at once, leaving just ten of his fifty Companions to guard Caerleon, while he took the rest to join Constantine.

He met the royal army as it passed through the high hills near Mons Ambrius. What he saw filled him with disquiet. Constantine was reduced to a pathetic figure, obscenely bloated, half-blind and almost bald, his youthful fairness a dim memory. Incapable of riding a horse, he was carried at the rear of his army on a litter, surrounded by his personal guard. Effective command of the army was given over to his Magister Militum, Geraint, and Pascent.

"Two thousand men," said Bedwyr, gazing at the moon, "dead now, save the few I brought here."

Two thousand, all Constantine could muster in a hurry, against three times their number of Saxons. Sweeping aside the cautious advice of Geraint, he had insisted on force-marching south, to meet the enemy before they could advance too far inland.

The Saxons had sailed their keels upriver, to the small harbour of Llongborth. Scored into Bedwyr's memory was his first sight of the Saxon camp, hundreds of tents spread across the marshy fields flanking the village; the noise of their drums and war-horns, sounding the alarm as the British advance was spotted; the rapid advance of their warriors under the black banners of no less than thirteen Saxon kings.

What followed was no battle, but a one-sided massacre. The British cavalry foundered on the unbreakable ranks of the Saxon shieldwall, and could do nothing to protect their outnumbered infantry, surrounded and overwhelmed as they tried to deploy in the marsh.

Bedwyr saw Geraint die, hacked to pieces as he tried to defend the royal litter, loyal to the last. Constantine was almost certainly dead, or worse, taken prisoner. Bedwyr did not know. When it became clear all was lost, he had done his best to gather up what remained of the cavalry and get them off the field. It was the disaster of Gaul all over again.

"I should have stayed," moaned Pascent, clawing at the sheets, his yellow face filmed with sweat, "I should have died beside him. He trusted me. Loved me. No-one save me."

"There was no sense in throwing your life away," said Bedwyr, "if all men fall before Saxon blades, who would be left to defend our land?"

Pascent shuddered violently, shutting his eyes and twisting his head left to right. Blood and pus leaked from the gruesome hole in his shoulder, staining the blanket. He wouldn't last long. If God was merciful, death would take him before the Saxons overran the fort.

Mount Badon's defences were weak. A single drystone wall, infilled with rubble, running around the roughly triangular summit of the hill. So far the Britons had beaten off a few desultory attacks. Osla, the war-chief of the Saxon host, was concentrating most of his efforts on reducing Aquae Sulis.

Bedwyr remained with Pascent until the first grey light of morning stole through the window. He slumbered fitfully, his back leaning against the wall. Not true sleep, yet rest of a sort, enough to get him through another day. If he survived it.

He was shaken awake by one of his men. "Lord," the soldier said, his bearded face white with strain, "you should come to the wall."

Bedwyr blinked. His mind was sluggish, and his head felt as though it was stuffed with wool.

He looked down at the bed. Pascent lay quietly now, his hands relaxed, eyes staring glassily at the ceiling. God had been merciful after all, and taken his soul during the small hours.

One less burden, thought Bedwyr. "The wall," he said, getting to his feet, "very well. Give me a moment."

He picked up his helmet, shield and sword-belt, and followed the soldier out of the hall. It was a dull grey morning outside, with rain clouds drifting closer from the west. Most of his men were gathered near the gate on the south-eastern side, crammed onto the rampart and walkway.

Many of them were silent, Bedwyr noticed. A few wept, while others threw curses down on Saxon heads. Beyond the gate, he could hear the infernal thump-thump-thump of drums, and raucous cheers mixed with laughter.

"Are they mocking us now?" Bedwyr said blearily, pushing his way onto the walkway above the gate, "let the pagans come closer, and we shall stuff their laughter down their throats."

His brave words rang hollow, a desperate gesture, aimed at pouring a little steel into his men.

Bedwyr gazed down over the battlements. To the south-west, across the river, he could see the torment of Aquae Sulis. Fires raged inside the town, destroying the timber buildings and scorching the marble walls of temples and bath houses. Ant-like figures scurried about with buckets, desperately striving to quench the flames.

Aquae Sulis, perhaps the last Roman town in Britannia to retain something of its old glory, was dying. The Saxons had broken off their assault for a few hours, allowing the citizens a brief respite. It wouldn't last. The gates were already half-broken, shored up with piles of earth and loose stones. One, maybe two, determined assaults would be enough to smash them down.

Bedwyr's eyes were drawn nearer, to the mass of enemy warriors drawn up under the steep slope of Mount Badon.

"Aelle," he said, picking out the familiar gigantic shape, bigger even than Wulfhere, standing in the middle of their line. Some men in tattered cloaks, their hair spiked with dung, pranced before him. Bedwyr assumed these were Saxon druids or priests, worshippers of their filthy pagan gods.

The druids were carrying stakes, brandishing them high in the air, to the bellowed approval of the men drawn up behind them.

There were things nailed to the stakes. Bedwyr rubbed his tired eyes to get a better look.

His gorge rose when he realised what they were. He clapped a hand to his mouth, willing himself not to vomit.

Constantine had been chopped up, his head and limbs fixed to the stakes. His bloated features and scanty fair hair were clearly visible. The golden wreath, symbol of the High Kingship, still adorned his brow. The druid holding the stake mounted with

Constantine's head also wore his gold-edged purple cloak, capering up and down in obscene mockery of the dead man's royal dignity.

"Curse them," muttered Bedwyr, leaning against the timber parapet for support, "curse them all. Vermin. Pigs."

There was a hiss of steel on leather to his left. "Let us ride out," cried one of the youngest Companions, his face dark with fury, "and take our king back from them. At least we may give his remains a Christian burial."

Bedwyr fought against the temptation to charge out of the gate at the head of his men, to go down fighting, taking as many of the Saxons as he could with him. Maybe even slay Aelle himself in single combat, as he had Wulfhere.

"No," he said with an effort, "can't you see the Saxons are trying to lure us out? Look at their numbers. We would be slaughtered."

The young soldier and his comrades scowled, but made no protest. Bedwyr hoped they could see sense. They had to hold Mount Badon at all costs. The Saxons had already swept through much of Dumnonia, swallowing up one fort after another. In a few short days they had all but destroyed the network of defences so painstakingly constructed by Ambrosius and his father.

If Aquae Sulis fell, as seemed inevitable, only Badon stood between the Saxons and the Roman road leading straight into the heart of Britannia. Not that there was much left for them to conquer. Once Dumnonia and its precious farmlands was in their grasp, the rest of the kingdom would be easy meat.

"So we just cower behind these walls?" protested another soldier, "and listen to the barbarians taunt us?"

"We wait," Bedwyr said firmly, "Artorius will come, with all the kings of Britannia at his back."

Mention of Artorius caused his men to stand a little straighter, and lose some of their woebegone look. The name alone was enough to restore some of their courage.

His name will not be enough, thought Bedwyr as he left the rampart, *we wait for Artorius, or a miracle.*

Shortly afterwards, while a grave was being dug for Pascent, the Saxons resumed their assault on Aquae Sulis. They dragged up more artillery; ballistae and catapults taken from the walls of captured British forts, and concentrated their barrage on the eastern gate.

The Saxons had no training in the use of siege weapons, and handled them clumsily. It mattered little. By noon the gates were little more than a pile of broken timber and iron, and the defenders were reduced to frantically piling up more barricades behind the wreckage.

Bedwyr watched helplessly as Osla threw his warriors against the weakened defences. Hundreds of spearmen swarmed forward with a great yell, carrying ladders and ropes to scale the walls, while others tried to force a passage through the ruined gateway.

The defenders fought with a desperation born of terror. Priests, women and children stood alongside the soldiers on the wall, hurling down pieces of masonry, broken spars, even furniture, anything to kill the enemy. Savage hand-to-hand fighting broke out, even as the artillery continued to bombard the town, fiery missiles streaking over the heads of the struggling mass of Saxons and Britons to add to the conflagration already raging inside.

"Christ save them," said Bedwyr, looking in vain at the misted hills to the north, willing the dragon banner to appear, "for I cannot."

The flimsy barricades thrown up behind the gateway couldn't hold the Saxons for long. Within moments the defenders were engulfed, driven back by sheer weight of numbers, the few survivors pursued as they retreated into the streets.

It was the end. Seeing his men win the gate, Osla poured in more warriors until not a living Briton remained on the walls. Howling for blood, the Saxons slew all they found, men, women and children, before carrying their relentless assault into the town itself.

Bedwyr witnessed the murder of Aquae Sulis. The butchery went on for the rest of the day and long into the night. When darkness fell, the town was lit by gouts of flame, leaping high into the air from the burning shops and houses: a sea of fire, illuminating at intervals the fighting in the streets, looting, rape, massacre.

It gave him no comfort to know his soldiers died hard. The old temple, built by the Romans in dedication to the goddess Minerva, was the last building to hold out, manned by what was left of his command, along with a few diehard citizens. Time and again, the Saxons were hurled back as they attempted to storm the temple.

In the end, there were too few Britons left standing to resist them. Bedwyr looked away when the final assault went in, though he could do nothing to block out the screams, the roar of flames, and the triumphant chanting of the enemy.

He got no sleep, and emerged before dawn, hollow-eyed and spent. His limbs felt like lead weights as he trudged towards the gate. Bedwyr forced himself to walk with a straight back, to assume a mask of cheerfulness, even as hope died inside him.

His men on watch were ghastly pale, their eyes red from weeping. Bedwyr gave them some wine from his flask, and looked down at the smoking corpse of Aquae Sulis.

At least the killing had stopped. Most of the Saxons inside the town would be dead drunk by now, passed out in a sea of gore and vomit. Any Britons still alive would have been taken as slaves, roped together and herded out like cattle, to be held under guard or marched down to the ships at Llongborth.

"Our turn soon," whispered one of the sentries, sitting hunched against the parapet.

"Courage," said Bedwyr, knowing mere courage wouldn't help them. Like Artorius, he had earned a warlike reputation, and strived to look and sound the indomitable hero his men needed him to be.

In truth, he was as tired and frightened as any of them. In a futile effort to induce sleep, he had drunk too much the previous night, and now felt ill. His head ached.

There was a sour taste in his mouth. His belly griped, but he could get no relief at the latrine pits.

Suddenly his chest tightened. He started to panic. *I am too tired to fight. Too slow. Christ, give me strength!*

Gulping in breaths of cold morning air, he tried to calm himself, hoping the sentries hadn't noticed. If they saw him weaken, the last shreds of their morale might dissolve.

The sentry was right. It would be their turn soon. Below the fort, at the foot of the hill, Saxon warriors were slowly moving into position. Osla had held back reserves from the final assault on Aquae Sulis, and was now deploying them to storm Mount Badon.

Osla *is no fool*, thought Bedwyr, *he is sending the pick of his warriors to finish us.*

The men below wore long coats of ring-mail, helmets with nose-guards, and carried the dreaded long-axe, capable of chopping a man clean in two. Their deep singing filled the air. Bedwyr saw horns brimming with mead passed among their ranks. The Saxons would drink deep before launching their assault, believing the mead gave them strength and courage. It certainly helped to reduce a man's natural fear of death.

"Make ready," ordered Bedwyr, though his men were already at their posts, strung out along the walls flanking the gate. They waited in silence, a long line of spears and shields, with a few bowmen and slingers among them. Twenty men on horses were stationed further up the hill, placed there by Bedwyr as a mobile reserve in case the Saxons broke through.

They were in no hurry to complete their victory. While the Britons sweated, the gesiths deployed at a leisurely pace, forming up into five great squares on the plain below Mount Badon. Bedwyr attempted a rough head-count, and stopped when he reached six hundred. Osla was using a mighty hammer to crack a nut.

Then Bedwyr saw the catapults being dragged up by teams of slaves. He felt sick. The Saxons were going to bombard the fort, perhaps in an effort to reduce the men inside to submission. Or perhaps because they simply enjoyed watching things burn.

"Keep your heads down," Bedwyr shouted while the crewmen busied themselves loading the catapults with flaming ammunition, balls of rags stuffed full of flammable material and set alight.

The first missiles streaked into the air, flying high over the drystone rampart. As he crouched under the wall, Bedwyr was reminded of the death of Vortigern, burned to death inside his last redoubt on the orders of Ambrosius. A horrific, shameful death: he could scarce imagine anything more painful, to burn alive like a human torch, skin peeling and sloughing from his bones while he yet breathed, screaming in unimaginable agony.

Bedwyr gripped his spear. *Almighty God, spare my courage*, he pleaded silently, *do not let me break at the last.*

Some of the missiles hit their targets, crashing onto the thatched roofs of the outbuildings and roundhouses. One hit the stables, terrifying the beasts inside. Their animal shrieks added a new horror to Bedwyr's nightmare.

The man to his right gurgled and toppled off the walkway, a white-fletched arrow sticking from his throat. Bedwyr peered through a gap in the wall, and saw Saxon archers loping up the hill, ahead of the companies of axe-men. The latter still hadn't moved. They waited patiently for the slaughter to begin, rank upon rank of men in glittering mail, banners waving gently in the breeze.

Osla's archers moved in skirmish formation, pausing to notch arrows and loose them high into the air, over the battlements. The few British bowmen and slingers, forced to stay under cover by the storm of missiles, could not respond.

Soon every building inside the fort was on fire. The roof of the hall itself, where Pascent had died, burned like a torch on the summit of the hill. Clouds of smoke wafted across the interior, getting into the lungs and eyes of the defenders.

Bedwyr coughed, rubbing his streaming eyes, croaking at his men to stand firm. A few more fell to the arrows. The heat was rapidly becoming unbearable. He feared they would roast, trapped inside like rats, while the Saxons stood back and warmed their hands.

However, Osla's taste for blood was not yet sated. The bombardment ceased, and was immediately replaced by the roar of Saxon war-horns. Bedwyr squinted through the gap, and saw a tide of iron and flesh tramping slowly up the hill.

"Archers!" Bedwyr shouted, showing his head over the parapet, "slingers! Bring a few of those bastards down. Thin them out!"

The Saxons broke into a run. They poured up the slope, screeching war-cries, heedless of the light rain of arrows and stones pattering among them. Here and there a warrior fell, swiftly trampled or kicked aside by his fellows.

Still they came on. Scaling ladders slammed against the wall. "Help me!" Bedwyr shouted at one of his men. Together they used their spears to push one back, making it topple down on the heads of the enemy.

Bedwyr hurled his spear into the horde below, hitting an exposed face. It blossomed red and vanished. He may as well have dropped a pebble into the ocean. Nothing could hold the Saxons back. They came swarming up the ladders and onto the walkway, axes swinging, swords jabbing at the hopelessly outnumbered British defenders.

Drawing his spatha, Bedwyr hacked at one of the gesiths climbing over the battlements, striking the side of his helmet and knocking him off-balance. The man cried out and fell backwards, onto his comrades toiling up the ladder.

Bedwyr sensed danger, and spun around in time to ward off a sword cutting at his head. The blades rang as they crashed together. For a brief second he found himself staring into a craggy, weather-beaten face, spitting like a wildcat, eyes bulging with hatred. He kicked the Saxon in the groin and slashed at him as he doubled over, pitching him off the walkway.

It was no use. The walls were already lost; his men hacked down or fled, retreating back up the hill towards the burning shell of the hall, as if it offered any refuge. There were Saxons already inside the fort, straining to lift the heavy bar on the gates and admit their comrades.

Bedwyr stumbled down the steps, determined to stop them. It was futile. Mount Badon was doomed, as was he, and all his men. Britannia would soon follow. All would go down in death and darkness, the light of Christianity snuffed out, along with the last feeble glimmers of Roman civilisation. The land would become a pagan wilderness, a play-pit for barbarians to sit in their smoky halls and lord it over the enslaved remnants of the British race.

Driven by despair, Bedwyr fought. Mustering his last reserves of strength and skill, he disarmed a gesith near the gateway and killed him with a sword-thrust to the eye. Three more turned on him. He retreated, somehow warding off their furious blows, sweat pouring down his face.

His shield was beaten to splinters. Shaking off the useless remnant, he stabbed at one of his attackers, opening a deep gash on the man's cheek. Another dived and seized him around the waist. Both men went down together into the dirt. Bedwyr hurled him off, and caught the flash of an axe as it swung down at his face.

He instinctively raised his left arm. The axe sheared clean through it, just under the wrist, separating bone and sinew and flesh. His severed hand, still twitching, fell to the ground.

Stunned, Bedwyr could do nothing but gape at the stump of his left arm. A Saxon fist smashed into his face, knocking him down. As he tried to crawl away, a boot thudded into his side, snapping a rib.

Bedwyr rolled onto his back, almost welcoming the death-blow. Instead a gobbet of stinking phlegm splashed onto his face. The Saxon who had cut off his hand laughed and moved on.

They left him to die, crippled, finished, not worth the killing. The screams of his men echoed dimly in his ears. Through a haze of pain, he watched clouds of black smoke funnel into the sky, like winding pillars carved from ebony, shot through with yellow sparks.

With his remaining hand, Bedwyr tugged at the hem of his filthy cloak, wrapping it as tight as he could around his stump. Blood pounded inside his skull.

The pounding became more distinct. A thundering and a racing of hoofs, rising like a storm over the hills to the north. The triumphant baying of the Saxon war-horns was echoed by others, more distant. These were higher, shriller, the prelude to the storm.

Cavalry bugles. Bedwyr's lungs were full of smoke and blood, else he would have laughed.

The dragon had come at last.

27.

The sun was rising. Artorius and his Companions saw the smoke in the south, and quickened their pace. They had ridden hard from Din Eidyn, gathering up fresh men and horses on the way. Word of Constantine's death was spreading across the land, inspiring men to fight or hide. Those who chose to fight joined Artorius.

There was no question of leaving the south of Britannia to its fate. Even the dullest of his followers realised that if the south fell to the Saxons, the north would soon follow. The tension among the Companions was forgotten, and Artorius was once again in full command.

As was his custom, he sent a band of light horse ahead to sniff out the enemy. They returned while his men had paused to rest outside the walls of the legionary fort at

Glevum, where Eidol Cadarn, now too old to fight, gave Artorius a hundred auxiliary cavalry from his garrison.

"All I can spare," the white-haired magistrate said, "you understand. If the Saxons take Aquae Sulis, my lands will be next."

Artorius didn't argue. He was grateful for all the reinforcements he could get. Too many of the remaining British kings and nobles had failed to send help. He cursed their selfishness. What did they think would happen, if the Saxons won? Did they hope to gain places for themselves under the new regime, to beg for scraps from Osla's table? Osla would make slaves or martyrs of them all, and parcel out their lands among his own followers.

No less a fate than they deserve, said a treacherous inner voice. Artorius stamped on it, hard.

His scouts, a band of Votadini, breathlessly poured their news. Aquae Sulis was besieged, and a few British soldiers holed up inside Mount Badon.

"Numbers?" snapped Artorius, "how many Saxons?"

"Many thousands, lord," was the reply. Artorius winced. His army numbered no more than twelve hundred men.

"You don't have enough men to break their lines," said Eidol, voicing his doubts, "forget Aquae Sulis. It cannot be saved. Attack the Saxons as they advance deeper into our territory. Whittle away their numbers. I will hold Glevum, no matter what Osla throws at me."

Artorius shook his head. "Our people are trapped inside the town and the fort. If I abandon them, what am I?"

He clasped Eidol's fragile hand, remembering how the magistrate had stumbled into Mons Ambrius, the only British survivor of the Treachery of the Long Knives. Artorius was still a boy then, and had wanted to grab a horse and ride alone to the stones, to fight Hengist and his Saxons single-handed.

Now the boy was grown, and his time had come.

The British horsemen cantered down the road, which led straight to Mount Badon before descending into the vale of Aquae Sulis. Artorius led them through the night, planning to use his old strategy of swooping on the enemy just before dawn, when most men were at their weakest. It was an old trick, picked up long ago from Ambrosius, and had served him well.

The night was lit up by a host of fires in the south. Artorius and his men pressed on in silence. When the sky started to lighten, they saw the blaze on the summit of Mount Badon. Artorius knew his men were inside the hill-fort, fighting and dying. Burning.

Summoning what he could remember of Badon and its terrain, he called a halt and gave orders to his captains.

"Gwalchmei," he said, "the road takes us directly up the hill to the fort. Take your squadron and drive away the enemy at Mount Badon."

He stabbed his finger in the direction of a little wood, cresting a knoll to the west of Badon. "Llwch, take two hundred men into those woods. They overlook the town. Remain there until you hear my signal. Three horn-blasts. Understand?"

Llwch nodded. "I will take the remainder," Artorius added, "and attack the Saxons outside Aquae Sulis. God be with us."

The Britons surged on, a single disciplined body of horseman riding at a canter. When they reached the slope of Badon, Artorius raised his arm for the bugles to sound. Once again their shrill wails echoed through the rolling hill country. His men spurred into a gallop.

Gwalchmei's squadron, four hundred strong, swung right and thundered towards the enemy infantry around the gate. Most of the Saxons were still inside, slaying the last of the defenders. Their comrades had heard the bugles and were hurriedly attempting to form a shieldwall.

War-yells erupted behind Artorius as he led the rest of his men past the fort, to a ridge overlooking the vale. Here he gained a clear view of the devastation below, where smouldering fires still burned inside the charred shell of Aquae Sulis.

The bulk of the Saxon host was camped on the plain outside the eastern gate. The plain was divided by the River Afon, and Artorius could see hundreds of their warriors drawn up at the foot of the hill, north of the river. Watch-fires burned like a constellation of stars among the tents beyond the southern bank.

Artorius couldn't afford to hesitate. War-horns were already sounding the alarm inside the camp. Soon the Saxons would come pouring across the river.

While Llwch's men peeled away and rode for the woods, he led the remainder of his army straight down the slope - bugles squealing, dragon banner to the fore. The Saxons below were hemmed in between the hill and the river. He willed them to break, to flee into the water, where he would have them at his mercy.

The Saxons stood their ground. Through the eye-holes of his helm he saw the glint of their mail, and knew these were some of Osla's best warriors, the personal friends and followers of Saxon kings.

Llamrei leaped, and he was among them, stabbing at pale faces with Rhongymiad, shuddering under the impact of axe-blows against his shield. The light was still poor. He could see little, and relied on his instincts, honed from years of campaigning, to carry him alive through the press. Rhongymiad broke off in a Saxon neck, so he threw away the useless stump and switched to Caledfwlch.

The shouts of his men echoed inside his helmet. They had followed, pouring into the gap he had created, casting their spears into the Saxons and then drawing their spathas for the close work. The reckless charge of the Companions would have broken lesser men, but the gesiths doggedly stood their ground, swinging their axes even as they were shoved back to the river. Many were trampled under-hoof, or cut down by the flashing spathas, yet still they fought on, inspired by the example of their king.

Artorius spotted this man, a stocky red-bearded brute in a coat of golden mail, wielding a thick-bladed sword. As long as he lived, his men would not retreat.

Cei had also seen him, and was trying to force a path through the knot of warriors, glutting his sword with their blood. An axe bit deep into the neck of his horse, half-decapitating the poor beast and flinging him out of the saddle. He was quickly up again, his face crimson under his helm as he hacked at the Saxons closing in to finish him off.

They left the king and his standard bearer exposed. Artorius kicked Llamrei into a gallop and rode at the banner. The young warrior holding it wore no shield, and was defenceless as Artorius cut downwards, shearing off four of his fingers.

The banner fell. A shout of dismay went up from Saxon throats. Artorius killed the wounded youth and turned on the king.

"Artorius!" yelled his foe, deep voice rising above the din of battle, "my name is Cissa, and I am your death!"

"Die, Cissa," Artorius grunted in response, cutting at the king's muscular neck. His opponent caught the blow on his shield and chopped at Artorius' knee. The blades met, Caledfwlch grinding against Saxon steel.

They cut at each other again, but the two men were well-matched. Cissa was as good a swordsman as Artorius, and took no risks, hunching behind his huge round shield whenever Caledwlch stabbed at his face. His yellow teeth were gritted in their thatch of greasy red beard, green eyes blazing either side of his nose-guard.

Those eyes suddenly widened in shock. His mouth opened in a silent gasp, and he slumped to the ground. The bloodied tip of a spear burst from his throat, lodged there by Cei, who had fought off his attackers and crept up on Cissa from behind.

Now their king and standard had fallen, the will to fight drained from the Saxons. A few stood firm, preferring death to flight. Many more turned and ran, casting aside their heavy shields and axes as they took their chance in the river. The Companions followed, baying like dogs at the kill, cutting and riding them down.

Artorius lifted his helmet and gulped in some air. He was breathing hard, as was Llamrei, her flanks rising and falling, soaked in sweat and splattered with blood and mire. Nearby Cei was swearing horribly as he tried to calm a riderless horse and heave himself aboard her back.

One Saxon king lay dead, and his warriors put to flight. Drums beat across the river as the camp sprang to life. Countless more of the enemy were hurrying towards the river, alerted by the sound of fighting.

Artorius thought rapidly. To lead his men over the Afon was sheer madness, unless panic did its work, spreading among the befuddled and barely awake Saxon warriors. With luck, they would think the Britons had attacked in great numbers, and the rout would become general. Then the real killing could begin.

He twisted in the saddle to look up at Mount Badon. Gwalchmei's men were still embroiled with the Saxons around the gate. In the semi-darkness of dawn, it was impossible to tell who was winning.

Artorius made his decision. "Back!" he shouted, wheeling Llamrei, "to the fort!"

The Companions turned and charged up the hill. Now attacked from three sides at once, the gesiths fought with grim ferocity until the slope was carpeted with dead and dying.

Osla sent them no aid. Instead he pulled his forces back across the Afon, the gesiths forming into packed shieldwalls around the standards of their kings, while the ceorls were pushed ahead of them or onto the flanks, until the Saxon host covered the width of the plain. More of his warriors streamed out of the town, roused from their mead-fuelled stupor by their chiefs and bullied into joining the battle-line.

When the fort was secured, and all the Saxons around it dead or fled, Artorius marshalled his cavalry on the brow of the hill. Bright morning sunlight was flooding across the hills, bathing them in gold.

He looked down at the enemy host. Company after company, file after file, gathered in iron ranks around the banners of twelve kings. Osla's banner, the largest, waved in the centre.

Artorius raised Calefwlch. "Charge!" he cried.

The bugles shrieked once more. He led his battered squadrons down, down, galloping over the bodies of the men at the foot of Mount Badon and crashing across the river.

Such a head-on assault against superior numbers was a terrible risk, but Artorius was faced with a stark choice of attack or retreat. Fall back, allow Aelle to seize Mount Badon and march on Glevum, and Dumnonia may as well be given up for lost. The Saxon advance had to be stopped, here, no matter the cost.

The ragged lines of ceorls scattered before the dragon banner, unwilling to withstand a single charge of the cavalry bearing down on them. The Companions ignored them and swept on to attack the core of Aelle's host.

They foundered. The enemy line held steady, and the long-axes swung in a murderous rhythm, hacking through men and horses. The Britons could do little save ride around the dense rings of shields, casting javelins at exposed faces and looking for any gaps to exploit.

Seeing it was useless, Artorius ordered the retreat. His men withdrew in good order, to the edge of the river. The gesiths remained where they were, rooted to their positions, jeering at the Britons and daring them to try again.

Another charge went in, and another. Both failed. Artorius fell back, leaving over a third of his men stretched out on the grass. A few of the horses belonging to the dead men stood mournfully over the bodies of their fallen masters, nudging at them to get up.

"Once more!" he shouted, riding back and forth before his bloodied followers, "one more charge, and they are done!"

His men had just enough spirit left to follow him in again. With a great shout, they hurled themselves against the unbreakable shields. The result was the same. The dreaded axes rose and fell, cleaving heads and limbs, felling the Companions like ripe wheat before the sickle.

"Flee!" yelled Artorius, turning away from the futile struggle, "flee for your lives!"

He bent low over Llamrei's neck and urged her into a flat gallop, flinging away his shield. The mocking cries of the Saxons rang in his ears, even as his men followed his example and retreated in complete disorder, all their discipline gone, brave men reduced to frightened children.

Their heads swimming with mead and bloodlust, many of Aelle's younger gesiths broke ranks and stormed after the fleeing Britons. The dense ranks of the Saxon shieldwalls eroded as more and more warriors abandoned their positions to join in the rout, ignoring the shouts of their chiefs.

Artorius risked all on this, his final throw of the dice. When he reached the edge of the plain he hauled back on Llamrei's reins and sat bolt upright in the saddle, flinging up his sword-arm.

The discipline and training of the Companions held true. While his allies carried on their flight, deserting the field, Artorius' veterans swung round and launched a counter-charge, tearing into the Saxons who had given chase.

Now the disastrous campaign in Gaul proved to have some worth after all. The feigned retreat mastered by Amorican cavalry, which Artorius had spent long years since drilling into his own men, came to his rescue. Caught in the open, too far from their banners and with no opportunity to re-form, the Saxons were doomed. The Companions simply rode over them, scores of warriors vanishing under the churning

hoofs, while the survivors had no choice but
to take to their heels.

The banners of the twelve kings still flew.
They had to be felled. In the midst of the
slaughter, Artorius seized the bugle from his
trumpeter and put it to his own lips,
throwing back his head to sound three shrill
blasts.

In response to the long-awaited signal,
Llwch's two hundred cavalry emerged from
the woods crowning the knoll opposite
Mount Badon. From the plain, their numbers
appeared far greater. Howls of fear and
dismay erupted from Saxon throats across
the battlefield as Llwch led his company
down the hill, bugles screeching like devils
in torment, pennons fluttering in the
morning breeze.

At last the banners started to fall as the
men holding them lost heart and ran,
forgetting their oaths in a desperate desire to
escape, to live. The Companions, wounded
and fatigued as they were, pressed their
attack to the last, butchering the Saxons as
they fled, closing in on the tattered rags of
the shieldwalls.

Osla and his fellow kings had their pride,
and refused to yield. Shoulder to shoulder
with their hearth guards, they stood and
fought and went to their gods with honour.
Fighting went on for hours, long into the

evening, and Artorius only counted the day safe when the gigantic figure of Aelle himself went down, pierced by innumerable blades.

When all was done, and nothing remained of the enemy save heaped piles of dead and wounded, Artorius wandered the battlefield on foot, leading Llamrei by the reins. She was every bit as tired as her master, and plodded along with her head bowed, all the spirit knocked out of her.

Artorius walked like a man in a dream, his head still ringing with the sounds of battle. Heedless of where he went, he trod on the entrails of the slain; wondering if any other still lived on this field of death. He had got cut off from his men during the last stages of the battle, and struck on the head by a sword. It split his helmet, and for a while he swooned, allowing Llamrei to take him where she would.

Cei and Gwalchmei eventually found him. They gently guided him to the river, where the dragon banner was stuck into the bloody earth. Some of the Companions had lit a fire, and were busy cooking bowls of porridge and bacon. Others were tending to the wounded, using their cloaks as blankets.

"Bedwyr," Artorius murmured, looking down at one of the grey-faced men on the blankets, "does he live?"

Bedwyr's eyes were closed. His left arm was bound up in a crude bandage and strapped to his chest. Artorius' heart lurched when he saw it ended in a stump.

"He hovers between life and death, lord," said Cei, his voice heavy with grief for his childhood friend, "we stopped the bleeding, but he is in God's hands."

Someone passed Artorius a cup of wine. He drank it all in a single swallow, and felt his head begin to clear a little.

"What are the numbers of our dead?" he asked, fearing the answer.

"Over half," replied Gwalchmei, "though the numbers are uncertain. We will know more in the morning."

Cei took Artorius by the hand, and led him towards the fire. Three more bodies were laid out next to it. They were not Britons.

"Aelle," said Cei, nodding at the silvery-haired giant laid out in the middle, "the others are Osla and Ebusa."

Artorius gazed down at the three men. He could hardly credit the scale of victory. The Saxon host was smashed beyond repair, thousands of their best fighting men ushered to Valhalla. Thirteen Saxon kings lay among the dead, including these, the chief of them.

It would be many years before their pestilent race recovered. Decades. In that time, Britannia might grow strong again.

"We plucked Osla's body from the river," said Cei, "hence his bloated look. He probably drowned trying to escape, trampled by his own men during the rout."

Aelle, Osla and Ebusa, thought Artorius, *three of Hengist's wolf-cubs. Where is the fourth?*

"Cerdic," he croaked, massaging his parched throat, "find his body. Bring it to me."

"Our men are searching for it," said Gwalchmei, "there was no sign of him among the kings. He may not have been here."

Not here? Artorius might have guessed. The half-breed always walked his own path.

I should have killed him at Caer Guinnion. He won't allow himself to be taken so easily again. Now his kin are dead, he is the only man of Hengist's blood still standing. How long before he becomes Over-King of his people? Clever, clever Cerdic!

Artorius became aware of men all around him: his men, the officers who had confronted him at Din Eidyn.

One stepped forward, holding a bloody purple rag fringed with gold. Artorius dimly recognised it as the royal cloak worn by Constantine, no doubt ripped from his shoulders when he died at Llongborth.

Another man came forward, this time holding the golden crown of the High King.

Both knelt before him, offering up the regalia.

"Artorius," said Cei, standing behind him, "we will have you as High King. No-one else."

"Artorius," echoed Gwalchmei, his voice rising to a shout, "Artorius!"

Others in the circle took up the cry. "No," said Artorius, backing away, "I can't...I won't..."

His voice was lost in the tumult. "Artorius!" shouted his officers, "Artorius! Hail Artorius! Artorius the King!"

His name swept across the field, echoed and repeated by the Companions until it bounced back and forth across the darkened hills.

"ARTORIUS! ARTORIUS! ARTORIUS THE KING!"

Swept along by a current he could no longer resist, Artorius allowed them to bind the tattered cloak to his shoulders and press the golden wreath down onto his brow. The touch of the cold metal sent a shiver through him. His flesh crawled with disgust. He wanted none of this power. Had never wanted it, never fought for it, never schemed and plotted and murdered for it.

He thought he heard Morgana's voice. *Which is why, my brother, you must be the one who wields it.*

Artorius stood alone among a world of dead or kneeling men, alone and afraid, abandoned by God and thrown onto the mercy of fate.

His name swelled until it filled the skies, greater than any storm, destined to sweep the land from sea to shining sea.

"ARTORIUS!"

END

AUTHOR'S NOTE

There are many theories relating to the 'historical' King Arthur, though he is generally thought to be a Romano-British warrior active a few decades after the withdrawal of the last Roman legions from Britain in the early 5th century. This is where the two earliest sources, the 9th century *Historia Brittonum* (History of the Britons) and the 10th century *Annales Cambriae* (Welsh Annals) place him. The Historia, a compilation of earlier texts attributed to a monk called Nennius, describes Arthur as a 'Dux Bellorum' rather than a king, saying that he 'fought alongside the kings of the Britons' against the Saxons and other invaders of Sub-Roman Britain, but he himself was 'leader of battles'. 'Dux Bellorum' was a late Roman military title, meaning commander-in-chief of all the Roman forces stationed in Britannia.

This Arthur, far from the later idealised monarch ruling from his glittering court at Camelot, is depicted as a military official in charge of whatever military forces remained in the country after the legions had left, and using them to fight on behalf of the various British kings and sub-kings. The Historia also supplies a list of twelve battles in which Arthur is supposed to have been victorious, culminating in his famous victory at Mons Badonicus or Mount Badon.

The Annales supplies dates for his career, giving 516 AD as the year of Badon and 537-39 for 'the strife of Camlann, where Arthur and Medraut fell'. Modern scholarship has cast doubt on the Badon and Camlann entries and their dating, though Badon is at least confirmed as a genuine historical event by one other source: Gildas, the 6th century monk who wrote of Vortigern and Ambrosius, mentions 'the siege of Mount Badon' as 'almost the last victory over the rascals (meaning the Saxons) though by no means the least.' Sadly, he neglects to mention the name of the British general responsible for this famous victory. Later tradition names him as Arthur, which at least suggests the reality of Arthur's existence. The location of Badon is unknown, though theories range from Little Solsbury Hill and Liddington Castle near Bath, Dumbarton Rock in Scotland and Mynydd Baedan in Glamorgan. I chose the first of these options, as being the most likely (in my opinion) and the best fit for my story.

In common with many other writers, I used the above sources as the basis for my version of Arthur's life and career. I also decided to try something different, and draw on the medieval Welsh tales of Arthur rather than the more familiar English/French traditions. Possibly the very earliest reference to Arthur occurs in the poem Y Gododdin, which celebrates the exploits of Welsh/Brythonic warriors in the northern kingdom of Gododdin. Here a warrior is described in vivid terms as 'glutting the black ravens on the walls of the fort with the blood of his enemies, though 'he was no Arthur'. In other words, he was a great fighter, but not as great as Arthur, already remembered as the superhero of the Welsh/British race.

The Welsh stories are dark and bloody, imbued with wild magic and strange, mischievous humour. The character of Gwrgi Wyllt, or Gwrgi Garwlwyd (which translates literally as 'Rough Dog Man Grey') to give him his full name, appears in the Triads as a terrifying figure in the habit of killing a Briton every day except Sunday. Why he hates the Britons so much is unclear, but his eventual death is described, unsurprisingly, as One of the Three Fortunate Assassinations of the Island of the Mighty. I decided to make Gwrgi one of my villains, since he is perfect villain material and has never - to the best of my knowledge - been depicted before in Arthurian fiction. Other characters, such as Melwas, Prince of the Summer Country, Ganhumara, and Rhitta of the Beards also appear scattered throughout Welsh sources. I have included them all, albeit in slightly changed circumstances: Rhitta and his gruesome cloak is originally described as a King of Gwynedd in North Wales, but I have relocated him north of Hadrian's Wall.

Rigotomos, King of the Amoricans, is one of the few definite historical figures from this era. He is described as a 'King of the Brittones', though whether this means the British in Britain or British settlers who had fled from the Saxon incursions to Amorica, now Western Brittany, is unclear. In about the year 470 he brought an army to help the Western Emperor, Anthemius, in his war against the Visigoths. The Romans failed to support Rigotomos, possibly due to the treachery of Arvandus, Prefect of Gaul, and the Brittonic army was destroyed in Gaul after a hard fight against overwhelming numbers. Intriguingly, Rigotomos was last seen retreating with the remnant of his army to the Burgundian town of Avallon - Avalon, of course, being the traditional place of rest King Arthur is despatched to after his last battle.

Some writers, the historian Geoffrey Ashe among them, have been tempted to identify Rigotomos as the historical inspiration for Arthur. Like almost everything relating to this subject, the theory is still hotly debated. 'Rigotomos' (also spelled Riothamus) was a title meaning 'Over-King' as well as a personal name, which doesn't help much. The date of 470 is a few decades earlier than the dates given for Arthur in the Historia, and there is no suggestion that Rigotomos ever fought the Saxons in Britain, though he may have brought his forces over the Channel into Gaul. All in all, I decided to keep the characters of Rigotomos and Arthur separate. Having them work together was a neat way of resolving the problem, at least in fiction.

The game of 'gwyddbwyll' played between Gwrgi and Aethelflaed was an ancient Celtic board game, and features heavily in several of the tales in The Mabinogion. The rules are lost to us, but it is thought to have been similar to an Irish game called Fidchell. Unlike Fidchell, there were probably an equal number of pieces on either side in gwyddbywll, though not in the version Gwrgi favours.

Part II of the Leader of Battles series draws on all the sources discussed above, along with others, and attempts to portray Arthur/Artorius the warlord, a complex and in some ways unattractive figure to modern eyes, but still Post-Roman Britannia's shining hope against the darkness. His story is not done yet.

Made in the USA
San Bernardino, CA
01 March 2016